COURTING EMILY

For a long moment, Kingsbridge gazed into Emily's eyes in the most innocent fashion. "You've not *fine* eyes," he stated, a smile touching his lips. "You've beautiful, even magnificent eyes. They are your very best feature, yet the rest are lovely, as well. Do you know how pretty you are?" His mouth fell slightly agape after that. "Is that a blush on your cheeks?"

Emily took another sip of the sherry, choked, and dabbed at the corner of her mouth with one of her gloves. He had disconcerted her completely. She knew that his compliments were offered not with any intention of arousing her interest. Yet that is just what they had done.

She was blushing because she was pleased. And she was pleased because with every minute that had passed since her initial meeting with Kingsbridge at the Scarswell masquerade, her delight in his company had increased steadily. She liked that he teased her. She liked that he didn't fawn over her beauty, but had detailed it so nicely. She liked that he laughed when she joked and that he didn't make a fuss as many of her previous suitors and beaux had done, reclining at her feet, staring at her with mooncalf expressions, writing her stupid sonnets, when all she wanted was to be kissed and loved a little.

And she wondered, if before their adventure was over, Kingsbridge would kiss her again . . .

Books by Valerie King

A Daring Wager
A Rogue's Masquerade
Reluctant Bride
The Fanciful Heiress
The Willful Widow
Love Match
Cupid's Touch
A Lady's Gambit
Captivated Hearts
My Lady Vixen
The Elusive Bride
Merry, Merry Mischief
Vanquished
Bewitching Hearts
A Summer Courtship
Vignette
A Poet's Kiss

Published by Zebra Books

A POET'S KISS

Valerie King

Zebra Books
Kensington Publishing Corp.

http://www.zebrabooks.com

ZEBRA BOOKS are published by

Kensington Publishing Corp.
850 Third Avenue
New York, NY 10022

Copyright © 1997 by Valerie King

Zebra and the Z logo Reg. U.S. Pat. & TM Off.

First Printing: November, 1997
10 9 8 7 6 5 4 3 2 1

Printed in the United States of America

For David Hetterly

*May your life be an adventure
tempered with wisdom, love, and an abundance
of self-knowledge.*

One

London, July of 1814

Emily Longcliffe tapped her foot to the lively music of a Scottish reel. She was dizzy with exhilaration as she peered from behind a gold-fringed, dark blue velvet curtain and watched a score of costumed revelers go down the dance.

She shouldn't be here, she thought, biting her lower lip.

A masquerade was in progress.

But not just a masquerade. A masquerade in which Lord Byron, that most notorious of rakehells—who was known to drink wine from skulls!—was said to be in attendance.

She closed her eyes and sighed with pleasure. Until this moment, she hadn't truly known how dull her life was, or how much she had blindly accepted the rigid nature of her existence, or how powerful and demanding were the true cravings of her mind and heart.

She was situated in the passageway that connected the magnificent ballroom of Scarswell House to a delightful antechamber near the stairwell. Her friend and cohort in mischief, young Lady Alison, was beside her. She, too, was delighting in the rakish air of the ball, a vision in the guise of a medieval maid.

Emily, on the other hand, was gowned as an East Indian Princess in a flow of blue, pink, and yellow muslin draped over a white silk shift that clung to her womanly figure quite scandalously. Covering her long, light brown locks were several feet of blue muslin secured by a gold circlet worn like a crown atop her head. She disguised her identity not by a mask, like Lady Alison, but by a gossamer pink half-veil which hid the lower part of her face.

What would her sisters think of her if any of them knew she had actually succumbed to Alison's persuasions and had attended the dangerous fete?

What would they think of the Scottish reel in progress?

What would they think if they knew the true imaginings of her heart tonight?

Oh, dear. Her sisters frowned on the waltz and the reel, both of which were felt to be too lively for truly dignified ladies of quality. Yet, she had already danced the waltz—twice—and if only she had been asked to go down the reel, nothing would have stopped her!

She disliked admitting as much to herself, but she could not recall the last time she had felt so elated by the festivities attendant at a ball.

Lady Alison drew close to her and also peered from behind the velvet draperies to observe the dancers. The tall pointed tip of her medieval hat frequently caught at other costumes and draperies, but for the present was laid gently against Emily's circlet and muslin headdress. "Do you see him?" she queried breathlessly. "There! Across the ballroom. Oh, that must be Byron dressed in Turkish garb. It is said the Ali Pasha gave him the entire costume as a gift. See how he stands back and admires the ladies? 'Tis a pity he cannot dance. He is very lame, you know."

Lady Alison was just eighteen, a full six years younger than Emily, but game for any lark. They had become fast acquaintances for reasons she could not as yet explain, but Emily rather thought it had to do with the fact that her new friend enjoyed a riotous, unorthodox existence which she herself had always been denied. The Duchess of Amesbury, Lady Alison's mother, was much less strict with her daughters than Mrs. Longcliffe, and was even now dancing the reel with an officer of the Horse Guards.

"Everyone knows of Byron's lameness," Emily breathed. She watched him closely, wondering how he bore his shrunken foot. She noted that several ladies nearby fluttered their fans in hopes of attracting his notice. Perhaps his lameness was one of his prominent attractions, she mused. If a lady's sympathies could be aroused, would her heart not follow soon after? Besides, he was ever so handsome and even taller than she had been told.

Lady Alison continued her observations. "Even with his mask on, he is a delight to the eye. Look what a noble chin he possesses." The ladies sighed together.

When his attention turned toward them rather suddenly, and he smiled broadly in their direction, Emily gave a squeak. "Oh, he has seen us ogling him! How mortifying!"

She withdrew quickly into the small passageway, but Lady Alison was not so easily intimidated and took up Emily's foremost position behind the drape. She continued her observations for a few seconds more, then turned back to look at Emily. She wiggled her eyebrows in a silly manner, which made Emily laugh, before giving her report. "He has left his place along the edge of the ballroom and is even now wending his way through the crowds. I believe he means to come to us." She glanced again about the fringe, then turned back to add, "How very odd, though. He does not seem to be limp—"

"Come away now!" Emily adjured her friend, grasping her firmly by the elbow and attempting to draw her toward the antechamber. "I wish very much to become acquainted with his lordship, but not in this truly schoolgirlish manner."

Lady Alison released the drapery which she had been holding back slightly with her gloved fingers and turned to scowl upon Emily. "Why are you being so missish now! You ought to be gratified by such a compliment. He probably observed you, or perhaps me, and has decided he wishes for an introduction! You are quite hopeless, you know. I vow you've been far too long under the dictatorship of your eldest sister."

Emily would not listen to her, but gave another tug on her arm. "Are you coming, or not?" she asked, exasperated. "We have but seconds!"

"I am not moving from this hallway," Lady Alison retorted firmly. "You may run away if you wish, but I shall remain steadfast. I have been dying to meet Byron this age and more!"

"Very well," Emily breathed. She released Lady Alison's hand and quickly left the passageway.

The antechamber of a deep burgundy silk smelled richly of roses. Four enormous vases, bearing pungent ferns and stuffed with an abundance of white blooms, sat in the corners of the room. The chamber was crowded with costumed revellers through which Emily had some difficulty forging a path. King Henry VIII spoke with a truly lovely Cleopatra, while a Roman soldier—the beauty of his legs scarcely concealed by the short skirt of his costume—whispered into the ear of a scantily clad milkmaid. Some still wore their masks, but some had already revealed their identities.

Laughter abounded in the warm, inviting home in which merriment and not intellectual conversation was the order of the day. How much her sisters—especially her eldest, Meg—would have disapproved of the teasing, flirting, and giggling that swirled about the mansion.

She finally squeezed her way out of the antechamber and found herself in a crowded hall lined with a rich wainscoting of marbled oak. Her heart was beating quickly, in part because of a fear that Lord Byron was on her heels, and in part because she had for so long wanted to meet the famous poet that the very thought of speaking with him set her nerves on fire. She could hardly breathe she was so excited.

Just as she left the hallway and entered the lofty entrance hall—also crowded with a myriad of costumed guests—she

chanced to glance over her shoulder. She caught her breath,
for above the heads of many of the guests she spied a Turkish
turban moving swiftly through the crowd.

"Oh, dear," she murmured. She sensed that she was being
pursued, a sensation so novel and so exhilarating that her
face became flushed in a warm wave of nothing short of
pleasure. For, if the truth be known, if Byron was indeed
giving chase, she was discovering how very much the experience pleased her. Her heart picked up its cadence further
and a delightful dizziness spread through her mind.

She opened her mouth and drew in a deep breath, then
continued her flight. Once having succeeded in reaching the
opposite side of the entrance hall, she found two choices
before her—a formal receiving room of a brilliant yellow
softened with white and midnight blue accents, or a second
hallway that led toward the back of the mansion.

She deliberated only for a second. Since she was unsure
if the receiving room led to other compartments, she chose
to turn down the hall.

Immediately she saw that the crowds had thinned and she
felt certain that the diminished number of guests indicated
her choice had been unfortunate. But there was nothing for
it now except to incline her head to several guests who eyed
her curiously, and proceed to the antechamber visible beyond
the hall.

She glanced behind her and saw that the Turk would soon
be upon her. Her heart thrummed in her ears.

Once she reached the antechamber, however, she discovered that only two gentlemen were present, neither of whom
were costumed. One was quite handsome with a decidedly
cleft chin and luminous, almost mesmerizing gray eyes. He
appeared to be arguing some point with his acquaintance. She
met the surprised glances of both gentlemen, inclined her head
slightly, then pressed on. A door separated the antechamber
from whatever lay beyond.

Goodness! What if she was approaching a closet of some

sort? But she had come this far and, when she heard her name called by a decidedly masculine voice from behind, she chose not to waver in her course.

Her decision made, she ignored the stunned silence of the two brangling gentlemen, gave the doorknob a hard turn, pushed open the door, and stepped boldly across the threshold.

She was greeted with a rush of warm, fragrant, humid air, and she sighed with tremendous relief as she closed the door swiftly behind her. She entered what proved to be a lofty, well-appointed orangery in which the smell of ripening citrus permeated the entire glass chamber. Pineapples, oranges, and lemons were all in evidence.

She did not advance far, however, since from behind the door she could hear the three men now talking together as though well acquainted.

Would the other gentlemen betray her, she wondered? Or would they even need to, since the hallway she had chosen to follow had ended in the orangery?

She could only wait, her heart ticking loudly in her ears, a hand pressed to her throat. She could even feel her heartbeat throbbing against her palm.

What foolishness!

Yet what delight!

There! She could admit as much to herself. She was delighted, she was enchanted, she was enthralled.

She was also dismayed, for the experience was exposing the truth of her unhappy existence to her, and the truth was smarting, for of the moment she did not see how she could change her life.

From the time she could remember she had listened to the strictures of her mother and her older sisters on just how she ought to conduct every aspect of her day-to-day employments. She must know three languages, so she spoke French, Italian, and German fluently.

She must be able to perform on the pianoforte, so she had

practiced diligently for years and was known to please even the most fastidious of listeners.

She must be able to manage her needlework with a precision of eye known only to Swiss clockmakers, and so her samplers were perfection itself.

She had a thorough knowledge of the globe; she painted in watercolors; she had studied Latin until her sisters made it clear it was unladylike to be considered a blue-stocking and to be entirely educated. Secretly, therefore, she had continued both her conjugations and her translations, as well as her study of mathematics and parallelograms.

She was well versed in the management of the household and knew to a nicety how to arrange menus for each meal, how to review the linen inventories with the housekeeper, and how to economize, to save, and to protect the fortune of an estate by not overpaying the servants or letting the tradesmen cheat her.

In short, she was a Lady of Quality.

In short, she was bored to tears and had been ever since she had purposely given off climbing trees when she was ten years old; her sisters had descended upon her, *en masse,* in order to show her the error of her ways.

She had submitted to their joint will, since she was a dutiful girl. Besides, they were only promoting their mother's purposes. But she had never told anyone how sad that day had been for her, when they had found her in the apple orchard at the uppermost branches of a tree. They had gathered about the tree trunk like witches around a bonfire, and insisted she change her ways. "Come down! Come down at once! You will disgrace our family! You are ten, now! You must come down! Come down and become a lady!"

She didn't like being a lady, even though she was quite good at it, she thought with a laugh. She excelled at taking on the form, yet her heart broke even now as she thought about how painful the descent from the apple tree had been. The wind in the afternoon always blew so delightfully, and

to be hugging a branch and letting the wind blow her around
was beyond every pleasant sensation known to her.

Every step downward, toward the earth, toward the embraces, encouragement, and admonitions of her sisters, with
the force of the wind decreasing steadily, was like being plummeted into the underworld and forced to serve Persephone
forever.

Perhaps that was why, after five years on the Marriage Mart,
she was still unwed. She had received numerous offers. Why
wouldn't she have, since she was the epitome of ladylikeness
and well dowered—thirty thousand pounds was an attractive
figure to any second-born gentleman. Yet none had tempted
her to enter the married state.

She sighed deeply, wondering why so many memories suddenly flowed through her. She turned to look at the door and
realized that in her reveries the room beyond had fallen silent.

They had gone!

What luck! she thought ecstatically.

Or was it?

She found herself disappointed that the game was over.
She felt as though she had descended the apple tree all over
again.

But this was absurd! Why was she torturing herself? Except that tonight she had had a glimpse of what life could
hold, at least in part.

Even the costume she had chosen for the masquerade reflected a sort of daring she had not employed since childhood. If Margaret, her eldest sister, had seen her in such a
costume, she would have lectured her for an entire decade.
Fanny, next oldest, would have fainted. And dear Pru would
have stammered and blushed for a twelve-month.

Why was she so very different from her sisters? Why
couldn't she be content with her lot and with one of the mild
gentlemen her sisters had presented to her over the years as
an excellent match? Why did she frequently awaken in the

middle of the night, only to throw open her window in order to see the stars and beg them to reveal their secrets to her?

She sighed again. If only she could believe that marriage might be full of fun and gig, of apple trees and peach trees and even orange trees that she could climb whenever she wanted to, without anyone demanding she do otherwise. Perhaps then she would not be so reluctant to take on the connubial mantle.

She blinked and became aware suddenly that in her reveries she had moved away from the door and had become lost in the midst of the pineapple plants, and orange and lemon trees. She was even now fingering the thick, prickly sides of a young pineapple.

"So, tell me," a man's deep, resonant voice called from near the door. "Just how does it come about that one of the famous Longcliffe sisters is in attendance at so indecorous a masquerade?"

Emily took a step backward and gasped. For there was Byron, or the man she supposed to be the famous poet, standing in his exotic Turkish garb, his hands planted on his hips and a crooked smile breaking up his face most attractively.

Two

Lord Kingsbridge was delighted as he watched the youngest of the Longcliffe sisters open her mouth and let out a gentle gasp. He was delighted because he was surprised, and with so many years experience among the *beau monde,* he was not easily surprised.

She was a vision, Miss Emily Longcliffe, in her East Indian costume. Every delightful curve of her figure was revealed enchantingly and, because her veil had fallen away, nothing of her considerable beauty was concealed from him. Her eyes were her best feature and distinctive from every lady he knew, for they were round and of a vivid blue that made the veil of her costume ineffectual in preventing her identity from being known—he had recognized her at the outset. Her brows were thin and curved prettily. Her nose was straight, her chin slightly dimpled, her cheekbones high and pronounced, her face oval. Her lips were bowed, giving any observer the sense that she held in her heart some extraordinary secret.

Why she was unwed, therefore, was a mystery to him. He would have supposed—given the Longcliffes' joint history of wedding the pride of the aristocracy and gentry—that Miss Emily would have long since accepted one of the numerous offers she had already received. Theirs was a noble familial history ranging back to the arrival of the Conqueror in A.D. 1066. A strong vein of common sense ruled the Longcliffes, whether male or female, and only rarely had a hiccough in the line sprouted to break up so much august continuity.

He wondered now as he looked at Miss Emily, if she was perhaps that aberration known occasionally to occur in even the finest pedigrees. If so, he had a duty to discover just what manner of aberration she was. He was certainly positioned well to do what he wanted with her, because he knew what she was thinking—that he was none other than Lord Byron.

He chuckled at the thought. Byron, a good friend, was famous for the Albanian costume he had brought back with him from his tour of Greece and the Levant. He was known to wear the costume at masquerades and even had had his portrait painted while wearing the splendid garb. Anyone who was familiar with Byron's costume would know at a glance that his was Turkish and not Albanian, and that he was anyone other than the famous poet.

Miss Emily, however, who did not frequent the circles of either Byron or himself, would not know the difference. What delight life could hold, he thought, as he moved slowly toward the beautiful woman whose blue eyes glittered in the dimly lit orangery. What an opportunity had presented itself, and at just such a moment when he had thought that there truly was *nothing new under the sun.*

This was new and fresh and very real—Miss Emily Longcliffe at a scandalous masquerade.

Miss Emily Longcliffe with her eyes glittering and her veil fallen away from her face.

Miss Emily Longcliffe watching him with a rapt expression on her face, ready and waiting to be kissed. Surely.

Emily watched the Turk approach and realized suddenly that he could not be the man she supposed he was, for he was not limping. Who was he then, and why did he approach

her as though he was a cat stalking a bird? But more impor-
tantly, why was she feeling entirely disinclined to run away?

Perhaps it was the Turkish costume, she mused. Or his
height, for he was certainly taller than Byron, who was
known to be five feet eight inches. This man was nearer to
six feet, of that she was certain. Who was he then?

She sought swiftly through her memory, reviewing the
men she had known and seen over the past several years,
especially those belonging to a fringe of gentlemen who
rarely visited the drawing rooms of the High Sticklers, who
were known to frequent the East End Hells, who took great
delight in boxing with Gentleman Jackson, and who held
membership in the Four-In-Hand Club.

Suddenly she saw the face, recognizing the visage of a
man she thought even more roguish than Byron—the Marquess of Kingsbridge. She drew in her breath in a soft gasp,
for surely she was in some danger of the moment.

Kingsbridge was a Nonpareil among sporting men and a
fierce gamester, if all the rumors she had heard of him were
true. The ladies in particular were known to throw themselves
at his head, visiting him scandalously at his rooms in James
Street in the full light of day. It was rumored that he, like
Byron, also drank wine from skulls. In short, he was a rakehell, a man of libertine propensities who pursued his vices
and damned his virtues, and who made any hopeful female
who crossed his line of sight the object of his attention. As
she looked into his smiling eyes, she understood exceedingly
well that she was his prey.

"Kingsbridge," she murmured.

His brows lifted. "Then you know who I am?"

She nodded slightly.

He was almost upon her. His eyes sparkled with ignoble
intentions, even though they were cloaked behind his mask.
She turned about suddenly and darted down a short row of
orange trees. She heard him laugh, a deep, low chuckle that
sent a shiver down her spine of something that was not quite

fright. She wheeled about to see where he was, knowing he hadn't followed her.

He was still standing beside the pineapple plant.

"You'll not escape without giving me a kiss as passage back to the masquerade," he called to her.

"You are being absurd, my lord," she whispered.

His crooked smiled reappeared.

"You're quite beautiful, you know," he returned softly.

"And you are a flatterer."

"I speak only the truth."

He took a step toward her and she darted to her right, away from the door, away from safety. Why had she done as much? If she had moved swiftly to her left she might have reached the door in time and found her escape.

Perhaps.

Perhaps not.

She knew—she could see—he was an athletic man. He carried himself upright, his shoulders well back, his proud chest giving the appearance that he could bear even the strongest wind.

He moved quickly toward her, at the same time tearing the mask from his head and letting it fall to the bricks at his feet.

She reached the glass windows, scooting behind a tall palm tree. A frond caught the blue scarf over her head and pulled it and the narrow crown off her long brown locks. She squealed as he tried to catch her to the right of the palm frond. She slid the other direction, she was almost away, but hesitated for the barest second thinking she ought to retrieve her scarf, then decided against it.

"Never hesitate," he murmured, catching her arm, as she tried to slip past him.

His hand was strong about her arm and to have resisted him would have given her a terrible bruise. He drew her strongly to him, and at the same time he gathered up one of her dangling curls in his hand, wrapping it about his fist.

He had captured her!

She was bound to him as surely as if he'd tied a rope about her neck.

He slid his arm about her waist and drew her hard against him. She opened her eyes wide, utterly astonished. Everything she had heard about him was true. His lips were pressed to hers before she could begin her protests and, for a long moment, she was too stunned to do anything but feel the pressure of his kiss.

Time drew to an abrupt halt. She didn't know whether seconds were passing, or minutes, or hours. The damp, warm air of the orangery held the clock trapped in humid silence. She felt the length of his body against hers, the heat of his skin, the strength of his arms and legs.

She was utterly astonished and *she would never see him again*.

If she never saw him again, what harm could there be in one reckless embrace?

That is what she began to tell herself as his kiss suddenly became a gentle search and still she did not commence her protests.

Oh, but she should have. She should have begun beating on his chest and insisting he release her. Instead, she was in her bedchamber, the windows thrown wide. She was pacing back and forth demanding the stars to reveal their secrets, and so they were. Next she was in the apple tree, the wind blowing her this way, then that.

When had her arms found their way about his neck?

His tongue touched her lips. She gasped. All was new, forbidden, and strangely wondrous. She parted her lips.

Oh, my!

Life opened up to her as it never had before. A new understanding came to her of Byron's poetry, which had formerly held mysteries beyond her comprehension. She tasted of the sweetness of love, yet not love, but nearly so. Surely.

No wonder Lady Alison spoke of kissing as being a heavenly sort of endeavor, for Emily felt as though she was rising from the earth and that her feet would never touch the ground again. She leaned closer to him, and felt his arms wrap about her more securely yet.

Ah, she thought. Therein lay the whole of the mystery, for never in her life had she felt so safe as when held tightly in the arms of this man.

His kisses became wild suddenly and her knees disappeared. The earth was gone forever. She would remain at the top of the apple tree until the universe turned to a white glow and disappeared once and for all.

He released her suddenly, frowning down upon her as though he was angry. He grabbed her shoulders. "You play with fire, Miss Longcliffe," he murmured. "Or is it possible you know precisely what you are doing?"

She didn't hear his words, at least not exactly. "The stars were speaking to me," she whispered.

"What?" he asked on a hoarse murmur.

"The stars. I have so frequently begged them to talk to me, and now I think they have."

"You are being foolish."

"And you, sir, have lost your soul in foolish pursuits."

He let his gaze drop away from hers, his mind drawing inward. "Perhaps," he murmured. "But you kiss like you've kissed a dozen men before."

"Only one," she said quietly. "I should go." But her feet wouldn't move. She couldn't quite feel them yet. She wasn't even certain where she was.

He reached down and retrieved her shawl and, removing the crown that had become tangled in the delicate fabric, settled the length of the blue muslin over her hair. He placed the crown carefully on the fabric. She reached up and settled it properly.

"May I call on you?" he whispered.

She shook her head. "No, you are too vile," she whispered.

"And you are unkind."

"If you had not been vile, you would not have kissed me."

"But you liked my kisses."

"You opened my eyes, but that does not mean I must like all that I see."

"Faith, but you speak plainly and boldly." He seemed offended, but not overly much.

"I am usually more circumspect, but you have stunned me."

"You ought to go now," he said. "For you are far too pretty to be hiding in the shrubberies with your lovely eyes and your cherubic lips begging to be kissed again."

She finally felt her feet, and without another word to him, turned away and headed back to the door. A moment more and she left him in the orangery.

An hour later, with the sounds of Mozart floating from the ballroom, Emily offered Lord Byron her hand as Lady Jersey introduced him to her. She found that her knees trembled slightly as she made his acquaintance.

Byron at last.

Yet how grateful she was that some time had elapsed between her encounter with Kingsbridge and the present, for the marquess's kisses had frayed her sensibilities considerably. She had required some few minutes to recover her composure, a circumstance aided by the fact that Kingsbridge left Scarswell House shortly after having kissed her. She had been intensely relieved. She would have preferred having left the masquerade ball herself, but neither Lady Alison nor her mother would hear of it, and in all fairness she had only herself to blame in having permitted the wretched kiss to have occurred in the first place.

So it was that she stared up into the face of the poet whose works had so fired her imagination, and offered him her compliments. "I have not had the pleasure of traveling abroad myself, so accompanying *Child Harolde* was of the sweetest

tance with Mr. Peveril. If her cousin lacked a certain *finesse* or consideration in doing so, she was sorry for Mr. Peveril, but she didn't see of what use she could be to him were that the case.

On the other hand, surely Mr. Peveril, whose connections and political involvements indicated a developed mind, would not have written to her in hopes of persuading her to become a liaison between himself and her cousin.

If assistance in his flagging flirtation was not the motive behind the missive, then what precisely might his *anxieties* be based on?

Her toes curled in anticipation at the fact that the only way she would ever know what Mr. Peveril's thoughts were would be to visit him in prison.

Newgate!

Her heart began to beat strongly in her chest.

Was this the start of a true adventure?

Yes, let it be the beginning, her mind and heart cried out together.

For a long time, as the gray light of dawn filtered through the slats of her shutters and the thin white muslin fabric over her windows, she grew drowsy in her ruminations about the meaning of the letter. She blew out her candle and closed her eyes. Her feet and legs ached most delightfully from dancing for hours on end. She was fatigued beyond belief and tomorrow she would begin an adventure.

On the following morning, Emily stepped down from her black and maroon town chariot and lifted her hand toward the postillion, bidding him to wait. She did not expect her interview with Mr. Peveril to take very long.

She stood on the sidewalk staring up at the bleak spectre known as Newgate Prison, named after the street on which it was situated. The tall, block edifice had been constructed in the 1770s by George Dance the Younger, an architect and

Clerk of the City Works. After a fire had consumed much of the integrity of the building during the Gordon Riots, a reconstruction was undertaken in 1780.

Since that time, little had occurred to disturb the tranquil appearance of the building that belied the horrors within. On Newgate Street itself, a scaffold was ever ready for the public hangings of those prisoners sentenced to death by the courts. Emily had never witnessed these executions, but for many the occurrence was treated with all the enthusiasm of an open-air fair. Rooms in the buildings opposite the prison were frequently rented out on hanging days at exorbitant prices.

Fortunately, there were no executions today, and a few minutes making polite inquiries of the prison officials soon saw her directed to Mr. Peveril's cell.

Upon approaching the cell, however, Emily was surprised to hear a lady's voice. "But Peveril," the lilting voice of the woman cajoled, "you promised you would not be angry that I was leaving for Brighton."

"He always favored you," Mr. Peveril responded throatily.

"I can manage Prinny and, if all goes well, I shall see you released before the hunting season."

"You are a baggage, Connie, but a beautiful one. Why do I trust you?"

"Because you love me, my darling goose."

Emily bit her lip, her feet stunned in place. A prison guard approached her from behind. "Is there a problem, Miss?" he queried politely.

She shook her head. "I didn't know he was entertaining a guest?" she offered by way of requesting enlightenment.

The guard smiled from one side of his mouth as though her query was both ridiculous and slightly embarrassing. "Er, he does sometime have visitors, Miss." He cleared his throat and brushed past her. "Here, here, Mr. Peveril. A lady to see ye."

He waved for her to step forward as the lady within protested. "A lady? Who has come to call on you—and in here? She can be no lady, then, surely."

Emily stepped into the square of dull light shining from a small, barred window at the top of the wall. Mr. Peveril's cell was small, but fitted with what appeared to be a comfortable bed and a desk. He wore gentleman's day dress.

"How do you do, Mr. Peveril?" she said, peering from between bars. "I beg you to forgive me for intruding, but I received your urgent missive last night from a—a friend of yours." She glanced at the lady, then back to Peveril, before continuing, "I most certainly would have informed you of my intended visit, but as I said, your letter seemed quite urgent in your need to see me as quickly as possible."

The guard interjected. "Will ye be leaving now, Mrs. Browne?"

The lady in question, standing close to Mr. Peveril, drew her veil of white gauze over her poke bonnet of a pretty fawn brown silk, and nodded by way of response.

"You are angry, my pet," Mr. Peveril whispered, catching her arm before she could move away from him.

She turned to look back at him and, even through the opaque fabric, her sentiments were clearly known to one and all.

The lady was displeased.

"You, Mr. Peveril, may send your explanations to Brighton—and your apologies as well, though I warn you I shan't forgive you this insult."

The guard unlocked the door, permitting Mrs. Browne to leave.

Emily met her in the hallway.

"Miss Longcliffe," the woman said, acknowledging her with a stiff nod of her head.

Emily could not return the compliment. She hadn't the faintest notion who she was.

The guard gestured for her to enter and, a moment more,

the barred door slammed shut. A terrible chill ran down her back.

"How horrid!" she murmured, turning around to stare at the scarred door. "I've never felt such a lonely sensation before in my entire existence. How do you bear it?" She whirled back to face the stranger who had summoned her.

He shook his head and turned his face toward the light. "With little enough grace," he managed bitterly.

Mr. Peveril was a rather handsome young man, she thought, perhaps of an age with her, but with long curling blond hair, styled in the fashion known as *à la Cherubim,* a romantic arrangement that would have appealed instantly to her cousin Evangeline. His nose was rather pointed at the tip, but his large brown eyes, the nice line of his jaw, and the lean, graceful appearance of his person could not help but please.

He looked back at her. "I shan't trouble you with my own difficulties, since for the present my only wish is that I might convince you of my concerns for your cousin."

He took a step to his right, which in the small room brought him next to his cherry wood desk. He opened a side drawer and withdrew a thick packet of letters tied with a black ribbon. "These I received from Miss Matford over the past several months, since my initial introduction to her last summer when I was visiting in Derbyshire. I was staying at a house of a friend situated not more than three miles from Aldwark Manor. I used to walk in the southern groves of that delightful mansion with Miss Matford nearly every afternoon during the course of my stay. The whole of it was quite idyllic."

"But not so idyllic as London?" Emily queried pointedly. Ever since she had become aware that Mr. Peveril, though corresponding steadily with Evangeline, had been entertaining a hopeful lady while incarcerated, she had begun to think that he might not be a very good man, and that her cousin was in some danger from him if she had expectations where he was concerned. She could not help but disapprove of Mr. Peveril's flirtations.

"You refer to Mrs. Browne," he said quietly. "Ah, well, there I believe you have found me out. I will admit that, though quite against my wishes or inclination, I have formed an attachment apart from your cousin. I was fully intending to inform her of the, er, situation, when her letters suddenly ceased—" He slapped the packet of letters against the palm of his hand. "And that, so abruptly, that I couldn't help but fear that some mischief has come about. You see, in several of her last letters she mentioned that her father had been locked up in his study with a certain Mr. Buxton, and that negotiations were underway with regard to her betrothal to Mr. Buxton's son."

"To Theodore?" Emily asked, stunned. "But Evangline despises Teddy Buxton! From all that she has told me, she holds him in immense dislike since she believes he hasn't the pluck of a dormouse. He is somewhat older than she, so they were never playmates when they were children, and in recent years their conversations have been more generally characterized by brangling than anything that might in any manner lead one to believe they would one day become engaged."

He set the packet of letters down on the table and untied the ribbon. Drawing apart the bow, he quickly flipped through the uppermost missives and separated three from the rest. These he handed to her. "The most recent ones," he explained. "If you will take a moment to read them, I'm certain you'll understand why I am as worried as I am."

Emily frowned at him, and when he gestured toward the bed, she took up a seat on the stiff mattress while he remained standing politely near the wall beneath the small, barred window.

The letters were written in Evangeline's sprawling style which she had affected from the time she had left the Nursery and taken on a governess. She wrote as she spoke and, in every syllable, Emily could hear her cousin's unusual mode of speech. Her affections for Mr. Peveril were presented time and again, leading Emily to fear the worst in that regard, that her cousin had become attached to a man who did not return her sentiments.

When Theodore Buxton's name was brought forward, however, some of the leisurely tone of her writing disappeared, and in its stead were clipped sentences and once or twice splotches on the paper that would indicate the shedding of tears. The last letter, dated most recently, exclaimed her horror that for the past two days her father had been pressing her most forcefully to accept Theodore's hand, and Theodore, now Major Buxton, had come forward to make a formal offer. She didn't know what to do. She had never been particularly affectionate with her father, for he had always been a strict, unfeeling parent. She felt that in the end she would be required to submit to his decision in the matter. Could Mr. Peveril possibly be of assistance to her?

Emily read the last line, which pleaded for Mr. Peveril to write to her so that she might know some comfort in her hour of peril, then lifted her gaze to Mr. Peveril. "You have heard nothing from her since?"

"Not a single line," he returned somberly, his arms folded across his chest as he leaned against the stone block wall. "I wrote to her, of course, encouraging her to oppose her father's coercion to the end; then her correspondence simply stopped. I had no way of knowing or even discovering what might have happened to her, nor could I find any way of helping her while locked up in this dreadful place, except to appeal to you."

She recalled to mind Lady Alison's prediction that she would soon experience an adventure because Lord Byron had kissed her fingers.

But this was absurd!

Yet what if certain magical forces were at work dictating the course of her life, of Evangeline's life? What if she was being called upon to render assistance in order to protect Evangeline from forming an alliance abhorrent to her? She knew perfectly well how she would feel in such a circumstance, that she'd rather tie a rock about her feet and jump into the River Thames than contract a marriage that could never be based upon love.

The more she thought on it, too, the more she became disgusted. Jasper Buxton was a local, wealthy cotton-spinning mill owner who had been grooming his son not to take charge of his business operations, but to rise in society through marriage. Theodore had been educated since birth in the finest institutions—Eton then Oxford—as well as with the best of tutors during the long summer months. To her knowledge, he had never been permitted to attend his father at the mill. When Mr. Buxton had bought his son a pair of colors and he became a lieutenant in Wellington's army, an inevitable future alliance with a Lady of Quality was as much as settled.

As for Lord Trent, Evangeline's father, his property was dear to him, perhaps dearer than his child. Undoubtedly he could make considerable use of an infusion of Trade wealth for improvements at Aldwark Manor. Emily felt it was no great stretch of the imagination to see that Lord Trent might have been swayed by Mr. Buxton to help push the alliance through.

"I can now understand your trepidation," Emily responded thoughtfully. "But what are you imagining has happened?"

"As to that," he said frowning slightly, "I fear I betray a confidence when I say that Mrs. Browne—who is connected to the theater, and who therefore enjoys a rather *broad* acquaintance—learned recently of a man and woman who were hired to remove a certain young Lady of Quality from her home until such a time as she capitulated in marrying a certain Tradesman's heir. They had left their small parts in a recent production at Drury Lane to travel north—*to Derbyshire.*"

Emily gasped.

"Just so," Mr. Peveril stated with a brisk nod of his head. He continued, "Mrs. Browne has no great opinion of either the man or his wife, and the coincidence of location seemed too specific to be ignored."

"Goodness!" she murmured, shocked. "Do you mean to tell me that you think Evangeline has been kidnapped?"

"Precisely."

"But it is all so barbaric, so unbelievable." She chewed on her lower lip for a moment, pondering the astonishing circumstances in which her cousin currently found herself. Yet, she was perplexed. "But why would any man go to such lengths to get his son married?"

"Mr. Buxton would not be the first toad-eater to steal his way into the gentry or the aristocracy," he suggested with a shrug of his shoulders.

Emily did not know why precisely, but she had the sense that something about the whole business did not ring true. Yet she was so far removed from Derbyshire, and any events that might be transpiring there, that she could hardly make a sound judgment one way or another.

She was not closely connected to her uncle, Lord Trent, and his Matford brood, though of course she had been at one time, delightfully so. Though she was cousin to Evangeline and to her older brother, Bertram Matford—who would one day inherit Aldwark Manor and his father's viscountcy—she no longer visited at the manor and had not for several years. Evangeline's mother, her own Aunt Sophia, had passed away many years ago. Lord Trent had remarried and his wife was not a congenial person. The Longcliffes had been unwelcome at Aldwark for over a decade.

Bertram, who she had not seen in as many years, had married Horatia Thornset and was now living in a snug property in Devonshire near Lord Kingsbridge's country mansion, known as Hollington Priory. Horatia Thornset, who Emily had never met, was sister to the present Lord Kingsbridge, the very man she had kissed last night.

Kingsbridge again! She shivered as though a spectre had just rushed through the chamber and touched her on the shoulder.

Oh, but what an absurdity to think it meant anything!

Bertram Matford was the logical connection in the entire business, she thought distractedly as she ran her thumb over the edges of the letters, flipping them absently. But he was too far away to be of any use.

"What do you wish me to do?" she asked suddenly, realizing that Mr. Peveril could not have written to her without at least having considered some course of action. "I mean, what do you think I ought to do?"

"I don't know," he said frankly. "But I have been thinking that if Lord Kingsbridge is still in town, he might have received some news from his sister, who I understand is married to Evangeline's brother."

Kingsbridge again! And so suddenly! Another spectre raced through the cell and again dragged icy fingers over her neck and shoulders.

"Are you chilled?" he asked, concerned, observing her shiver.

"No," she responded. "Not at all. I am merely overwhelmed by your news. As for Kingsbridge, it is so odd that you would mention him, for I met him for the first time last night."

"I would have supposed you to be well acquainted with Kingsbridge, given his connection with your cousins."

She shook her head. "I have seen Evangeline once in the past three years, and then not in Derbyshire. As for Bertram, I have only corresponded with him during the past decade, and that somewhat irregularly. His step-mother, Fanny Linton, was not interested in the Longcliffes. Once she contracted her marriage to Lord Trent, Evangeline's connections were dropped completely in favor of promoting the Lintons' interests."

"A common-enough occurrence, I suppose," he murmured.

"Yes, but quite unfortunate since I was very fond of Aunt Sophia—Evangeline's mama—and I regretted that I could no longer enjoy the extensive gardens at Aldwark."

"They are magnificent, aren't they?" he offered with a soft smile.

"Truly extraordinary," she responded. And the best trees in the world for climbing, she thought, sighing. Her gaze then dropped to the packet on her lap. As for Evangeline, whatever was she to do about the possibility of a kidnapping? "I suppose," she continued slowly, her heart picking up its cadence, "I had best seek an interview with Lord Kingsbridge."

"I believe that might be best given the circumstances," he returned quietly. "I only regret that I can be of so little assistance. I—I was very fond of Miss Matford. You will inform me of whatever it is you discover?"

"Yes, of course," she responded, rising from the bed. "May I keep these with me?"

He looked at the letters and a faint, remorseful line creased his brow. He took a deep breath and responded, "Yes, of course. Given the circumstances, that would be best."

Four

On the following morning, Emily stood at the foot of her four-poster bed, one hand planted on her hip and the other fingering the soft, purple velvet bed curtains as she surveyed the four gowns her abigail, Gwendolyn, had laid out for her.

She could not remember having experienced so much indecision in her entire existence. Ordinarily, she knew her mind to a nicety, but ever since she had awakened and realized that very soon she would be receiving a visit from Lord Kingsbridge, her mind and heart had known a disunity that had kept her undecided about everything—how she should fashion her hair, which jewels she ought to drape about her neck, wrist, fingers, and ears, whether she ought to wear a pretty lace cap, or astonish his lordship by sporting an ostrich feather before noon, and most particularly, which beautiful, summer gown she ought to don.

One part of her was determined to behave sensibly, demanding she wear a modest, unassuming gown in order to convey to Kingsbridge at the outset that she was disinterested in any manner of flirtation. On the other hand, there was another part of her—a quite wretched, hopeless part—which wanted to dress engagingly, the same part of her that had permitted Kingsbridge to continue kissing her the night of the masquerade, when at the very least she should have set up a caterwaul of protests!

Back and forth her mind wavered.

How many times in the course of the past hour alone had

she reprimanded this heedless, almost reckless inclination of hers, only to find herself still unable to resist the notion of wearing the most daring gown of all?

She approached the creation now and sighed deeply. She had been waiting for just the right event at which to dazzle the *haut ton* with Madame Matilde's extraordinary gown—a boat ride on the Thames, perhaps, or an excursion to Vauxhall Gardens. But nothing as yet had presented itself and, given the fact that summer was now fully upon London and daily the *beau monde* was seen to be leaving the Metropolis, she knew that if she waited much longer for the right opportunity to wear the gown, she would lose the moment entirely.

Then fashions would change, another year would pass, and the exquisite confection of cherry red silk and white muslin would grow *passé*. She ought to wear it now. Truly she should or the gown would simply disappear into her wardrobe never to be seen again.

What foolishness! She was merely attempting to justify her strong wish to sport the gown for Lord Kingsbridge with such silly reasonings!

She chewed on her lip. The creation was of a beautiful red silk undergown over which white muslin, trimmed along the edge of the bodice with a delicate red point lace, floated like a gossamer web. The hem of the muslin overdress was caught up in little billows of fabric and held in place by pretty red bows, exposing several inches of red ruffles about the hem of the silk underdress. The sleeves were puffed and the neckline enjoyed a daring *décolleté*. The overdress was clasped at the bosom with three red bows. The effect was charming, summery, and utterly tantalizing.

The other gowns on the bed were matronly and dull by contrast—a green sprig muslin round gown, a white cambric undergown topped with a white spencer trimmed with violet bindings, and a patterned Indian cotton dress of pale yellow and brown. All so very dull—or at least dull against the red and white muslin confection!

She glanced at Gwendolyn, who was watching her in astonishment. "Yes, yes, I know what you are thinking, that I ought to wear the modest yellow or the uninteresting green."

"I beg pardon, Miss, but I were thinking something else."

"And what would that be?" Emily queried, a little surprised.

"I hope I doan give offense, Miss, but I've nevuh seen ye so concerned 'bout pleasin' a gentleman afore."

Emily drew in a sharp breath. "Is that what I'm doing?" she asked.

A smile played upon Gwendolyn's lips. She was a pretty young woman with a gentle disposition, a round figure, and a round face dominated by large green eyes. She had an excellent ability to manage curling tongs and hairpins. She also had an unerring eye for fashion. Her judgment, on every score, generally proved sensible.

"I believe it is," Gwendolyn said, her gaze sympathetic. "Would ye object if I made a mite of a suggestion?"

Emily felt a rush of relief pour through her. "Yes, please do, for I am at a loss as to what to wear. Lord Kingsbridge is beyond fastidious in his tastes, for whatever else he might be that is abhorrent, I find that I am reluctant to appear like an unmarriageable dowd before him."

"I quite understand," Gwendolyn responded with a nod of her head as she, too, scrutinized the gowns, her gaze landing last on the red silk and white muslin *ensemble*. "But the cherry silk would be too *temptin'* for such a man, if I am not mistakin' the situation, would it not—the cut bein' as low as 'tis?"

"That it would."

"So, I wuz thinkin', Miss, that yer pretty white lace fichu, trimmed with the tiny silk ruffle, might win the day, so t'speak."

Emily pressed a hand to her bosom, sudden excitement rising in her breast. "Oh, it would indeed! And such a simple notion. I don't know why I didn't conceive of it before! Yes, yes, fetch the fichu." She glanced at the ormolu clock on the mantel. "Goodness, I have spent so long deliberating that we will hardly have time to dress my hair properly."

At that, both ladies began to race about the bedchamber, collecting quickly all that would be needed to complete Emily's toilette.

A half hour later, when a carriage was heard to stop in front of the town house, Emily was ready to greet his lordship. Her light brown hair was drawn up into a tidy chignon, but left bereft of all enticing ribbons, pearls, and feathers. She wore small ruby drops on her ears, an ivory cameo dangled from a gold chain about her neck, and red silk slippers adorned her small feet. She was utterly pleased with the result and knew instinctively that Lord Kingsbridge could not possibly find fault with her appearance today.

A few minutes more and she strolled easily into the crimson drawing room, fully aware that the chamber complemented her *ensemble* to a nicety.

Lord Kingsbridge was situated across the chamber, his elbow settled on the mantel over the fireplace and a booted foot poised on the edge of the red brick hearth. He was frowning into the empty grate, a finger stroking his chin in a thoughtful manner. In fact, he was so lost in thought that he did not immediately perceive her, which afforded her an excellent opportunity to observe him.

He was dressed to perfection, as always, his shirt points of a medium height and his white neckcloth arranged in the symmetrical folds known as *trone d'amour.* His hair was a dark brown and brushed forward at the temples *à la Brutus.* He wore an elegant coat of blue superfine, a silk waistcoat in alternating stripes of buff and white, and breeches of a fine soft doeskin that fit his muscular thighs snugly. His top boots were a glossy black and she wondered if he followed Beau Brummell's lead and used champagne in creating the glimmering appearance of the leather.

Within the confines of the darkened orangery, she had not been able to scrutinize his features. But now that he was so deeply entrenched within his own mind, she was able to do so.

She knew his eyes to be a fine hazel color, but presently was intrigued by their light gold-green appearance, a hue reflected in contrast to the red silk damask that covered the walls and most of the furniture. He wore neither side-whiskers nor a moustache. With a laugh she noticed the ear he was presenting to her was nicely formed. She had never paid the slightest attention to the shape of ears before, and the novelty of it made her giggle. Her amusement at her thoughts was having the beneficial effect of reducing her nervousness in meeting a man who had so thoroughly kissed her two nights before.

She was smiling fully when he suddenly caught sight of her and turned in her direction. He slid his boot off the bricks of the hearth and his elbow from the mantel. He was quite a handsome man, she realized with a start, something surely she had known before, yet had not quite assimilated. His skin was sun-bronzed—probably from his numerous excursions out-of-doors as a member of the Four-in-Hand Club. His brows were dark and arched nicely over expressive eyes. His nose was straight and his jawline firm and angled. His chin, however, seemed stubborn in its set, a fact which did not surprise her, given his determination to kiss her the night of the masquerade. A certain unwelcome yet quite excited fluttering of imagined butterflies began to dance in the center of her stomach.

In response to her, he smiled as well, but his smile was with perception and understanding. Were her butterflies so easily perceived then?

His smiled broadened as she reached him and offered her hand to him. He bowed over her fingers, then placed a warm, lingering kiss on her gloveless hand.

What a rogue, she thought, smiling inwardly.

"Good morning, my lord," she offered in what she hoped was a voice of indifference.

"Good morning, Miss Longcliffe," he returned. He released her hand but only after giving her fingers a significant squeeze. He glanced purposefully about the chamber. "Your companion is not present? Dare I hope, then, that the kiss we shared two nights past will be the first of many?"

"No, you may not dare to engage such a hope," she responded simply, refusing to take up his bedeviling line of thought. "But pray sit down, for I have not brought you to Upper Brook Street without a purpose. As it happens, I have a matter of some import to discuss with you." She took up a seat on a settee covered in a fine crimson silk situated nearest the fireplace, and gestured to a black lacquer Trafalgar chair opposite her. The chair was upholstered in a white silk damask.

He set aside the tails of his blue coat and sat down. A smile teased his lips. "A matter of some import?" he said. "I believe I understand you, but let me say at the outset that I never offer a *carte blanche* to a maiden."

If she was supposed to be shocked by his having said something to her of such an improper and risqué nature, she schooled her features to indifference. "I have no interest in becoming your mistress," she returned flatly, unwilling to even address the roguish suggestion.

She was pleased to see the quick dart of an eyebrow. She *had* surprised him.

"Ah," he murmured. "Then I am terribly confused. I am a man of some reputation, as you are most certainly aware, yet you invite me to your town house and greet me in a chamber in which neither a maid nor your companion are present? Besides, the kiss you gave me has led me to hope."

Emily thought it wise to address both his arguments. "Two nights ago I fear I was caught entirely unawares by a libertine, and I shall take great care that it doesn't happen again. As for the unchaperoned state of our interview today, I will only defend myself by saying that I wish no one—including my companion—to know the substance of our conversation."

He sighed and seemed to affect strong disappointment. He slipped a hand into his coat pocket and withdrew a letter folded into a tight package. "Are you perchance referring to the odd predicament in which Mr. Matford's sister now finds herself?"

He held up the missive. She stared at it, afterward her gaze sliding to his face. "You have heard from my cousin Bertram?" she asked, stunned.

He shook his head. "No, from Horatia."

"Your sister, then," she stated. So Mr. Peveril may not have been mistaken in his suspicions, as she had hoped.

He nodded. After a long silence, he said, "You have grown pale, Miss Longcliffe. You are not going to swoon, are you?"

"No, of course I am not," she returned impatiently. "But you have given me a shock. Initially, I had supposed, that is, I now believe that I had been hoping that the person who caused me some concern as to the whereabouts of my cousin had been suffering dark imaginings not based on fact, but only on his suspicions. If Mrs. Matford has received some intelligence to verify these suspicions, I find myself gravely disconcerted. What did she relate to you, or do you feel bound to keep her revelations private?"

"Not in the least," he said, referring to the confidentiality of his sister's letter. "As it happens—and here I must confess I find myself mystified by the odd nature of such a coincidence as this letter presents to me—Horatia begged me to search you out and to lay the particulars of her letter before you. The message, it would seem, has been sent through Horatia and me—to you."

He rose, crossed the small space between them, and offered the letter to her. Emily took the missive between her fingers, not surprised that her hand trembled in doing so, since her heart was now hammering unhappily against her ribs. Was it possible Evangeline had indeed been kidnapped? Kingsbridge bowed slightly, then turned to resume his seat.

Emily unfolded the letter slowly. She mentally noted that he had folded the missive eight times into a small square—so much like a man not to care in the least for the general beauty of a letter, but to compact it to suit his needs. It looked like a pillbox.

A thought struck her suddenly and she lifted her gaze to meet his squarely. "One thing first," she posed through narrowed lids. "Precisely when did you receive this correspondence from your sister?"

A wicked smile curled the edge of his lips. "The day of the masquerade."

She gasped. "Then you knew full well that you—that I—that we should undoubtedly meet again!" she cried.

He nodded, his lips twitching.

"Well!" she cried, huffing her astonishment as she lowered her gaze to the unfolded letter. Before she began to read, however, she promised herself that never again would she underestimate such a man as Kingsbridge had just proved himself to be. The wretched rogue!

Once the promise had been made, however, she quickly ran her gaze down line after line of the brief correspondence. Mrs. Matford's script was easily deciphered and quite beautifully scratched onto the fine vellum. The words, however, were less lovely, and confirmed Mr. Peveril's darkest worries. Evangeline, it would seem, had been compelled to become the *companion* of a tall dark man and a woman who wore a red wig, though whose real hair seemed to be blond, for her cousin had once caught sight of her unawares. Mr. Buxton had been making a strong push for a betrothal between his son, Major Buxton, and Evangeline. She had refused unwaveringly all the arguments and persuasions her father had used. Having remained steadfast in her purpose to the end, since she was in no manner in love with Major Buxton—in fact she even hinted her affections were engaged elsewhere—

she found herself roused in the middle of the night and taken to an unknown location in the company of two strangers, known to her as a mere Mr. and Mrs. Smithe, who would not let her out of their sight for even a moment. Her father had entrusted a letter with her captors, stating that when she had come to her senses she would be brought back to Derbyshire. Only by using the greatest care and waiting for precisely the right moment was she able to have a letter sent to Devonshire, in order to beg for help in her unhappy circumstances.

Emily's name was mentioned in the context of seeking that help, *Miss Matford would be forever indebted to you if you could contact some member of her family, on her mother's side, and beg for assistance. I would do so myself, but I am approaching my confinement and cannot possibly leave Devonshire. Miss Emily Longcliffe, residing in London, may be of use for, according to Miss Matford's missive, she was used to hold Evangeline in great affection. Miss Matford speaks of her as a bold female, which makes me think, dear Kingsbridge, that she is the very person needed. Besides, if my suspicions prove correct, you might even know a little pleasure in this situation, and for at least a particle of time you will be relieved from the tedium of your existence.*

These last words intrigued Emily, because they confirmed her own opinion of Kingsbridge as the sort of fellow who finds most everything about his life boring in the extreme. The final farewell intrigued her even more. *Do what you can, dearest brother. I am fond of the Matfords, more than I can say. The new Lady T. is an abominable creature and is probably glad to be rid of her stepdaughter. Bertram would lend his assistance, but I am afraid my own fears for my forthcoming labors have kept him pinned to my side. We are weekly in hopes of making you a proud uncle. Whatever you decide, please don't leave Albion's shores before you have kissed my babe.*

Mrs. Matford's signature was even prettier than her fair

copperplate and her farewell flowed with several tender affections for her *dearest pug*.

Emily bit her lip.

Dearest pug.

She lifted her gaze, wide-eyed, to Kingsbridge. "Pug?"
she queried.

He narrowed his eyes playfully. "If I ever hear of that pet
name being bandied about on anyone's lips other than my
sister's, I shall know precisely who I may call to book for
the gossip having gotten round."

Emily placed a hand at her bosom. "Oh, sir," she responded,
"I pale at the thought! Surely you do not believe that I would
be capable of such a transgression of confidence?"

He eyed her more narrowly still, crossing his arms meaningfully over his chest. "I don't know yet of what I believe
you capable." His gaze slid over the delicate fichu covering
her full bosom, the pretty bows holding the white muslin
clasped tightly over the red silk, and of the exposed red silk
ruffles at her ankles. He smiled suddenly, "Except excellence
in fashion. You clearly have a judicious eye."

She was pleased. He had given her a charming compliment,
one that might have turned her head except that she was too
sensible a female to permit a man of Kingsbridge's stamp to
do more than flatter her a little. Therefore, without anything
but a little regret, she turned to the strange matter at hand.

"So tell me, my lord, what is your opinion of your sister's
letter? I can't help but feel there is something strange about the
situation, especially with regard to my uncle. The whole—"

But before she could utter another word, voices were heard
in the entrance hall below. She turned her head to listen intently and, upon realizing who had come to call, she jumped
up from the settee, a hand to her cheek, and cried in a frightened whisper. "Dearest *Juno,* 'tis my odious sister Meg!"

Lord Kingsbridge, in response to her sudden agitation,
rose to his feet as well, a look of amused surprise on his

face. "Margaret is here?" he asked, in just such a manner as to cause Emily to turn sharply toward him.

She eyed him askance, then doubled back for a second, perusing the wicked smile on his face. "Kingsbridge!" she cried, wondering whether to be horrified or in awe of him in that moment. "Do you say—does your expression tell me—that you—*you* vaulted at least one of her castellated walls?"

"I stole a kiss from her at Vauxhall," he whispered teasingly. "Of course it was a long time ago."

"I don't believe you," she returned, dumbfounded. She heard her sister's footsteps on the stairs. "You must hide," she added quickly, gesturing to a door at the far end of the drawing room. "In the antechamber beyond." She gave him a playful push and he chose to follow her lead, hurrying in the direction of the door.

"Your sister Prudence was with her," he whispered over his shoulder. "She can verify that Lady Chaddeley was not entirely indifferent to my, er, attentions." When he reached the door, he added, "But won't your maid tell her that I am with you?"

"Only if she wishes to be dismissed."

"Ah," he said, opening the door and stepping across the threshold, "Very wise, very wicked, very foresightful. I begin to want to know more of you, Miss Longcliffe."

She scowled at him. "Do stubble it, Kingsbridge, and not a peep from you or, or—"

"Or what?"

"Or I'll think of something nasty, never you fear!"

"Oh, Miss, I pale at the thought," he returned, mocking her earlier remark.

She smiled and giggled, then closed the door hurriedly on his teasing face. She turned just in time to move quickly to the pianoforte, seat herself, open a piece of music, and pretend to be studying it just as Margaret strolled proudly into her drawing room.

Five

Emily looked up from the music, feigning an expression of surprise as the maid dipped a curtsy and announced the arrival of the formidable Lady Chaddeley.

"How do you go on, Meg?" she queried nervously, knowing full well that Margaret never called on her except to come the crab. "I was preparing to practice Bach fugue in F# just now," she said, glancing at the music and noticing it was upside down. "But I am always so happy to receive a visit from you." She rose abruptly from her seat, rounded the pianoforte, and stood waiting for her sister's first pronouncement.

Margaret was a little taller than Emily, but seemed to tower over her because of her proud bearing and the height at which she held her nose. She never failed to appear to Emily as one of the famous Amazon females come alive from mythology. Her pale blond hair was caught up in a tightly braided chignon, her blue eyes scrutinized the drawing room carefully—Emily rather thought her sister might be looking for dust—and her nostrils flared when her gaze returned to land with a jolt on Emily.

"Do sit down," Emily said brightly, leaving her place beside the pianoforte and moving toward the settee of red silk she had inhabited only moments earlier. She gestured for Margaret to follow her.

Margaret, however, had a different notion entirely, and swept toward the pianoforte in a stately, yet leisurely manner, tugging on the cuffs of the long sleeves of her elegant morning gown. Her gaze was again rotating in a scrutinizing pattern over everything, the various landscapes displayed on the walls, the music scattered haphazardly atop the pianoforte, the bronzed bust of Mozart placed in the corner opposite the doorway leading to the antechamber. She noticed the upside down music and, as though it was the most natural occurrence in the world, turned it right side up and began retracing her steps.

"What is going forward?" Margaret queried coolly as she advanced toward the fireplace. She seated herself in the chair his lordship had recently occupied and, with a careful tug here and a gentle pressing of her hand there, smoothed out the skirts of her gown of gray patterned silk. "And don't bother pitching the smallest portion of gammon, for you must remember that I have known you all your life. You tell whiskers abominably. And don't think I have not been fully informed of your, er, activities."

A faint half-smile touched her sister's austere lips, an expression Emily could not fail to construe as anything other than it was—a preamble to lecture and pontification.

Emily knew she must prevaricate, for it wouldn't do to tell her sister that Lord Kingsbridge was in the next chamber and that she was receiving him without benefit of a chaperone. "I will confess that I have been contemplating begging Lord Kingsbridge to call upon me," she said, choosing to tell a half-truth. "I was hoping I might have a good effect upon his character."

Margaret's face drew up into a sudden, tight frown.

"I knew you wouldn't approve," Emily said, giving her chin a purposeful lift.

"Not approve?" Margaret queried facetiously. "There are so many things wrong with asking Kingsbridge to call upon you that I hardly know where to begin, except by assuring you that you can have no effect on that libertine's character. You must instead protect yourself. You have already done sufficient damage to your currently threadbare reputation by having been observed flirting with him at the Scarswell masquerade. I cannot conceive why you would even consider jeopardizing the remains of your worn-out mantle of indiscretion by inviting him to Upper Brook Street. Which brings me to an even more incomprehensible subject—how was it possible that you permitted Lady Alison and her wretched mama to beguile you into attending such a masquerade? You must explain yourself to me, or I vow I shall instantly go off on a fit of apoplexy."

Emily felt a familiar rage begin to boil at the top of her stomach. She wanted to tell Margaret that she could please herself and blow out all the vessels of her brain if she was so disposed, but little would come of such a tactic except to bring forward pursed lips, a pinched nose, and flared nostrils. Meg's sermonizing would begin, and subsequent lectures would not end for a fortnight.

Besides, she knew Kingsbridge well enough to comprehend fully that he would not be in the least content to sit about her antechamber, kicking his heels while Lady Chaddeley prosed on and on.

She did the only sensible thing she could, therefore, and began to weep. She forced her lips to tremble and carefully controlled the onset of several quite pretty sobs. She pressed her hand to her mouth and her other hand to her stomach.

"It was very wrong of me," she murmured weakly. "I have been regretting the whole of it ever since I first crossed the threshold of Scarswell House."

She wiped away the tears that began to flow down her cheeks, first with her right hand, then her left hand. Two more infinitesimal sobs.

"I was never more mortified than when Kingsbridge began pursuing me. He is such a *terrible man,* almost as bad as that, that *odious* Byron who also cast out lures to me." She would have to do penance for these wicked lies. Well, at least part of what she said were lies, but Margaret wouldn't know the difference. "And then," she continued, noting with delight that her sister wore an utterly astonished expression, "Kingsbridge had the audacity to tell me the worst whisker of all—oh, Meg, it was horrid. A terrible abomination against, well, against our family. He is such a despicable man!"

With that, she threw herself facedown into the cushions of the settee and, with her shoulders and back shaking in such a manner as to make the great Sarah Siddons turn pea green with envy at so much dramatical talent, she entered into a series of heart-wrenching sobs.

She felt Margaret's presence before she actually knew her sister had left her chair and was now kneeling beside her couch of feigned misery.

Yes, her penance would have to be great indeed for this piece of mischief!

"There, there, Em," Margaret murmured soothingly, her hands gently upon her shoulders. Emily felt a kerchief being slipped over her right shoulder and she took it gratefully. Her sister's fragrance of delicate lavender was on her cheek as she began awkwardly swiping at her false tears.

Margaret continued, "I had no notion that I would find you so completely overset by your recent experience, and I certainly did not mean to give you further distress by coming to you this morning. I can see that you have repented your conduct—only, only what was this particular abomination that Lord Kingsbridge said to you? In what way did he malign our family?"

Emily was smiling into the soft dark red silk of the settee. Her ploy had worked to perfection, for clearly Margaret's attention was now fixed on what Kingsbridge had said rather than her own conduct in attending the masquerade.

Schooling her features, however, she turned toward Margaret and saw that her sister wore an expression of deep concern—almost of fear.

Sobbing twice more and blowing her nose soundly, she

said, "Well, it really wasn't against our family, precisely, rather, it was about you. But I didn't believe him for a second." She sobbed again and noted from over the top of the lavender-scented kerchief as she held the wisp of cambric and lace up to her nose, that her sister's complexion had paled ominously.

"He told you something about me?" she queried in a voice that faded with each word she spoke.

"Yes," she replied, nodding and blowing her nose. "Kingsbridge told me he had kissed you once and that you had taken great delight in being accosted in such a rough, out-of-hand manner, and that Pru had watched the whole of it!"

Margaret blinked three times rapidly in succession, her cheeks turned pink, and her mouth fell slightly agape. For the briefest moment, a certain distant light, full of memories, entered her eye.

Emily felt as though she was being given a glimpse into her eldest sister's soul. She drew in her breath sharply, but hid her surprise behind her kerchief, for even though she understood that Margaret's mortification was acute, there was something more in her reaction than just embarrassment.

So, Meg had enjoyed being kissed!

Well! Well! Who would have thought!

Emily pressed her with the information. "Wasn't that just wicked of him to have said something so ignoble of you? Especially you, for I vow, Margaret, you are the most virtuous female I have ever known."

All right, so she couldn't help but punish her sister a little.

"You mustn't pay the least heed to the ramblings of a man of Kingsbridge's stamp," Margaret returned, composing herself quickly. She rose from her knees and crossed the room carefully to take up her seat again.

"Of course I won't," Emily assured her sister firmly. But giving her voice an extra push in order to make certain Kingsbridge could hear her, she added, "The truth is, I found his lordship to be a perfect idiot, a braggart, a sore excuse for a gentleman, a poor dancer, and a lagging conversationalist. In fact, I thought him stupid."

A loud crash was heard from the antechamber and Emily bit her lip.

Margaret jumped in her seat. "Goodness!" she cried. "What was that?"

"Well 'pon my soul!" Emily cried. "That must be the new maid Mrs. Monroe hired only a sennight past. She has already broken a clock in my bedchamber, and downstairs she dropped one of my favorite vases on the entrance floor tile. I believe I am going to have to dismiss her, for she is the clumsiest female I have ever known."

"Yes, I would suggest you do so immediately," Margaret agreed. "Perhaps you ought to tend to the business now?"

Emily bit her lip. Her sister seemed so utterly hopeful of the event and so wishful to leave, that only with the strongest effort could she keep from smiling. Evidently, the subject of Kingsbridge's kiss was a little more than Margaret could bear and still sustain her queenly, self-righteous dignity.

"I believe you are right," Emily said, rising from the settee. She then wiped her cheeks one final time and began the process of easing her sister from her house. "As for Kingsbridge, I now see I must avoid all social intercourse with him. How happy I am that you came to help me adjust my purposes. I won't even consider his attending me here in Upper Brook Street. What an imbecile I was to think for even a moment that I could have a good effect on his character. You have shown me that I must do all I can to protect myself from both his advances and the hateful attentions I would call down upon my head, simply by my association with him."

Margaret had thoroughly regained her countenance and rose from her seat with a satisfied expression on her face. Clearly she believed she had accomplished her purpose. Emily began walking slowly toward the doors of the drawing room and saw to her delight that her sister did not hesitate to follow her. How odd to think that Margaret, the regal, self-composed Lady Chaddeley, could be so easily managed.

Well! Well! She had learned at least one significant lesson today.

Margaret spoke hesitantly, her voice lowered considerably, "As for anything Kingsbridge might have said to you where I am concerned—"

"He is a liar, Meg. You needn't reproach me further on that score. You have shown me the error of my thinking where he is concerned. I promise you." She then smiled sweetly on her sister and escorted her down the stairs and to the front door, where a hackney was awaiting her. "Are you returning to Staffordshire with Chaddeley?"

Meg shook her head as she began drawing on her gloves. A beautiful July sunshine poured down upon the lovely Mayfair street and the rumble of carriages, gigs, and coaches on the cobbles was a pleasant counterpoint to the whinnying of her horses, which were ready to be going.

"No," Margaret said. "As it happens, you will never guess who has invited us to enjoy a sennight's leisure in the country."

Emily could imagine several well-connected personages who would be more than happy to have the prestigious Chaddeleys call upon them. "Who?" she asked, aware that Margaret was pleased with the invitation.

"Bertram," she said simply.

Emily caught sight of an odd expression in her sister's eye, of affection and true delight.

"Our cousin?" she asked.

"Yes, isn't it marvelous? I know that his wife—and how odd that she is Kingsbridge's sister, when we were just speaking of him—is approaching her confinement, but not for a month or more yet. I believe he wishes a lady of some experience nearby during these last weeks. I understand that Mrs. Matford has been in the sullens a bit." Margaret had herself been delivered safely of seven children.

"Bert was always a favorite of ours, wasn't he?" Emily queried, a sensation very much like affection rising in her breast toward her sister.

"Yes," she said, "though he was of an age with you, I still always felt as though I understood him as I believe he did me. Odd, isn't it?"

Emily tilted her head and queried. "Have you perchance received any recent tidings from him, oh, of his wife's progress or his own delights in the Devonshire landscape?"

"Only a missive about three weeks past, indicating how much he was looking forward to the visit."

Emily was relieved. She didn't want Meg informed of even the smallest mite of Evangeline's predicament. "Are you taking the children?"

She shook her head. "My attention will be all for Horatia. Well, I will say goodbye then, Emily. Again, I am sorry if I caused you too much distress."

"You did not," she assured her honestly, but added, "You merely confirmed my own convictions." Yes, a number of penances were most certainly in order.

Meg embraced her briefly and then climbed aboard the hackney. "I shall see you at Christmastide, then."

"Indeed," Emily murmured as the coachman gave the horses a brisk slap of the reins. All the Longcliffe sisters met at Ockbrook Hall, Margaret's home, for the holidays. She sighed as she watched the hackney slip round the corner.

For the first time in many years—perhaps because Kingsbridge's revelation had confounded Margaret—Emily felt a true affection for her sister. She saw her, for these precious few seconds, as possessing a genuine and even passionate heart. She held onto the sentiment for a long time as she remained standing on the sidewalk, the July sun warm on her face and shoulders. She wanted to think of Margaret this way, of being not just a sister to her, but also a flesh-and-blood woman.

The sensation, however, could not last, not with any of a

thousand memories soon rising to torture her. She would never be on an equal footing with any of her siblings. She was the youngest, she would always be viewed as an infant, and her sisters must always take an instructing role with her.

She didn't despise them for it, because she was convinced of their true affection and devotion to her. But frequently their kindly meant interventions in her life and thoughts felt more like manipulation than love.

The truth of her situation with her family was that when she actually reached Ockbrook in December, each of her sisters would begin their campaign against her unwedded state. They would insist she was letting her best childbearing years escape her, and why wouldn't they say such things, for Margaret had seven children, Prudence was in possession of eight babes, and dear Fanny was increasing with her tenth, having given birth to two sets of twins among the others in the seven brief years of her marriage!

The Longcliffes were, if nothing else, a fertile clan.

She did not begrudge her sisters their chosen paths, however, she knew that never in a million years would they understand her own desires and longings. Never!

On that note, she turned on her heel and reentered her town house.

She laughed suddenly at all she had just done to poor, unawares, self-congratulatory Meg.

And to Kingsbridge, too!

"Oh, dear," she murmured, as she ascended the stairs. She knew full well he had heard her indictments of his character, and that he had undoubtedly been the source of the loud crash in the antechamber. What would she find when she returned to him?

She strongly suspected he would be in the devil's own temper! And if not, she knew full well he had a number of modes by which he could torture her for her slanderous words.

Six

"What a baggage you are!" Kingsbridge cried as Emily entered the drawing room. "And quite pleased with yourself if I do not much mistake the sparkle in your eye."

Emily scrutinized his expression for a long moment and was grateful to find that he was not on his high ropes after all.

"More than you will ever know or imagine," she responded with a proud lift of her chin and turn of her shoulders. She held his gaze, silently reading each feature and trying to see into his mind. "I wish you to know," she added, her lips quivering with amusement, "that though I spoke so disparagingly of you earlier, I find myself in profound admiration of your most evident yet peculiar talent."

He frowned slightly, and she could see that he was uncertain as to her meaning. "And what would that be?"

"When I saw the look—a deep, guilty glint—in Meg's blue eyes as she was reviewing her memory of your assault on her at Vauxhall, I became awestruck with your abilities! For the barest second a kind of fond regret rippled across her face. If you could reach even my sister's heart—"

She left the rest to his imagination until he chuckled. He did not believe her.

"Kingsbridge," she said insistently. "You don't know my sister, else you would comprehend the grandness of my compliment."

He did not seem as pleased as she thought he ought to be.

"Thank you—I think," he returned, eyeing her askance, "but I do not wish for you to think, even for a moment, that I am at all appeased. Lady Chaddeley may be susceptible to your theatrics and fulsome compliments, but I am not. You spoke harshly of me—and at just such a time as I was performing a favor for you. You owe me at the very least an apology."

For the second time in scarcely fifteen minutes, she was dumbfounded. First by the fact that her stoic eldest sister could actually have been enchanted at one time by a man such as Kingsbridge, and now by the fact that she actually saw hurt in the eyes of the man before her.

She grew very quiet and let out a deep sigh. She could not help but feel repentant. She had used him ill. She might be a bit of a baggage, but she did not have a mean heart. "I am sorry," she said softly. "I said several things I oughtn't to have said, especially when you were not only so kind as to remain hidden so that I might not have to bear the brunt of my sister's tirades for the next three years, but also because you have so kindly attended me today in order that I might find a way of lending assistance to my cousin. I'm very sorry. Will you forgive me?"

"That is much better," he said, almost like a schoolmaster. He moved back to the hearth where she had first seen him upon entering the drawing room initially. He brooded for a moment, then his lips twitched.

She gasped and could not help but cry out, "Why, you *devil!* For the barest moment I had supposed—I had believed I had wounded your sensibilities. Now I can see you were only shamming it."

He grinned broadly. "Well, I had to bring you down a peg or two. Good god, you were preening like a peacock when you walked in. Though I must admit you had something of a right to your self-congratulations. I've never heard such an abundance of tears without cause before! And your little sobs—I vow for a moment even I was affected!"

"The deuce you were," she retorted, strolling toward him, her hands behind her back. That funny feeling in the pit of her stomach was returning to her, of excitement, of enchantment, of growing interest. Kingsbridge intrigued her and the fact was, she was enjoying his silliness.

He smiled, a soft light in his marvelous hazel eyes. "Do you know, that just for a moment, you sounded like your cousin Bertram."

"We grew up together," she confessed. "Bert and I were always in scrapes. He was the brother I never had."

"Three sisters, eh?"

She nodded. "And I had become their mission. I can recite you a dozen strictures alone on the value of economies in housekeeping. Do you wish to hear them? Or some of them, or one of them?"

He chuckled. "Not today."

A warm silence fell between them. He had for a few minutes been her companion in mischief, and a kind of intimacy had risen up between them. After a moment, she turned and took up her seat on the crimson settee once more.

Goodness! She had nearly forgotten her initial reason for asking him to Upper Brook Street in the first place. Without looking at him, she said, "I suppose I ought now to address my cousin's current predicament and why I asked you to see me."

She glanced at him and saw that he was watching her thoughtfully. "Yes, I suppose so," he said.

He wore a curious expression, as though he were trying to understand her more completely. Or maybe he was just bored. She couldn't tell.

Taking a deep breath, she carefully revealed the whole of her conversation with Marcus Peveril, noting in particular the many ways Mr. Peveril's recital dovetailed with Horatia's letter. He frowned slightly as she mentioned that a certain Mrs. Browne knew of an actress and actor who had recently quit the Drury Lane Theater ostensibly having been hired to remove a young Lady of Quality from her home until she agreed to marry a certain unnamed Tradesman's heir.

He regarded her intently as she finished her history. "Everything you've said has confirmed my sister's letter. But I am curious about this pair from Drury Lane. You believe there is a connection?"

She nodded. "They must be the very ones Evangeline wrote of in her letter."

"Perhaps."

"But tell me, what is your opinion of this strange kidnapping?"

He shook his head. "I don't know. I've never heard of any *gentleman* resorting to such desperate stratagems to get his daughter married."

"Exactly what I was thinking. There seems to be something havey-cavey about this situation."

She saw a faint smile on his lips and a warmth blossomed on her cheeks. She had spoken a cant expression that Bertram had frequently used, but one which a young lady of quality did not necessarily employ in conversation.

Setting aside her blushes, however, she watched Kingsbridge carefully for a long moment. She thought of his roguish reputation and marvelled that he was speaking so sensibly and calmly about Evangeline's bizarre circumstances. She recalled the kiss at the masquerade and balanced his amorous assault against the rather composed creature he currently appeared to be. He seemed like two different people, yet the same. The truth was she had never known anyone like him before.

Perhaps for these reasons she suddenly blurted out, "I was wondering if you would lend me your assistance by accompanying me to Aldwark?"

He blinked and stared at her, utterly speechless. "To Derbyshire?" he asked, stunned.

She nodded in response.

For a long moment, he again didn't speak, but continued

to regard her as though she'd gone mad. "You can't be serious," he cried at last. Clearly, he believed she was as mad as Bedlam. "Miss Longcliffe," he continued in a stern manner, much like a father reproving his hopelessly addled child. "Did you not hear a word of your sister's advice? Your reputation would be shattered were it known that we were travelling together, no matter how noble the purpose. Have you no sense about you? It is no wonder then that your sisters were forever attempting to instruct you."

At that Emily rose from her seat and moved slowly to the windows overlooking the street. A fine muslin underdrape allowed the sunshine to pour in a delicate warmth through the gauzy weave of the fabric. Beside each of two windows facing south, matching dark red damask draperies hung in bold contrast to the light muslin. She ran her fingers down the smooth fabric and sighed. "You are right of course," she said quietly. "It would be most nonsensical to travel together."

But I vow I am sick to death of being sensible and wise and always proper, she thought morosely.

"I am glad to hear it," he responded quietly. "So, I will tell you what I am willing to do for you, given the circumstances. I shall go to Drury Lane and speak with Byron, who is well known among the actors and actresses there. He will have a greater knowledge of the man and woman you have described. Certainly, he will know their names, since I would suppose *Smithe* is a false one, and perhaps their reputations, which in turn might further elucidate your cousin's plight."

She then turned to him. "Are you acquainted with Mrs. Browne?" she queried.

The fact that his expression grew very still spoke volumes, though she was not entirely certain of the nature within the covers of those tomes. "Yes," he offered carefully. "A widow who enjoys a certain amount of attention from the very highest circles . . ."

"She spoke the Regent's name in her conversation with Mr. Peveril."

"Ah," he said, the look in his eye still guarded.

"A Cyprian?" she queried.

"You are bold," he said, frowning slightly, but not necessarily in disapproval.

"I only venture to discuss her because I have cause to believe that my cousin, Evangeline, is in love with Mr. Peveril."

She watched him shift his boot on the hearth ever so slightly, as though an eggshell had just crunched beneath it. "Are you saying you have no great opinion of Mr. Peveril?" she pressed.

He was weighing the whole conversation in his mind. She could see as much, and for that reason waited patiently for his response. When at last he spoke, his words were brief and to the point. "Your cousin would be wise to break her connection with Mr. Peveril. He is young, he does not show the greatest sense in the world—otherwise he would not be in jail—and his heart is quixotic at best."

She could not help but smile a little. "For a man supposed to be a rakehell, you certainly can speak like a prig."

He smiled and chuckled. "And you, Miss, for a Lady of Quality, have broken more rules with me than I care to enumerate. You do not disapprove of Mr. Peveril or his conduct?"

"I disapprove very much, except of course in his wish to help my cousin. But I did not expect a man of your habits and inclinations to disapprove of Mr. Peveril."

"Would you be shocked now to discover how deeply you offend me?"

"Very."

"Perhaps I deserved that, then. As for accompanying you to Derbyshire, the answer must be, unequivocally, no. I will only add that given all the information which has presented itself, through Mr. Peveril as well as through Horatia, I hold some reservations as to the nature of this kidnapping. Mr. Buxton can't possibly believe he can coerce a young lady who is past her majority into a marriage she clearly abhors. Something is amiss with the whole of it . . . something un-revealed as yet."

At that she left her post by the window and returned to stand near him by the hearth. "Do you know, that was my very thought once I left Newgate—that all was not right, which only strengthens my wish to be of use to Evangeline in whatever way I can. Thank you, Lord Kingsbridge, for attending me today, and I will thank you in advance for any assistance you can lend me in seeking out Lord Byron's knowledge of these people who appear to be involved."

She extended her hand to him, and he, as before, slid his foot off the hearth, then closed the small space between them to take her hand in his. She was not surprised when he lifted her hand to his lips and placed another lingering kiss on her fingers.

The butterflies, the enchantment, the excitement she had known earlier and on the night of the masquerade, returned in full force as his gaze met hers over the curve of her fingers. His lips parted as though he wanted to say something to her.

"What is it?" she murmured.

He held tightly to her hand as a small frown became fixed between his brows. He seemed to be deliberating just what it was he wanted to say.

"Oh, the devil take it!" he muttered, at last. The next moment he had drawn her swiftly into his arms and his mouth was again slanted over hers in a demanding kiss that sent her butterflies roaring upward in a dizzy, spiraling flight. Up and up they soared, causing her mind to lose all bearings. She was flying now as his lips began a firm, purposeful search. She parted her lips and, as before, his tongue became a melody against her own, increasing the tempo of her ascent.

She heard an odd murmuring and only after a long moment realized that the sound was coming from her own throat in a long series of dovelike coos. And how had it come about that her arms were now fixed so firmly about his neck?

After a tense moment, he drew back from her, but she could not quite bring herself to release his neck. He held her arms tightly, as though also unwilling to end the embrace. His eyes searched hers hungrily, yet warily. "You play with too much fire, Miss," he said hoarsely.

"You kiss like heaven, Kingsbridge. I vow I would follow you to the ends of the earth, just to know such kissing every day."

He laughed and chuckled and smiled as though delighted and disbelieving all at once. "And I should take you with me if I thought for a moment that there truly was even a night of eternal happiness destined for us. But there isn't, my fiery one."

"No, of course there isn't," she agreed. She wanted him to kiss her again anyway, but instead he began pulling her arms from about his neck and returning them to her sides.

"I must go now," he said, a little unsteadily.

She nodded. "Yes, that would be wise, best, and sensible."

Oh, why did sudden tears spring to her eyes?

He turned away from her and her throat grew constricted with even more tears. She was stunned by how she was feeling as though in letting him go, she was losing something of infinite yet incomprehensible value.

The fading of his footsteps across the blue and red Aubusson carpet told her that he was nearly to the door. Suddenly she turned toward him and called out, "Kingsbridge."

He paused, then turned, but only to look back at her.

"You must come to Derbyshire," she said. "You must. I feel it in my bones that you are meant to come."

He gave his head a long, determined shake. "Too much fire, Miss Longcliffe."

And then he was gone.

Seven

Just past noon, Lord Kingsbridge found Byron at the Drury Lane Theater, sitting several rows back from the stage and observing the rehearsal of *The Merchant of Venice*. Edmund Kean, an actor of extraordinary abilities, was at present pacing briskly about the stage, evidently working through the coordination of his movements and his lines in the role of Shylock. He was a gifted actor whose performances Byron described as *Reading Shakespeare by flashes of lightning*.

Kingsbridge seated himself one row behind the poet and flung his arms over the row of seats in front of him. After exchanging greetings with Byron he laid his concerns before him in a series of quiet whispers, relating most of his singular conversation with Emily—including details of his sister's letter—and the odd circumstances in which her cousin Evangeline now found herself. But once this information had been broached, Byron eyed him curiously and begged to know if he was tumbling in love with Miss Longcliffe.

"I don't know," he whispered. "She intrigues me, but—good god!—she is, after all, a Longcliffe."

Byron laughed softly. "Then she's not for you, old fellow," he murmured. "She might have allowed a kiss or two—but then in my experience even the most innocent of them will, when properly cajoled—but in the darkest part of her heart she will become like *Lady* Chaddeley or *Lady* Broughton or *Lady* Mickelover." Emily's three elder sisters had each gotten a handle to her name through marriage.

"I know," he murmured, glancing up at the stage in front of him. "Damme, don't I know."

"She would not be the first to pursue you in order to enjoy the privileges of rank in wedding you, or even to outdo her siblings."

Kingsbridge responded in a low voice, "But she didn't strike me as giving a fig for that sort of thing. If she had, she would have married at least three lords before me."

"Yes, but not a *marquess*," Byron whispered pointedly. "Even Lady Chaddeley, the eldest of the brood, is only a countess."

"You are a cynical one," he stated with a half-smile. He heard Lord Byron sigh. He had been often enough in the poet's company to have come to understand him a little. For a man so young, he was already world-weary. Though he was known to have enjoyed a long sojourn in the Mediterranean and Albania, he never spoke of these places with so much sadness as of his current connections in England. Byron had told him recently that his only true contentment was to be found at Six Mile Bottom, where his half sister, August Leigh, resided.

"Then go to Derbyshire," the poet said, continuing their conversation about Emily, "if you doubt my perceptions. Perhaps Miss Longcliffe is different, but how rare that would be."

"Indeed," Kingsbridge said, sighing deeply.

Byron turned to look at him, holding his gaze firmly. "You are smitten," he stated baldly. "Damme, who would have thought! Kingsbridge snagged by a Longcliffe! Now there's an irony for you. I had laid odds with Davies only recently that some scandal would send you abroad before ever Cupid could strike deeply enough to keep you fixed here in this tight, little island."

"I have not said I intend to marry the chit!" he cried, leaning back in his seat. His strong voice however carried to the footlamps and brought the actors on the stage turning to eye the intruders with hostility.

After a long moment, when Kean was once again pacing the stage, his lines held gripped in his hand, Byron turned around and pressed him. "But you are interested in the possibility," he whispered. "You must at least admit that much true."

"Perhaps. Maybe. All right, yes. She has something unusual to offer . . . a playfulness, and at times I have observed a longing in her eye . . ."

"Amore."

He shook his head. "No, not a longing for love. Something else. I felt love, passion in her kisses, but in her eye was something more. She begged me to attend her to Derbyshire, but not because of love and that, my good fellow, is why I am finding I want to go."

Byron shook his head, a wry smile on his lips. "If you go, it will be a lamb to the slaughter, mark my words."

Kean's voice suddenly rose to a brilliant height as he delivered, quite strangely, part of one of Romeo's speeches.

> "By Love, that first did prompt me to inquire:
> He lent me Counsel and I lent him Eyes.
> I am no Pilot, yet wert thou as far
> As that vast Shore wash'd with the farthest Sea,
> I should adventure for such Merchandise."

Byron chuckled and whispered to Kingsbridge, "Is this your answer, delivered by the Fates? We are rehearsing *The Merchant of Venice,* yet he speaks the words of Romeo. Or does Mr. Kean discern your indecision?"

"Miss Longcliffe said it was my Fate."

Again Byron chuckled. "She has already entrapped you within her silken web, my friend. I have only now to wish you Godspeed."

Kingsbridge felt the decision deeply within him and was

stunned by it. At three and thirty he had long believed himself impervious to such romantic enticements, and certainly one coming from a Lady of Quality who was most definitely still a maiden. She might have great fire in her kisses, but he sensed she was a complete innocent. Yet, here he was, about to act against all sense and all reason, like a stripling not yet out of his salad days. He sighed, bemused. "I suppose I must go then," he said, shaking his head as one stupefied.

With his mind settled, he then posed the question Emily had suggested to him. "Mrs. Browne told Mr. Peveril that an actor and actress left Drury Lane—on a summons to perform some service in Derbyshire. She believed there was a connection between the kidnapping and their departure."

"Mrs. Browne, eh?" Byron said, narrowing his eyes. "What mischief is she brewing, I wonder."

"I believe she was merely gabble-mongering, one of her favorite pastimes. But do you think there might be some truth to the matter? Do you have any particular knowledge of a tall dark man and a woman who prefers to wear a red wig? Horatia's letter referred to them as Mr. and Mrs. Smithe."

"If I do not much mistake the matter, you have described the Glossips—Harold and Maria. He is tall, adequate in his way as an actor, but not much liked. Twice he has been accused of cheating at whist or faro, I do not remember which. Mrs. Glossip flirted with me once, but I found her hard and cruel." He paused for a long moment, his gaze fixed to the stage.

Kingsbridge knew he was pondering the characters of each and once again he leaned forward across the back of the seats in front of him, waiting.

Byron whispered. "I am recalling now that there was some unfortunate gossip about Harold, something that doesn't quite come to mind, but it was unpleasant. Something about that famous crime of some time past—do you remember the murder involving a Mr. Hunt?"

"Only vaguely. Something about a man being buried alive in a ditch, or something."

"The very one."

"Are you suggesting Mr. Glossip is somehow connected to these men?"

"Perhaps, if only I could recall the particulars. Oh, yes, now I remember. It was rumored that he had visited the murderer in prison."

Kingsbridge felt as though a door had just opened and a cold, wintry gust of wind had blown across the back of his neck. A series of chills snaked down his spine, and he again leaned back in his seat. If this reading of Harold Glossip's character was true, then Miss Matford might be in more trouble than at first would be presumed.

Was theirs a double-game? Even Emily had felt all was not as it should be, and she was on her way to Derbyshire to discover for herself what had actually happened to Evangeline.

"I believe it is time I harnessed the bays to my curricle."

"Yes, I daresay it is," his friend murmured. "And perhaps procure a Special License along the way."

"You are a damned fellow, *my lord*," Kingsbridge responded, chuckling.

"And you delude yourself, *my lord*. Only tell me this, if love awaits you in Derbyshire, do you intend to sell your newly refurbished East Indiaman?"

Kingsbridge was stunned, not by the question, but by the fact that he had forgotten all about his ship, which was now awaiting him in Falmouth. For three years he had been planning his journey and except for the final provisionings of the vessel which would require two or three more weeks, all was in readiness.

Yet here he was, prepared to make a cake of himself by chasing a female to Derbyshire on what might just be an absurd wild goose chase, and his ship was waiting for him in the south.

At the very least, he ought to be sensible and simply send her word regarding the Glossips.

"There you see," Byron murmured. "In the end, we are always ruled by our hearts, rather than our heads. In the end, we are all *damned fellows.*"

Emily stared at the landlord of the Swan Inn and could not credit what he was saying to her. She had arrived at a village west of Milton Keynes which was in possession of two inns, in which the Swan was decidedly the better facility. "I don't understand you, my good man. The inn you are suggesting I remove myself to is quite inferior. I passed it before proceeding here. You cannot mean to suggest that your rooms are full, for I will not believe it. When I drew into the yard, there was only one other conveyance present—a curricle."

The landlord, a short man with balding black hair, a pointed, aquiline nose, and thick lips, folded his arms over his chest. He lifted a brow. "You've not even a maid with you, and that to me, Miss, means a great deal—in particular that they've accommodations at the George, whereas we do not."

Emily felt her cheeks burn at his insinuations. She had never been so livid in her entire existence. "But it is as I have said. My maid will be along directly, perhaps in two or three hours since she is frequently carriage sick and must travel in easy stages, while I am of such a constitution that to travel slowly sets my teeth on edge."

He narrowed his gray eyes at her. He was clearly unmoved. "The George will have a room fer ye. Good night, miss."

She was about to remonstrate quite heatedly with the landlord of the inn, when a masculine voice intruded. "Good god, Horatia, leave the man in peace and attend to me. Mama and Papa are mad as fire that you left London when you did."

Emily whirled around and found herself staring in astonishment at Kingsbridge, who had emerged from a private parlor of the inn and who was holding a glass of what appeared to be a fine sherry in his hand. "Kingsbridge!" she called out. "What are you doing here? You said you weren't coming!"

"And you lied to me, and to Mother and Father." His expression was cold and hostile. Emily wasn't certain what he meant by it, precisely, but she understood enough to remain mute for at least the next few minutes until she could follow his lead more precisely.

She glanced back at the landlord, whose expression was now bemused as he narrowed his eyes at Kingsbridge.

"Do ye know this lady?" he asked.

"M'sister. Wouldn't you know it?" He strolled down the hall and brushed past Emily to address the landlord in a whisper.

The landlord eyed Emily and the marquess several times as though trying to determine just what manner of whiskers were being told to him. But when Kingsbridge drew a sovereign from the pocket of his waistcoat, the landlord's suspicions faded entirely and a rather rapt expression overtook his face. He bowed to Kingsbridge and ambled toward the kitchens.

Only then did Kingsbridge turn to address her. "Mama was in hysterics when I left her," he stated harshly, taking her up by the arm.

Emily now knew precisely what to do. "Oh, don't touch me, you beast. I've always detested you and now you've shown your true colors. Papa always favored you and treated me as though I was a dormouse, and Mama—well I'm sick to death of her hysterics and faintings and I won't do what she says anymore."

By the end of her speech, which she hoped was broad enough to encompass whatever whiskers he had told the landlord, she was passing across the threshold of a lovely private parlor. "Oh, but how delightful," she said, her tone altering suddenly as Kingsbridge shut the door behind him.

"Yes," he murmured. "Now it is."

Emily shot a surprised glance toward him and frowned him down. "If you begin immediately flirting with me, what will you do tomorrow?"

"I shall think of something," he responded, a wry smile on his lips.

"You are incorrigible, aren't you?"

He nodded and his smile deepened.

Emily's heart began to flutter about in a pleasant way. "So," she mused, "am I to infer by your presence here that you are inclined to help me after all?"

"Yes," he responded. "Byron gave me certain information which led me to believe that the Smithes—otherwise known as Harold and Maria Glossip—may not be as innocent as my sister's letter would indicate. Mr. Glossip, for instance, seems to be something of an unsavory character. At the very least, I thought to come in order to warn you to be careful in your dealings with them, should you cross their path."

"Oh," Emily murmured, slightly taken aback. "Does Byron know them, then?"

"Only by reputation."

"I see. Then I do thank you for coming."

He smiled crookedly. "I ought also to warn you that I did not come merely to tell you as much."

Emily untied the ribbons of her poke bonnet of light blue silk, but did not remove it from her head. Her curls were undoubtedly sadly flat and she would not for the world appear with a creased coiffure before Lord Kingsbridge. "Do you mean to say, then, that you came for me?" she queried, drawing off her gloves of a soft, yellow kid.

"In part," he murmured. He took a sip of the sherry, his warm hazel eyes meeting her gaze over the rim of his glass.

Emily felt her heart turn over in her breast. She stopped mid-tug on the index finger of her left hand. "Indeed?" she murmured. "Kingsbridge, I hope you don't think—I mean, I am not disposed to tumbling in love. In fact, I've—I've never been in love to my recollection, except with Bertram when I was nine. We were used to play in the orchards together at Aldwark when we were young." She chuckled and continued drawing off her gloves "Knights and ladies, of course. We had more tournaments and jousts and feasts than you can imagine, though we rode on the backs of our dogs— you know, not sitting on them, but poised over them while walking when they walked. Lord Trent would never have permitted us the use of his cover hacks. Bert's favorite game, however, was Henry VIII." By now her gloves were off her hands and she clapped them together. "I have been decapitated more times than you can imagine. What do you think of that?"

She chuckled, but heard no answering laugh from Kingsbridge. She thought perhaps she had revealed too much to him and that of the moment he held her in some disgust, especially since there was an odd light in his eye as she met his gaze.

An awkward silence followed and she felt wretchedly uneasy. When he remained mute as he continued to stare at her, she couldn't help but press him as to why. "Have I offended you?" she asked, turning more fully toward him.

"What?" he responded, frowning slightly as his gaze descended to her lips, then roved her cheeks, her forehead, her nose, and her eyes. Whatever was the matter with him?

"I said, *have I offended you?*"

"Offended me?" he asked, as though not comprehending her question.

"Yes, you have a very odd look on your face and I wondered if when I spoke of decapitations if perhaps I hadn't somehow caused you distress and perhaps offended your sense of propriety and decorum."

At that, he burst out laughing and continued to laugh as he crossed behind her and settled his empty glass of sherry on a table to her left. "No, you've not offended me," he said, taking her by the arm and drawing her toward the fireplace, near which were settled two comfortable, winged chairs of a dark forest green leather. "It is just that I have never known a female like you, to speak so forthrightly and so affectionately of her childhood games."

Emily sat down on the chair to the left.

"Would you like some sherry?" he asked congenially.

"Yes, thank you, that would be lovely."

She watched him retrace his steps and noted again how well he carried himself. His shoulders were quite broad and his legs were nicely shaped with a strong, muscular appearance. She had a sudden image of him poised with his feet planted a good foot and a half apart as he balanced himself on the deck of a sturdy sailing ship, the waves lifting the craft in a steady rise and fall. He seemed fit for the sea, she thought, or for any rigorous physical employment. She had a sudden sense that he was not happy in England.

How odd to think of him in that way.

He poured the sherry, carefully and slowly.

So, he had decided to come after all. But not *for Evangeline*. And not, she suspected, merely to flirt with her, though he initially gave her that impression. For what then?

He brought the sherry back to her, which she accepted gratefully, the fatigue of the journey from London suddenly washing over her. She sipped the nutty wine and her gaze fell to the empty blackened grate. "How terribly romantic," she mused. "The black stains of burnt wood and coals and thou!"

She turned to lift her glass to him and he burst out laughing again. He had a fine, deep, resonant laugh. "Yes, very romantic," he agreed.

"So why did you change your mind?" she queried. "And pray do not tell me it is because of my fine eyes."

For a long moment, he gazed into her eyes in the most innocent fashion. "You've not *fine* eyes," he stated, a smile touching his lips. "You've beautiful, even magnificent eyes. They are your very best feature, yet the rest are lovely, as well. Do you know how pretty you are?" His mouth fell slightly agape after that. "Is that a blush on your cheeks?"

Emily took another sip of the sherry, choked, and dabbed at the corner of her mouth with one of her gloves. He had disconcerted her completely. She knew that while he had been describing her features so dispassionately, as one might observe a painting at the British Museum, his compliments were offered not with any intention of arousing her interest. Yet that is just what they had done.

She was blushing because she was pleased. And she was pleased because with every minute that had passed since her initial meeting with Kingsbridge at the Scarswell masquerade, her delight in his company had increased steadily. Her heart was fluttering, as she took another sip and watched him smile at her discomfiture, yet she did not want him to know the true source.

"I am not used to being stared at and having each feature scrutinized and catalogued," she stated at last. She lifted her chin feeling a little unsafe, then averted her gaze to the hearth.

"You pout prettily, too," he murmured. "How do you find the grate now? Is it still *romantic?*"

She couldn't help but smile. She liked that he teased her. She liked that he didn't fawn over her beauty but rather had detailed it so nicely. She liked that he laughed when she joked. She liked that he didn't make a fuss as many of her previous suitors and beaux had done, reclining at her feet, staring at her with mooncalf expressions, writing her stupid sonnets when all she wanted was to be kissed and loved a little.

She wondered if before their adventure was over, Kingsbridge would kiss her again.

She looked at the darkened, cold grate and thought that never had her heart been so warmed at a fireside before. "Yes, exceedingly romantic," she responded, not untruthfully.

Eight

"No! No!" Emily cried, laughing. Kingsbridge had just handed her the reins while the pair harnessed to the curricle were galloping along a narrow stretch of the King's Highway. She shoved them back at him. "You are frightening me half out of my wits! No, I tell you! No!"

"I will not be happy until I see you master this skill. You are very close to doing so. Don't give up now!" He threw the reins back at her, scooted closer to his side of the curricle, and folded his arms over his chest.

Emily shrieked. She was a pretty whip, but not an accomplished one. Kingsbridge had been trying to teach her how to handle the ribbons a little better and especially how to manage such a lopsided team as the one presently dragging his curricle toward Derbyshire, but she was proving a slow student.

However, she had already taken Kingsbridge's measure and knew that he would no more take the reins back now than he would jump off the careening vehicle. Besides, the reins were drooping down and would soon be caught up in the pole and traces if she did not have a care.

"Oh, very well!" she exclaimed.

Taking a deep breath, she quickly gathered up the reins and took up the dangerous slack. She felt the team tremble in stride, uncertain as to the messages they were being given. Lacing the leather through her fingers as Kingsbridge had shown her, she began to draw firmly on the reins and brought the horses steadily to a slower, more comfortable trot. By now, beads of perspiration dripped down her neck.

"Excellent," he said, reaching over to take the reins from her.

"You dare and I shall see you drawn up by your thumbs! You forced this on me, and so I shall see your carriage through to the next village or be damned!"

She didn't know what manner of effect her unladylike speech would have on him, but of the moment she didn't care. She knew two things—she was mad as fire at him for having forced the issue in the first place, and secondly, she was thrilled at having just discovered that she could handle a lively pair on the open road. The most she had ever been allowed to do as a young lady was tool a low phaeton about the grounds of her father's home.

Here, on the King's Highway, with every manner of cart, lumbering wagon, gig, carriage, coach, and post chaise ready to block the road, lose a wheel, break a trace, overturn, or slide dangerously off the side of a hill, she had to keep her wits constantly about her.

The worst of it was, however, she liked the sensation prodigiously!

She was reminded yet again, as she had been several times since having made Kingsbridge's acquaintance, of how wondrous her childhood had been with her cousin Bertram. So many former sentiments came back to her—of the thrill of learning to swim, of climbing tree after tree after tree, of crawling about all the fine hills and tors of lovely, craggy northern Derbyshire, of exploring the caverns, and of engaging in dozens of make-believe games of adventure—that her heart was enlivened all over again.

The globe had become her second-best friend after Bertram. Together, they had plotted sea adventures by spinning the orb, closing their eyes, and letting their fingers blindly locate whatever spot they were to travel to next. The library at Aldwark Manor, Bertram's home, was very complete and contained many worthy tomes of history and travel. They read them all.

These delights, however, had been steadily replaced by each of their mounting responsibilities. Bertram went to Eton and she was relegated to the strict guardianship of a fusty old governess. Her childhood had soon become a misty place like Greek or Roman mythology—alive but dead, a place of visitation and observation but not of *doing*.

Years later, in 1812, when Byron's poem, *Childe Harold,* appeared, detailing the adventures of the hero, she relived all her early fantasies. Was it any wonder that with such a rich beginning, she should doubt deeply her ability to become any man's wife, to stay sequestered in the country, to occupy her time with only the most elemental aspects of housekeeping and of childbearing and raising?

She drew in the horses further as a heavily laden wagon appeared on the horizon. The road stretched before her. She could see a gig in the far distance, though she did not doubt it was travelling at a spanking pace. The thought occurred to her that she could pass the wagon before the gig reached her if she had the bottom for it. But should she pass? Did she have sufficient time to do so without incident?

She made her decision without knowing she had done so. She gave a quick, hard slap of the reins and called out to her team. Brown ears flicked. She guided the horses to the right. The oncoming lane opened up. The gig approached swiftly. She raised her voice again.

"Good god," Kingsbridge muttered.

"Never fear, my lord," she returned quietly but confidently. "Although I hasten to inform you I am but following your lead!"

Again she shouted. The horses responded, straining in harness. The gig loomed larger still. She glanced back to her left. The oxen drawing the massive transport were slow and plodding. A moment more. She drew the reins to the left. She heard the driver of the gig shout a loud *whoop*. The curricle slid neatly into the proper lane and the gig rushed past.

She heard Kingsbridge let out a fulsome sigh, but afterward his deep-throated laugh resounded into the countryside.

Emily was satisfied as she again drew the team up a little more. She glanced back and saw that the driver of the gig was waving his hat appreciatively. The oxen became smaller and smaller figures. She had learned something about herself. She glanced up at Kingsbridge and saw that his eyes were narrowed slightly. There was no fear in him, no condemnation, only an expression of understanding and almost of compassion.

"Well done," he murmured, a half-smile blooming on his lips.

His accolade was welcome but unnecessary, she realized.

"Thank you," she responded. "And not just for your compliment."

His smile blossomed fully. "Do I apprehend a kindred spirit of sort?"

She smiled. "Of sorts," she responded happily.

The travelling chariots carrying Emily's abigail and Kingsbridge's valet were still several hours behind the curricle, so it was that when they chose to stop at an inn situated in a village northwest of Rugby for the night, they had already determined just how they should proceed in hiring rooms for the night.

They entered the inn brangling.

"But this is where I wish to stay, Evan, and so we shall. You promised that I might choose next. I wish Mama was here. She would not permit you to bully me as you do. You are the most hateful of brothers."

"I said you might choose the inn tomorrow night," he said. "And do stubble it, Em. Here is the landlord and you will give him the worst notion of us if you continue your quar-

relsome arguments. Mama always dotes on you, petting and
spoiling you, until you are about as worthless as a horse
without legs. I'd like to see the man who would marry such
a termagant as you!" He turned to the innkeeper, and letting
out an impatient huff, said, "Two rooms, if you please—one
for myself and my valet, and the other for m'sister and her
maid!"

The innkeeper did not blink an eye, he did not question
their relationship, he did not even seem surprised they appeared to be arguing. Instead, he bowed politely to them both.
"Very good, sir," he said. "And will ye be wanting a private
parlor for dinner? We've a haunch of venison on the spit,
and m'wife has made an excellent pigeon pie."

Kingsbridge drew off his gloves in quick jerks as though
still irritated with *his sister* and engaged in a brief discussion
of the other delicacies to be had at the posting inn. When he
was satisfied with the arrangements, Emily was shown to
her chamber where, with a bandbox containing a few grooming implements slung over her arm, she took her time in
arranging her flat curls for dinner.

At last satisfied with her efforts, she joined Kingsbridge
in the private parlor, which had been nicely laid with covers
and presented a wondrous array of dishes that greeted her
senses like a heavenly bouquet. The exertions of the day had
given her a monstrous appetite. Even though every muscle
in her body ached from the natural effects of having driven
half the journey and the less-pleasing results of having been
bounced around as a passenger for miles on end, her whole
being craved a hearty meal. She was starved and said so.

He smiled at her in complete understanding, and rather
than forcing her to take up her seat and wait until a maid
arrived to serve them, he suggested they attack the sideboard
together.

"How very wicked," she said.

"Tell me you and Bertram did not do so on more than one
occasion during your medieval feasts."

She had elucidated too many of her childhood experiences, she decided, and felt a blush rise on her cheeks. "You know we did, but I take unkindly in you that you must mention it now. I begin to feel like a barbarian."

"But a beautiful one," he whispered appreciatively.

"I will allow your flattery to persuade me," she said, smiling up at him.

He handed her a plate, then took up one for himself. Side by side, they began to heap their plates with abandon, partaking of the venison and the pigeon pie, as well as escalloped oysters, sausages, salad, fresh baked bread, carrots, celery, roast onions, olives, oranges, cheese, and butter.

Later, as Kingsbridge cradled a glass of port in his hands and watched Emily sip her tea, he thought back over the day's journey. Something in his heart began to burn ever so lightly, a small flame kindled by the remembrance of watching Emily take up his challenge and then go him one better by passing the wagon. He had known a quick lightning bolt of panic as the gig approached his own curricle. But Emily hadn't flinched, not even a mite, a circumstance that had sent his admiration for her soaring.

She had been in complete command of her actions, then as now, as though she possessed some inner guidance beyond his comprehension, a compass true and strong.

He was drawn to her, just as he had confessed to Byron, and of the moment he knew his heart was burning with something unexpected and new. But what? And to what purpose should he encourage such a bright licking of flames? To what end? That they might murder one another in the boredom and insipidity of married life? Never, even though he knew he should be thinking of his estate and of the perpetuation of his title. Emily Longcliffe would make a suitable wife; she might even amuse him for a time.

But, instead, all he could think about was the ship anchored at Falmouth, waiting for him to depart for a score of ports of call.

Yet here he was, being tempted—yes, that's what it was— tempted by a Longcliffe, *a Longcliffe,* to remain forever in England, to never know the borders of other principalities, to never taste the strange fruits of a foreign land, to never see the brightly colored clothing of exotic peoples.

He watched Emily and sighed deeply, disappointment in the nature of life rolling over him in a hard wave. She held her cup and saucer in hand—very ladylike. She was seated opposite him in a matching, comfortable winged chair of a heavy blue twill, her gaze somewhat absent as she stared into the empty grate. Fatigue was settling into her face, her shoulders, and her limbs.

She blinked several times, gave her head a shake as though to clear her mind, then turned to look at him. "I'm afraid I'm not lively company for you this evening, Kingsbridge."

"I don't need lively company, not after a day of travelling. Your maid is probably arrived by now. Why don't you see to your bed?"

She could not suppress a yawn and, after settling her cup and saucer on the table at her elbow, rose to shake out her skirts. Her travelling gown of a pretty violet silk was sadly creased, but she didn't seem to notice nor to care. She had made no apologies for her appearance, which he found pleased him, though he had had to smile upon her return to the parlor earlier. She had attempted to arrange her curls, but in so doing had let fall a portion of her hair so that it dangled down her back. He wasn't sure she had even noticed the discrepancy, though he strongly suspected that even *had* she noticed, she wouldn't have been overly distressed by it.

He rose as well, intending to bid her a pleasant good night, but the narrow proximity of the chairs brought her too close to the bright burnings of his heart. Before he could stay the impulse, he had closed a hand about one of her arms, thereby preventing her from moving past his chair.

She looked up at him surprised. "What is it?" she asked, her large, blue eyes luminous in the soft candlelit chamber.

"You were magnificent today," he murmured. "When you challenged the gig—I thought the world had stopped spinning on its axis." Why was he saying such things to her? How would she interpret such words? As a flirtation? Or worse, as some warm professed sentiment of his heart?

To his surprise, to his dismay, to his delight, she giggled. "I was inordinately foolish—you know I was. I don't even know why I risked your neck and mine by passing that wagon as I did, and you are very wrong to encourage me by admiring my daring."

The burning within his chest grew stronger still as he gazed into her laughing blue eyes. The bare skin of her arm was warm and soft against his fingers. He could feel the skirts of her gown against his leg. He watched her smile dim and her lips part as she caught her breath. She had read his thoughts.

Dear god, he couldn't kiss her again!

"Kingsbridge," she murmured.

Her voice was a delicate melody to his ears. He already knew what a delight she was to hold in his arms. They shouldn't be alone in the parlor. He was finding it too easy to take sore advantage of her and of the situation.

But she was so deuced pretty and engaging and he liked her.

Damme, he liked her too much!

He leaned toward her and found that she lifted her face sweetly to his in response.

Well, he must kiss her now. To do otherwise would make him look like the fool he felt himself to be.

He placed his lips on hers, a light touching of the senses, except that her lips were still parted so enticingly. He wanted more, but he felt himself poised on a decision he didn't quite understand. He should draw back.

So, he did.

Her expression was dark with desire, yet a confused light was in her eye. He understood the question she couldn't pose.

She drew in a deep, long breath. "I don't expect you to marry me, Kingsbridge," she whispered. "Not after a few kisses and one or two quite scandalous embraces. I am not such a stupid female as to believe that, nor am I a chit just out of the schoolroom. As it happens, I am not particularly inclined toward the married state. So kiss me, if you will, for I won't tell a soul of your—of our—indiscretions. Besides, I want you to kiss me ever so much."

"You play with fire," he breathed hoarsely.

"Then throw a little water on it, if you must, but I defy you to do so now."

With that, she turned more fully into him, slid her arms roughly about his neck, and planted her lips hard against his.

Kingsbridge had never been kissed like this before, at least not by an inexperienced miss. Everything she did seemed to surprise him, and he did the only reasonable thing he could do. He caught her up fully in his arms and when her lips parted he fulfilled her sweet invitation and began a gentle, exotic search of her. She began her dovelike coos almost immediately, trilling a song that caused the fire in his heart to roar like the wind.

He held her tightly against him, hoping she would not be frightened by the ardor of his embrace. His desire rolled over him in a sweeping blaze. How he wished she was his wife, that he might let the fire burn uncontrollably for a long, long time.

But she wasn't his wife. She was Emily Longcliffe, and no matter what road his passion for her might take there could be only one end, an end he abhorred—marriage!

The fire of his passion met the sea of his common sense and soon he found the fire turning to embers that at last burned out, at least sufficiently for him to take his arms from about her. He stood knee-deep in the cold surf of reason, yet still he burned as he looked into her eyes.

She lifted her hand to his cheek. "You were with me in the apple tree," she murmured incomprehensibly.

"Whatever do you mean?" he queried, a smile on his lips.

"The wind was blowing us around ever so gently. I didn't want it to stop."

He thought he began to understand her metaphor a little, though not fully, but enough to respond, "It must always stop, little Em."

"Yes," she nodded sadly. "That is what I hate most about the lives we lead."

"Emily," he murmured. He thought of Falmouth and his sailing vessel, loaded and waiting, ready for him, ready to provide him everything he had wanted that did not exist for him in England. "Why couldn't everything be different?"

"I don't know," she replied softly, her eyes brimming with tears.

Why did she cry, he wondered. Was she crying for him or for herself? If for herself, then why? He didn't understand her. Her path was the easy one—to tumble in love, to marry, to bear a passel of children, to care for a home. All women longed for these occupations. Yet she had said she was not inclined toward the married state.

Pshaw! All women were. She merely deceived herself.

She leaned up to him and placed another kiss on his lips, only this one was gentle. "Good night," she murmured.

Once she was ready for bed, Emily cried herself to sleep for reasons she didn't understand.

Nine

The next morning, Emily rose early and dressed with great care. Her eyes were still a little puffy from her tears, but she hoped that if her maid was able to arrange the curls on her forehead prettily enough, Kingsbridge might not notice her red-rimmed eyes.

When at last she descended the stairs, she was gowned to perfection in a dashing bonnet of cornflower blue silk, ornamented with a curled ostrich plume. Her carriage gown was of a matching silk, bearing three rows of lively ruffles about the hem. The sleeves were puffed and trimmed with a small white point lace, and the bodice, though cut low, was made modest with a white lace fichu. Over her elbows she carried an orange blossom shawl of fine silk. She wore matching white lace gloves, though she had tucked a pair of yellow kid gloves into her reticule in case Kingsbridge wanted to share the driving again today.

He was waiting for her at the bottom of the stairs, his arms folded across his chest. Having previously arranged with him that they would once more conduct themselves like brother and sister, she exchanged only the frostiest of greetings with him when she reached the lobby. The innkeeper did not even lift a brow as she flounced from the inn. A few moments later, Kingsbridge left the hostelry having settled the bill.

A morning breeze blew across the cobbles and whipped up the ends of her shawl. When he moved to stand beside her, she glanced up at him and smiled, and he in turn winked. What a great joke to be sharing with him.

He pulled on his gloves and said, "Are you well, Miss Longcliffe?"

Emily clucked her tongue. "I was hoping you would not notice."

He chuckled. "I hope it is only fatigue, then?"

She shook her head. "I am not at all tired. The fact is, I cried my heart out last night, but it is nothing to signify, I assure you." From the corner of her eye, she could see that he was staring at her and that he was frowning.

"Nothing to signify?" he asked, disbelieving.

"That is what I said," she responded.

"I hurt you then," he stated.

She turned toward him. "Why must you think that? You've done nothing wrong."

He opened his mouth as though startled. Throwing both hands wide, he whispered, "I kissed you last night, again, and that was very wrong of me."

Emily bit her lip. "Yes, it was, wretchedly so, especially since I was conducting myself with perfect propriety throughout the whole of it."

"Oh, stubble it, Em," he whispered, a crooked smile on his lips.

"Only if you stop tormenting yourself where I am concerned. I'm not a chit out of the schoolroom. It's been six years since I had to listen to the lectures of my governess, so don't treat me as though I'm a completely fragile, inexperienced young miss."

"Yet, still you cried," he pressed her.

"But not because of a kiss or two. Well, perhaps it was, but not as you might think. I do not regret last night. The past does not torment me. Only the future." The wind buffeted her bonnet and fluffed the curls on her forehead. She secured the ends of her shawl by holding them together, an action that caused the shawl to billow out behind her like a sail.

Kingsbridge popped his hat more securely down on his head. "Then in what way were the kisses we shared the cause of your unhappiness?"

"I don't know if I can explain, and even if I could, it would be of little use." When her travelling chariot appeared from the direction of the stables, she asked, "Where is your curricle?"

"I sent it ahead to Derbyshire by postillion. I wish to travel in a closed carriage since we are so near Lord Trent's home. I thought it best."

She nodded in agreement. "I think you're right."

Kingsbridge ushered her toward the waiting town chariot and assisted her in alighting. Emily settled herself on the squabs and, glancing down at her feet, noticed that a basket sat on the floor. A moment more and the smell of freshly baked pastry rose to fill the confined space of the cab. "Kingsbridge! How delightful! How thoughtful!"

He was closing the door as he looked back and noticed the basket. He chuckled and snapped the door shut. "I told the innkeeper that if you didn't have something to nibble on during the journey, you were likely to cast up your accounts."

"Oh, you didn't," she responded, laughing. "How wretched of you, but how very considerate. Thank you."

For the next several miles, Emily enjoyed the travelling picnic, especially the apricot tartlets.

By noon, the coach had passed the flourishing town of Leicester. "I've been thinking," she said, "that we ought to settle you in an inn far enough from Aldwark Manor to go about relatively unnoticed, yet close enough for me to get messages to you. Do you think you could manage going about *incognito*, perhaps as a mere honorable? Or would that be beneath your dignity?"

She couldn't help teasing him a little.

"I won't dignify that remark by rising to the fly even the littlest bit. Your plan is sound. I think I shall take on the name Biron, with an *i*. What do you think?"

"I think Childe Harold would like that."

He smiled. "I would agree."

In the end, they settled on the village of Kegworth, just inside the Leicestershire border near the southeast border of Derbyshire. The great town of Derby would have been a better choice except that the Marquess of Kingsbridge had frequented the ancient city's major hostelries. The proprietor of the black and white Dolphin Inn located in Queen Street, for instance, would know him at a glance. Besides, he could easily meet one of his acquaintances in the simple comings and goings of staying at the famous inn.

Kegworth it was, therefore, and once Emily had enacted her sisterly farce with Kingsbridge yet again, she headed northwest, toward the village of Aldwark and nearby Aldwark Manor, a trek which would require at least two hours to complete.

Sometime later, as her coach lumbered up the neatly raked drive of the manor, Emily looked up at the mellowed Tudor mansion and a sensation of nostalgia swept over her in a sweet wave of pleasure. The manor, facing west, caught the slanted afternoon rays of the sun and appeared to be smiling at her arrival. The shrubberies were pruned tidily, any decay in the stones of the building were neatly repaired, and the many windows glinted merrily in the sunshine.

Whatever else the current Lady Trent might be, she saw that the property was kept in good order, for she knew that Lord Trent's occupations were less homey. He spent most of his daily hours either in his library or in the stables and kennels, seeing to his hunting horses and hounds.

How odd to think that neither Evangeline nor Bertram were particularly welcome in their home, yet their home could appear more welcoming than most. She wondered, therefore, just what she would find once she crossed the threshold of the fine old house.

The postillion drew her coach to a stop on the gravel by the front door. He sounded the knocker for her, then returned to let down the steps to her coach, open the door, and hand her down.

Just as she arrived at the shallow flight of steps to the front door, the heavy wooden door opened. She recognized the butler at once, though she had not seen him in at least ten years. "How do you go on, Mr. Boyles?" she queried, barely restraining a smile.

Mr. Boyles peered at her, blinked rapidly several times, opened his brown eyes wide and cried, "Well, if it isn't Miss Emily!" He held the door wide for her. "Do come in! How happy I am to see you, though I do believe ye've come at a time when we were begging for the angels to send us a little help."

"Indeed," she murmured, both gratified and alarmed by his greeting as she crossed the portal. A closer scrutiny of his face revealed tight lines beside his ancient eyes, indicating that all was not well at Aldwark, notwithstanding the careful tending of the stones, the gravel, and the shrubbery. She slowly began to draw off her white lace gloves and glanced around the elegant entrance hall. Everything was as it should be. The long table nearby, waiting patiently to receive hats and gloves, canes and whips, was polished to a dazzling shine. A vase of sweet peas, ferns, and roses was settled on an inlaid table placed in the curve of the elegant staircase. The frames of the large portraits lining the stairwell were free of even a mite of dust or grime. All was beauty and order. Yet in the air was a strain of tension as real as the fragrance of the lovely sweet peas and the aromatic roses.

When she had given her instructions to her postillion, she held her gloves in her hand and turned to Boyles. "Whatever is amiss here? I can feel that something terrible has happened."

Mr. Boyles lowered his dark gaze to the planked wood at his feet. He sighed and shook his head, seeming all the while to deliberate within himself as to precisely what he needed or ought to say to her.

She took a step toward him. "I have come to help," she murmured. "Evangeline sent word to me through her sister-in-law in Devonshire. You may trust me, Boyles."

He drew in a deep breath, clasped his hands behind his back and bowed slightly to her. "They've got Miss Matford. A ransom is what they're demanding. We only heard of it just afore nuncheon, not two hours past."

"A ransom?" she cried. Then the worst had happened. The Glossips—if indeed it was them—had kidnapped Evangeline in truth. "Does anyone know who it is that has abducted her?"

"That be the worst of it," he murmured, tears sparkling in his eyes. "They were hired by his lordship to keep Miss Matford till she agreed to wed Master Theodore—I mean, Major Buxton. Now it seems the whole game has changed and not much anyone can do about it."

"Where is my uncle?" she queried softly.

"With my lady, in the library."

"I shall go to them," she said. "Please announce me."

He nodded, but grimaced. "Be careful, Miss Emily. Nought is as you would remember."

"I know, Boyles. You needn't fear for me on any score. I took *her* measure a number of years past, and I have no misplaced fancies where she is concerned."

He seemed relieved as he straightened his shoulders and led the way to the staircase. He wore the elegant blue and gold livery of the manor and, as her gaze took in his slightly slumped back, she realized he had shrunk since she had last seen him. Whether it was his age or the dictatorship of the current mistress of the house that had caused the bending of his spine, she couldn't be certain, though she rather suspected the latter.

When Boyles announced her, she walked firmly and briskly into the library before Lady Trent had the chance to refuse her admittance.

The chamber was situated facing the west, so that the afternoon sunbeams poured into the long, elegant, and well-stocked room in a flood of golden light. The floor was covered in a gold and dark blue patterned Aubusson carpet, accentuated by matching dark blue velvet draperies flanking the four windows of the immaculate chamber. A scattering of overstuffed chairs, also in dark blue, and two spindly settees, covered in a white silk damask, invited all who were of a mind to settle their souls between the covers of a book for an hour or two. The walls between and opposite the windows were lined with row upon row of leather-bound books, placed on shelves that rose from floor to ceiling.

"Emily!" her uncle called to her, clearly startled by her sudden appearance.

"How do you go on, dearest Uncle," she called sympathetically and confidently to Lord Trent. How stunned the poor man was as she descended quickly upon him, kissed his cheek, then turned to address his wife.

"Dear Lady Trent!" she cried, summoning the most anguished expression she could manage. "I have heard the news and I cannot begin to imagine how you bear such wretched tidings, especially when Evangeline is not even your own child." She peered down at the cold, unfeeling woman who sat with her fingers clutched tightly about the arms of the chair in which she was situated. Her right hand held a crumpled paper in a talonlike grasp.

Lady Trent's mouth was slightly agape. She could not for a long moment find her voice. When she did her tone was venomous. "What is the meaning of your conduct, Miss? And who are you, though I would suppose by your wretched manners that you must in some manner be related to the former Lady Trent."

"I am, my lady," she said, feigning a sorrowful tone to her voice. "My name is Longcliffe. Emily Longcliffe. I have come to speak with your husband on a matter of some urgency. Would you mind if I steal him away from you for an hour or two? It is regarding his daughter."

"What's that!" Lord Trent cried. "Do you know something, then? Have you heard from Vangie?"

Emily turned to stare at her uncle. For the first time since she could remember, he actually spoke of his daughter with some affection and perhaps even a little regret. Certainly, she had never heard him refer to her as *Vangie* before.

"Yes, Uncle. I've news of a sort, but I don't know how much more I know than you. A little, perhaps."

"If you are involved," Lady Trent cried intrusively, "then you ought to at least be apprised of the current *debacle*. Here! Read this!"

Lord Trent glared at his wife and took the paper from her which she had thrust toward Emily. "You would do well, Madam, to temper your conduct."

"So the pot will call the kettle black, eh," she remarked, rising from her chair. She was gowned in a violet silk dress that complemented her peppered black hair, giving her a regal appearance. "It is you who have gotten all of us in this fix— you and that absurd Mr. Buxton. I told you times out of mind not to become involved in any scheme a man of Trade might lay out before you. All you had to do was take Evangeline to the church and *make* her sign the wedding papers. Nothing could have been simpler. Instead, you must concoct this most stupid scheme of hiring a person of low breeding to steal her away until such a time as she relents and marries the major. Of all the bungling I have witnessed since I wed you, this is the worst. But I will tell you one thing, I'll not allow you to spend a groat on that worthless child of yours so that mine might starve, merely because she would not do as she was bid. That manner of disobedience in a child should be punished, and those who are obedient shouldn't have to suffer for her willful, hateful actions. As much as I disapprove of your ridiculous schemes, I cannot help but think that she has brought the whole of this mischief down on her own head because of her refusal to wed Buxton."

She drew in a deep breath through flared nostrils, and

Emily could see how the marriage conducted itself daily, of
will battling will. She sensed they were a match, these two,
and of the moment she wished herself anywhere but with
them. What next would happen, she couldn't begin to guess.

"You will kindly leave us now, my dear," Lord Trent said
to his wife. His voice was firm, his expression not less so.

Emily was stunned and bit her lip to keep from gasping
audibly.

Lady Trent narrowed her eyes meaningfully, as if to say
that she would have her revenge and that he ought to beware
if he was at all wise. She then kicked the demi-train of her
violet silk gown behind her and walked slowly from the
chamber.

Lord Trent watched her go, his lip curling.

Emily, however, felt little sympathy for her uncle. Perhaps
he was experiencing some remorse where his conduct toward
Evangeline was concerned, but every indication was that he
had treated his daughter unkindly over the years and was at
best an indifferent parent. Any man who would attempt to
manipulate his daughter into a marriage she clearly abhorred
deserved the sort of wife Lady Trent had proved herself to be.

He drew Emily more deeply into the chamber, toward the
sunshine and away from the doors. She suspected he did so
because his wife might be eavesdropping. Whatever the case,
when she was seated on the settee nearest the fireplace, he
drew a chair forward so that they might talk in secretive quiet
tones.

He began in a hushed voice. "I told Lady Trent a whisker,"
he said confidentially. "I never composed such a scheme,
nor did Buxton. Evangeline was kidnapped, but not at either
of our instigations—I promise you."

Ten

Emily was surprised by what her uncle had just told her, yet not surprised. From the first she had felt something was amiss with everything Marcus Peveril had told her.

She shook her head. "When I first heard she had been kidnapped through some odious design," she said quietly, "I could not credit it as being true. Only tell me what has happened. Is it what I suspect, that Evangline has been caught in a web of her own making?"

He nodded. "I think so."

Emily saw the distress in her uncle's face, but felt little pity for him in that moment. "And in the web of your making as well. Were you really trying to force her into a match she despised?"

Again he nodded, hanging his head a little. "But it's not as you think. She is in love with Theodore. She has been since times out of mind."

"What?" Emily cried, startled and laughing all at once. "My dear Uncle, you are badly informed if you believe such a thing! For the past several months, Evangeline has written to me of a certain Mr. Peveril and of her attachment to him. Her lines have been crossed and recrossed with a dozen strongly expressed sentiments. Whether she had truly formed a *lasting* passion for Mr. Peveril I could not venture to say, but to tell me now that she is in love with Teddy, I will not believe. She was always used to brangle with him."

Lord Trent eyed her thoughtfully for a long moment. "You've never been in love, have you?" he asked cryptically.

Emily was thrown out of stride a bit. Her thoughts turned suddenly to Kingsbridge and the truly reprehensible kisses and embraces they had shared on their equally scandalous journey into Derbyshire. More than once the thought had crossed her mind that her willingness, even her eagerness, to fall into his arms, might be construed by some as certain evidence that Cupid's arrow had struck home at last. But she was not so easily convinced or persuaded by such thoughts. She was drawn to Kingsbridge in a manner that she had never experienced before, but did she love him?

She gestured helplessly, before answering, "I don't suppose I have been in love, but I can't imagine what that has to do with Evangeline and your belief that she loves Theodore."

"Everything," he stated baldly. "And believe me when I say that I know a great deal about falling in love and marrying—versus wedding for convenience's sake—and I would not wish the latter on anyone, least of all Vangie."

Emily felt her whole being stop dead at his words. She crinkled up her brow in an effort to make him out. Was it possible he was referring to Evangeline's mother in contrast to the current Lady Trent? Surely there could be no other interpretation. If so, was it also possible that he both understood and loved his daughter better than she had ever supposed?

She sought back in her mind trying to determine at what point she had drawn her original conclusions about Lord Trent and his disposition toward his offspring, but no particular event came strongly to mind, only Evangeline's complaints. But her grumblings had been catalogued only after her mother had passed away and a new mistress had been brought to Aldwark in her stead.

The formerly warm, inviting atmosphere of Evangeline's home had been instantly transformed by Lady Trent's arrival.

The new mistress of the manor had proved cold, calculating, and unfeeling. Lord Trent, escaping as he did into the hills beyond Aldwark with his gun and his hounds, nine minutes out of ten, had apparently left his children to bear the brunt of the unhappiness moving about the ancient halls of the manor in the form of his new bride.

So Lord Trent had become an indifferent, unfeeling father, in Evangeline's words. Emily scrutinized his face and began to readjust all of her previous opinions as though she was resetting a clock.

He had said he had married for convenience.

Poor Lord Trent.

Poor Evangeline and Bertram!

"Yes," he began quietly, leaning back in his chair, his jaw working strongly. "I see the questions in your eyes, I see the workings of your mind, and yes, you are right. I married in too great a haste following my dear Sophia's demise, and a day has not gone by that I have failed to regret my actions. I was only hoping therefore to make certain that Vangie did not suffer as I did. Theodore—Major Buxton—had laid his heart before her and she spurned him so cruelly, that I—"

"One moment," Emily called out to him. "Do you say that Theodore actually had the bottom to offer for Evangeline?"

"He is much changed since you knew him. He is, after all, a man of thirty now, not the moonling you were used to know."

Emily shook her head. "You are right," she murmured. "I have not seen him for ten years, and when he was twenty I thought him a sallow-faced weakling."

Lord Trent smiled. "You are forgetting. I bought him a pair of colors that same year. He has campaigned in the Peninsula alongside Wellington these many years. He is now an officer in the Horse Guards—soon to be made Lieutenant-Colonel if I do not much mistake the matter."

Emily was stunned. Of course she knew that he had joined the army, but her opinions of Theodore Buxton—*Major* Buxton—had been formed early when he was still a young man in his salad days, and she an ungovernable chit of just fourteen. Besides, most of her notions about Major Buxton were based on Evangeline's numerous complaints of how Teddy was always pinching at her, if not about how she fashioned her hair, then how she walked, or danced, or conducted herself at the local assemblies, forever moralizing and prosing on and on.

Emily considered these things and realized that there was some small likelihood, given Evangeline's current prank, that she might be in some need of instruction after all. Though whether Theodore was the person to inflict the morals on Evangeline's heedless ears was another matter entirely.

"You said Major Buxton had proposed to Evangline. Is he here, then, in Derbyshire?"

The major's father—a widower—lived some seven miles from Aldwark Manor in a newly built mansion known as Buxton House.

"Yes. He is staying with his father for two months before returning to Europe. Wellington, it would seem, has no great opinion of how prosperous the conventions in Austria may prove, nor of how long Napoleon will remain fixed on such a small island as Elba."

Emily nodded, her brow furrowed as she lowered her gaze to her hands which she realized were clasped rather tightly in her lap. Her thoughts returned abruptly to her cousin's current predicament. "What is the major's opinion of the kidnapping?" she asked, lifting her gaze to her uncle's once more.

"I haven't told him yet, but I expect him sometime this afternoon. As soon as I received the ransom note, I sent for him. But how does it come about that you arrive at just such a time? Did you know of this?"

"I know this will seem very strange to you, Uncle, but three days past I received a missive from, well, from a man with whom Evangeline had been corresponding for some time. He spoke of Aldwark and of walking in the groves beyond your gardens and how beautiful they were. Do you recall a Mr. Peveril calling upon my cousin last summer? I mentioned him earlier."

Lord Trent shook his head, his eyes taking on a faraway appearance as he searched his memory. At last he said, "Was he a rather tall fellow with curling blond hair who enjoyed striking poses?"

Emily bit her lip, trying to think of the man she met at Newgate behaving so foppishly. "He has brown eyes," she offered hopefully. She supposed it was possible that Lord Trent might view the flirtatious Marcus Peveril in that manner.

Lord Trent snapped his fingers. "The very one!" he exclaimed. "Agreeable manners, pleasant in the drawing room, but a little lacking in any reasonable occupations."

These observations seemed true to the mark.

He wrinkled up his nose. "And my daughter is in love with the fellow?" he asked in disgust.

"As to that, I'm not certain. She was certainly smitten, but as I said before I never quite determined if she *loved* him."

"But you say he wrote to you?"

"Yes," she responded, treading warily. She was not in a hurry to inform him that she had visited him in Newgate Prison. "He begged to make my acquaintance that he might share with me his concerns for Evangeline's safety. Naturally, I obliged him and was stunned to learn that her letters to him had ceased altogether and quite abruptly."

"What did he tell you that sent you flying to Derbyshire?" he asked, a little surprised. "He cannot have known of her kidnapping?"

Emily shook her head. "He knew that she was being pressured into accepting the Major's hand in marriage, so when her correspondence stopped—and that so suddenly—his imagination filled in the spaces."

"He suggested then that you come to Aldwark and seek me out?"

"Not precisely. He suggested that I discuss the matter with the Marquess of Kingsbridge."

She noted the sudden flight of one of his gray eyebrows and the quick parting of his lips in a silent gasp. "Kingsbridge, eh? And what, pray tell, did that rascal have to say?"

Emily could be in no doubt of Lord Trent's opinion of her travelling companion. Somehow, his opinion amused her but she bit her lip to keep from smiling. "Oddly enough, he had news for me from another quarter—from your daughter-in-law in fact. Mrs. Matford had been encouraging him to seek me out in order to inform me that she had received a letter from Evangeline—ostensibly mailed without the knowledge of her kidnappers—that she was being held against her will and until such time as she agreed to marry Major Buxton."

Lord Trent's shoulders sagged a little. "The little minx," he murmured, shaking his head slowly. Emily saw concern and affection mingled in his aging blue eyes. Regret was in every line of his face. "It would seem she was seeking support against me from her brother and from you. Then her schemes rose up and bit her."

"May I see the ransom note?" she queried.

"Yes, of course," he said. He rose from his chair and retrieved it from the table where Lady Trent had left it. He returned to Emily and handed her the crumpled sheet of paper. She glanced at the signature first and had all her suspicions confirmed, for the note was signed *Harold Glossip*.

She read the demands, as well as subsequent instructions for the exchange of largess for Evangeline, and thought that if nothing else, the criminals had arranged everything to a nicety. Miss Matford could be retrieved by leaving a portmanteau containing ten thousand pounds in a hotel room at the Black Bear Inn, in Tewkesbury, Gloucestershire. Upon arriving at the hotel, Lord Trent was to request a room for himself posing as a Mr. Renbow. He was to leave early the following morning, but the portmanteau was to remain behind and would be examined forthwith. If everything was in order, a letter would be mailed to *Mr. Renbow* indicating where his daughter could be found. If the ten thousand pounds were not within the valise, Miss Matford would never be heard from again.

"How horrid," Emily breathed as she read the final warning. Several thoughts occurred to her. "What do you mean to do, Uncle? Will you follow the instructions to the letter? Have you considered hiring a Bow Street Runner?"

"I don't see that we have time," he responded.

"You should go to Derby then, and secure the ten thousand," she said firmly. "And afterward proceed to Tewkesbury."

He nodded, frowning. "I suppose you are right."

A dozen thoughts occurred to her about how he ought to arrange the matter, how he could involve someone unknown to Evangeline to spy on the transactions, how he could send a person beforetimes to the specified inn, how he should mark the portmanteau in some manner. She wanted to suggest these things to him, but she could see he was not in a state to work through the details of how to proceed. When at last she suggested one or two of these notions to him, he smiled in a patronizing manner and said, "Don't worry your pretty little head, my dear niece. I shall see everything settled. I intend to consult with Major Buxton as soon as he arrives, and between the pair of us I'm sure that we shall see Evangeline safely home."

"But surely I might be of use in some manner," she suggested hopefully.

"Don't be absurd, Emily. You would only be in the way, I'm 'fraid. It is enough that Evangeline is in danger. I would be driven to distraction if I also had to worry hourly about your safety as well."

Emily knew a sense of disappointment so keen that she could hardly speak. She was a female, an object to be protected only, but not to be considered of the least use. Anger rose bitterly in her breast.

This was always the way, she thought. From the time she could remember, save a few years with Bertram in the apple orchard, her place had been made abominably clear to her. Seen, not heard, except when playing the pianoforte or singing a pretty country ballad or speaking French or Italian or German.

She handed the letter back to him.

"I must be going," she said quietly.

"Whatever do you mean?" he asked, attempting to smile. "You are staying here, in my home, of course."

She shook her head and rose to her feet. "You are very kind, but I have already made arrangements in Kegworth to stay for the night. My maid was taken up with a fit of the ague during the last few miles of our journey." Oh, dear, she was telling whiskers again. Where would all of this end, she wondered guiltily. "She is quite ill and I do not wish to leave her alone in a strange inn. I would ask, however, that you send word to Kegworth with regard to your efforts to rescue my cousin. I am very sorry to have found the situation as grave and as dangerous as it has proven to be."

He nodded, accepting her sympathies, but added, "Won't you at least stay for a little tea, or lemonade perhaps?"

"A little lemonade would be delightful, but just while my carriage is being brought round."

Sometime later, and after having exchanged with her uncle a few anecdotes about Evangeline and her penchant for getting into scrapes, Emily descended the stairs to the entrance hall. Her travelling coach awaited her. As the butler opened the door for her, Major Buxton stepped across the portal at the very same moment.

She was astonished by the change in him as he shook her hand and smiled in a friendly, concerned manner. He was nearly as tall as Kingsbridge and certainly as broad of shoulder. He carried himself in much the same manner as the marquess, since he spent much of his time in the saddle as a cavalry officer. His hair was blond and even lighter than she remembered, probably because of his years enduring the sun and heat of the Peninsula. His complexion was deeply and ruggedly sun-bronzed, his eyes were a clear, light blue, and tiny lines fanned out from the edges of his eyes. His nose was slightly aquiline and his lips were a straight, almost grim line, as much by habit she mused as by the dire nature of the situation.

He was not wearing his uniform but had rather donned the simpler, less restrictive clothes of a country gentleman, sporting a brown coat, buff breeches, a white waistcoat, top boots, and a neckcloth creased in the careful folds known as the Mail Coach. He was very handsome, almost as attractive as Kingsbridge.

"It has been many years, Major Buxton," Emily said, smiling. "I would not have known you."

"I don't suppose you would," he responded, a twinkle growing in his eye. "For if I recall, the last time we met you gave me a terrible set-down, calling me a sallow-faced halfling."

"Pray don't put me in mind of anything I might have said when I was still in the schoolroom. I hope I have long since outgrown my tendency to speak my mind too freely."

"So long as you do not remind me overly much of what a prosy bore I was on more than one occasion."

"Agreed," she said. "And now," here she glanced at her uncle, "though I would prefer to remain and learn of all your adventures, I know that the difficulties besetting Evangeline must by their nature prevent such a conversation. I shall leave the pair of you, therefore, to resolve as best you can the truly wretched troubles before you. Remember, though—I shall expect to hear word from you as soon as possible."

Lord Trent nodded vigorously to her. "I shall send you word daily, regardless of where we are or what has transpired. Kegworth, you say?"

"Yes, that's right."

"Very well, then."

With that, Emily left Aldwark Manor and climbed aboard her travelling chariot.

A little less than two hours later, having told her postboy to *Spring 'em,* Emily arrived at the inn in Kegworth. Her spirits were utterly low on two counts. First, that Evangeline was now truly in some danger of her life, and secondly, that she would have to remain, as always, kicking her heels at the inn and fairly going mad with worry and frustration, while the gentlemen—*the gentlemen!*—were galloping across the countryside, taking all the action necessary that was in no manner allowed to her.

When she entered the inn from the direction of the stables, however, she was met by Lord Kingsbridge, wearing travelling gear and an expression that told her all was far from well.

"What is it, Evan?" she asked, taking on the form of *sister* again. "Don't tell me you have refused to pay the shot for some reason and now the innkeeper means to eject us both!"

"Hush!" he cried, then caught her by the elbow, whirled her about, and dragged her toward the cobbles.

She was stunned. She knew that he was in part playing his role in order to allay suspicions about their true relationship, but she also sensed that something had gone amiss.

Once the door to the inn was closed behind him and he had barked an order for his curricle to be brought round, he looked down at her and let out a heavy breath of concern. "I saw the Glossips, not a half hour ago."

"The Glossips?" Emily was stunned, her eyes opening wide. "Did they see you? Would either of them know you if they did?"

"Yes, both of them would know me, but I don't believe either were aware of my presence. I was partially hidden behind the half-curtain in the parlor and was able to observe them from inside without too much fear of being discovered.

They were busily engaged with a young female who I must presume was your Cousin Evangeline. Besides, Glossip was arguing with the hostler the entire time."

Eleven

Emily blinked rapidly. "But that can't be," she whispered, not wanting her conversation overheard by anyone.

"The young woman I saw was devilishly pretty, but not exactly in the common way. She had dark brown hair, dark eyes, a pointed chin, and a slightly retroussé but quite enchanting little nose. Her brows were thickly arched and she had a tendency to bite at her lip—just as you are doing now—when she is worried. And she appeared to be quite worried. When she spoke to Mrs. Glossip, that lady took strong hold of her arm and gave her a shake. The young woman's face crumpled ominously."

"Without a doubt, you are describing my cousin," she said. "But, oh, Kingsbridge, it is worse than you know—Lord Trent received a ransom note and the kidnappers, well, Evangeline hired them herself as a sort of prank to stop her father and Mr. Buxton from pressing her into a marriage she disliked."

"Good god!" he breathed. "I would guess then that once they had her in their power, they thought to take advantage of the situation."

Emily nodded. "My uncle had only a few hours before my arrival at his home received a ransom note. He showed it to me of course, once I revealed all that I knew of her circumstances, so that at least we know in which direction they are travelling. The Glossips were quite specific—Tewkesbury in

Gloucestershire. You did see them leaving by way of the high-way to the southwest, did you not?"

"No," he responded softly, meeting her gaze. "Not to the southwest but the northwest—the road leading to Brailsford and Ashbourne. Two hours past."

"But that's not possible!" Evangeline cried. "Gloucester-shire is southwest, not northwest. I could not have been mis-taken."

"Hush," Kingsbridge warned her. "I'm sure you weren't."

Emily placed a hand on his arm. "The ransom note stated that my uncle was to take ten thousand pounds to Tewkes-bury. Why would Evangeline's kidnappers head northwest?" She paused, her heart thrumming loudly in her ears. "Do you suppose they are misleading them to a purpose?"

"Yes," he murmured, nodding slowly. "What is ten thou-sand? Buxton is worth a quarter million pounds alone on the exchange."

"Oh, dear god!" she whispered. "I must warn my uncle at once!"

She would have begun crossing the cobbles toward the stables immediately in order to urge the hostler to harness the horses more quickly, but Kingsbridge stayed her with a hand on her arm.

"Wait," he whispered.

She turned to look at him, a little surprised that he was not responding with a similar urgency, but a considering light had entered his eye. "I don't think going to Aldwark would be wise. We would lose another two hours and more by doing so. If we begin a pursuit now, we might overtake them, if not by this evening, then tomorrow."

She met his hard, forceful gaze and quickly thought through his reasonings. "Of course you are right," she said, her voice still conspiratorially low. "But I ought at least send word to my uncle, though the more I think on it, the more I believe it would be possible that by the time a message could be sent to Aldwark, he will have already left for the Cotswolds."

"Then we've precious little time to lose."

He turned back to the door, opened it for her, and escorted her to the lobby where she seated herself at a writing table and quickly penned a note for her uncle. She described the essentials of her conversation with Kingsbridge, informing her uncle that *a friend* of hers who knew Evangeline had seen her in the company of a questionable pair by the married name of Glossip. She further wrote that *her friend* was certain Evangeline's coach had taken the northwesterly route toward Derby and Ashbourne, and not the southwesterly highway passing through Measham, Tamworth, and Burmingham. She indicated as well that she was following in the wake of Evangeline's carriage and hoped to do all she could to disrupt the kidnapping scheme. She was entirely reluctant to reveal that though she had her maid in attendance upon her, she was in effect travelling in the company of the Marquess of Kingsbridge.

What would her uncle say to that, she wondered with a slight shiver that shot down her spine! He would likely suffer an apoplectic fit!

When she completed her letter and a rider was sent galloping north to Aldwark Manor, Emily returned with Kingsbridge to the inn yard where his curricle was now fully harnessed, as well as both travelling chariots.

Emily saw the brief train of vehicles and was not a little pleased. "I see that you've all my baggage neatly stowed!" she cried. "It would appear you've thought of everything." She fell into her sisterly role and added, "I am so very proud of you, Evan. For a brother, it would seem you've at least half a brain at times."

He laughed outright, then offered his hand to her to help her alight his curricle. A moment more and he had the brown pair moving at a spanking pace up the High Street toward Derby and Ashbourne.

At each stage of the journey, Emily's task was to leave word for their servants, while Kingsbridge made discreet inquiries regarding Evangeline's coach. The hostlers and one or two of the stable boys at Derby, Langley, and Brailsford were able to confirm that a young lady of Evangeline's description was travelling in a yellow town coach along with a man and a woman. One of the stable hands at The Green Man and Black's Head Inn, in Ashbourne, noticed the yellow bounder because of the beautiful young lady who sat in the coach staring quite forlornly out at the countryside. It would seem her cousin's beauty was becoming a sort of guidon on the horizon, a north star they could follow with at least some ease.

From Ashbourne the curricle quickly crossed the border into Staffordshire The countryside swelled and dipped with beautiful green hills, and the wheels of the carriage rolled across more than one stone bridge as they made their way toward the town of Leek. Inquiries at Winkhill and Bottom House revealed that their course was true—Evangeline's beauty might prove to be the undoing of her captors, for hardly an hostler or stable boy failed to notice the sad young lady whose complexion was like cream and her eyes ever so doelike, who waited so patiently in the town coach while the horses were changed.

Upon leaving the village known obscurely as Bottom House, Emily began to feel the effects of having travelled most of the day. She hated admitting as much, but fatigue was settling into every joint and she was beyond famished. Not for the world however, would she say as much to Kingsbridge.

The sight of the ancient town of Leek, known to have been in existence before Roman times, was so welcome to Emily that she inadvertently let out a deep sigh.

"Never fear," Kingsbridge murmured. "I shall see you fed and tucked between the sheets before much longer. You must be fagged to death."

"Not by half," Emily responded brightly.

"What a rapper!" he cried. "I don't like to mention it, but you haven't said two words since the wheels of my carriage rolled out of Bottom House. I am not used to so much silence."

Emily glanced up at him a little stunned. "Do I talk so very much?" she queried.

"Incessantly," he said. "No, no! Don't look repentant, for I have not enjoyed myself half so much in, dare I say, years?"

"You are being kind," she said. "And I do chatter a deal too much, I know I do. If your ears grow tired, Evan, you must tell me to hold my tongue. You will not offend me, I promise you."

Kingsbridge drew his horses a little to the left to keep his equipage from locking wheels with a cart that was being drawn by a man he suspected was in his cups. When he was certain they weren't in the least danger of an accident, he turned to glance at Emily. She had again fallen silent and her eyelids drooped ominously. Did she even know she had called him by his Christian name? Did she know that he liked it . . . very much?

Of course not. He drew in a deep breath and forced himself from releasing an equally forceful sigh. He was in a state of great confusion, he realized, about Emily Longcliffe and about what the devil he was doing travelling in this scandalous manner all about the English countryside in pursuit of a female he'd never met in his life.

He chuckled to himself, for he had a strong suspicion he was making a great cake of himself in doing so. But did he have any regrets? Not especially. Not when he was in the company of such a pretty young woman, whose liveliness matched his own restless energy. She was certainly greatly fatigued of the moment, but then she had been travelling for nearly fourteen hours with hardly a rest in between. While he had been relaxing at the inn, in Kegworth, she had travelled northwest to Aldwark Manor. If anything, he was surprised she had not simply collapsed entirely.

When he had first seen the Glossips with a pretty young woman in tow, he had wanted to race from the inn and wrest her from her travelling chariot. But he knew he couldn't possibly reach the vehicle in time. So, instead, he had watched the wheels spin along the cobbles of the village and awaited Emily's return. He comprehended her sufficiently well to know that she would at the very least wish to follow in her cousin's wake. She was impatient to be helping her cousin, she was impatient about life, and he was becoming impatient about wanting to take her in his arms again.

Faith, but he couldn't believe how strong his desire for her was—and she a Longcliffe, a chit who travelled in the circles of the High Sticklers, a pure maiden, but whose kisses were as sweet as nectar.

He watched her head nod and then she lifted her chin quite suddenly and blinked several times.

"You may rest against my shoulder if you wish for it," he offered hopefully. He wanted her to lean against him a little. He wanted her close to him.

She smiled, a little shyly perhaps, and shook her head. "No, I thank you. We are very near to Leek now. I can see the lights in the distance." She glanced about the countryside, the tall trees lining the highway and the hedgerows covered with a white dust from the traffic of the road. "Night is nearly fallen. I wonder if the Glossips will have taken rooms for the night in Leek?"

"I should think they would have ventured a little farther along their journey, if they are at all wise."

She looked at him, a slight frown between her brows. "What if they are staying at The Red Lion and we chance upon them? Evangeline will make our presence known, and then who knows what might happen?

"Never fear. I shall make discreet inquiries first. If they

are at The Red Lion, then we shall take up rooms at The Swan."

A half hour later, when they drew into the yard of The Red Lion, Kingsbridge spoke briefly with the hostler and discovered that their prey were not fixed at the inn. Emily was a little surprised when he jumped lightly down from the curricle and extended his hand to her as though to help her descend. When she lifted a brow, he said, "Come! Em, if you mean to argue with me I shan't assist you at all. Mama said we must put up at The Red Lion."

Emily immediately took up his hints. "But I want to stay at The Swan. Besides, don't you think we ought to at least see if there are *rooms* available or not?"

"No," he answered firmly. "Though tomorrow I intend to fully scrutinize their accommodations for future trips."

Emily appeared satisfied but put on her best, most petulant, expression. "But you promised we could stay there," she whined, like an annoying sibling.

"I did not," he retorted brusquely.

"You did, too."

"You must come anyway," he stated firmly and eyed her with hostility. He was fully aware that the hostler and an attendant stable boy, who were busily unharnessing the horses, would repeat the whole of their conversation later. "I'm not going another foot, Em, until I've had my supper and a good night's sleep."

"Oh, very well!" she cried. "But I think you're a beast!"

He offered his hand up to her again. She took it and alighted, but not without stumbling a little as her halfboots touched the gray stone cobbles of the inn yard. He caught her up with a hand about her waist. "You are nearly dead with fatigue!" he cried.

"I am not," she said, pushing him away.

"Well, I'm sorry that I did not stop in Ashbourne," he said quietly.

"Don't be silly," she responded, placing one careful foot

in front of the other. "All right, I will confess I have been wanting my bed these two hours and more, but I'm glad we've pressed on."

"Then at least take my arm," he said.

She did not hesitate to slip her hand about his arm and lean on him. He felt his chest swell with unexpected pleasure as he guided her into the inn.

When he had ordered supper for them both, he found she was protesting that all she wanted was her bed, but he insisted she eat. "For I will not have you fainting on our drive tomorrow from starvation."

"I shall be happy to eat an excellent breakfast," she countered in defense of her wish to retire immediately to her room.

"It will not do," he said. "You need sustenance now, and tomorrow's repast ought to be light."

She huffed an acquiescing sigh. "You are right, of course. Lead me to the parlor, then."

When she had eaten a few slices of roast beef, brussel sprouts in a light lemon sauce, and a couple of spoonfuls of potatoes, he escorted her to her bedchamber. Halfway up the stairs, however, she nearly stumbled again, which prompted him, quite oddly, to simply pick her up in his arms, sliding his left arm beneath her knees, and cradling her like a child.

Only, she was not a child, he thought as he walked slowly up the narrow staircase. For there was not a curve of her body that was not soft and inviting to his touch.

He glanced down the stairwell, then up it, for fear that he would be observed in such a wretched indiscretion. But the hour was late and the inn was quiet. No one was about to see how sweetly she slipped her arms about his neck.

He paused on the darkened stairs and gazed deeply into her eyes.

"How chivalrous," she murmured softly, her bowed lips curved in a half-smile as she held his gaze.

He knew a strong impulse that was not at all *brotherly*.

He wanted to kiss her and to go on kissing her until the sun rose on the morrow. He wanted to hold her in his arms as he had done twice before, to feel the length of her delightfully pressed against him, to experience again the sudden passion that blossomed within her when he would kiss her, to hear the delicate, soft moans that rose from her throat when she was thusly entangled in his arms.

"I should put you to bed," he murmured.

He felt a shiver ripple through her and he saw a light in her eye that was not in the least innocent. He drew in his breath and began a purposeful march up the stairs. He found her bedchamber, turned the doorknob, then pushed open the door with the toe of his boot. A candle burned at the foot of a pleasant, four-poster bed. The covers were turned down, the pillows had been plumped, and the cherry red bed curtains were tied back invitingly.

He groaned as he closed the door behind him and let her slide out of his arms, only she didn't leave him entirely. He still held her cradled against his right arm.

He should leave.

He should leave her bedchamber on the instant.

Every instinct warned him that he was in danger, but of what?

She placed her hand on the lapel of his coat. He felt the gentle pressure against his heart as though she was touching his soul. He looked down into her luminous, blue eyes, so dark in the dim light of the chamber, so beckoning, so hopeful that he would kiss her again.

He wanted to.

He placed his left hand over the fingers pressed against his heart. He took her hand in his and lifted her fingers to his lips. He began kissing each finger tenderly in turn, his gaze never straying from hers. He watched her brow become furrowed as though each kiss was causing her pain, yet he knew it was not pain that he was seeing but the same frustration he was feeling.

He turned her hand and placed a warm, wet kiss on the palm of her hand. He heard her gasp, he felt her draw closer to him as she leaned her head against his shoulder. He should stop kissing her hand. He should leave her bedchamber.

Instead, he kissed her wrist and felt her entire body quiver against his. He drew her more tightly against him and she turned into him, sliding her left hand up about his neck, which brought her lips against his cheek as he continued his assault of the palm of her hand.

All he had to do was turn his head and capture her lips with his own.

He should go.

To stay was madness.

But a fire had blossomed in the pit of his stomach, spreading upward through his heart and his chest. He turned quickly, caught her lips with his own, and at the same time released the hand he had been kissing to draw her fully and tightly against him. He kissed her hard, almost violently, realizing as he did so that he had been wanting to kiss her in this way ever since he had last kissed her. She held him fiercely in return, her body trembling against his. He couldn't breathe, he couldn't think, he couldn't reason away how he was feeling. A madness must have come over him. He could not seduce an innocent, and he could not allow her to seduce him, for there was only one end with a Longcliffe—marriage.

And he did not want to be married.

He stopped kissing her, but drew her into a crushing embrace. She was panting lightly, her head turned away from him and resting on his shoulder. She clung to him as though she was clinging to life itself. He couldn't imagine her thoughts. Was she hoping now that he would offer for her?

By god, he should, because he had compromised her so thoroughly by kissing her like this, by being in her hotel room unchaperoned.

"Hold me forever," she whispered.

Dear god, how he wanted to, but he knew he couldn't. He knew there was nothing he could offer her beyond a little kissing and cuddling. But why was he dallying with her in this wretched manner, causing hope to rise in her young, inexperienced breast, when his intentions were nonexistent if not ignoble.

"The wind is blowing again," she murmured.

He turned his head slightly to hear if the windows were rattling, but only silence returned to him. "Whatever do you mean?" he said, curious.

"When I was used to climb trees in my family's orchard, I would sit at the very top, especially when the wind was blowing. It was so delightful, just as this is, beyond anything I have known."

"So I am as the wind in the trees."

"In the top of the trees."

He felt his heart swell with something he thought might be affection mixed with a little wonder. Emily Longcliffe could have said many things to him in this moment, she could have upbraided him for his libertine conduct, she could have become nervous and chattered at him in her anxieties, she could have demanded that he marry her, and he would have deserved any of these.

Instead, however, she had offered him a sweet, womanly compliment, likening his embraces to the wind. Deep within his mind, he heard a crashing sound and he laughed aloud.

"What is it?" she queried, drawing back from him to look into his eyes.

He smiled down at her. "Didn't you hear that odd noise?"

She shook her head. "The inn is so silent, pleasantly so. I heard nothing."

"I heard it distinctly—as though someone just took a hard tumble."

"You mean, like someone falling down the stairs?" she asked. Her brow was furrowed with perplexity.

"Something like that."

She shrugged prettily. "I heard nothing."

"Then it must be the lateness of the hour. I will bid you good night, Emily. I think I ought to see if someone has hurt themselves on the stairs."

"Yes," she nodded, still a little bemused. "I suppose you should."

With that, he stole from the chamber into a deserted hall and entered his chamber across the way from her. The sound he had heard had come from deep within his heart, only he could not have said as much to Emily. In truth, he knew he was in a damnable fix and he hadn't the least notion how to go about getting himself out of it.

Twelve

The night had given counsel.

Emily stood at the top of the stairs, waiting as though stayed by a firm hand on her elbow as she gave herself to thought yet again. The kiss she had shared with Kingsbridge of the night before had been born of what? Of her fatigue? Of the undercurrent of excitement that had carried the journey forward even from London? Of the fact that from the first, from the kiss he had so brutally planted on her lips at the Scarswell masquerade, her relationship with the marquess had been characterized by a scandalous measure of attraction and sensuality?

She could not be sure, but she rather thought it was a combination of all these things.

Yet, when she had awakened this morning, her thoughts had been disrupted by a brilliant twinge of conscience that had fairly catapulted her from her bed and sat her attending to her morning toilette with unusual violence. The skilled hands of her maid had created another smooth chignon and a frill of curls across her forehead, both so suitably adapted to travel and to the constant wearing of a bonnet.

She had donned a gown of fine-grained patterned violet silk shaded with diamond shapes, which sported puffed sleeves, an Empire waist, a simple hem, and a bodice cut high at the neckline. Her bonnet was a simple poke design in a white silk stiffened with whalebone and bore a flattened back that would allow her to recline her head while travelling in the town coach. Across the brim were several staggered sprigs of violets, creating a summery effect that did not precisely match the tenor of her mood.

As she waited at the top of the stairs, she wondered yet again what the kiss between them had meant, for it was unlike the others and held an edge of desire that had sent her scurrying beneath the bed covers last night as though she might be safe there from the strength of her feelings.

What had it meant? And why did she feel this morning as though her entire being was thrumming with a sensation not unlike the way the air feels before a thunderstorm—alive and electrified?

What would Kingsbridge have to say to her this morning? And what should she say to him?

Was she tumbling in love with the handsome marquess?

She pressed her eyelids closed, praying that she was not. She didn't want to know love, or to love, or to be loved, or to have love dictate the direction of her life.

There it was, she thought, her eyelids popping open suddenly. She understood herself, at least in part. Love was a thing to be avoided, which might best explain why she had rejected all her suitors. Of course, Kingsbridge had never been a suitor, and had their paths parted following the masquerade she had little doubt that she would never have seen him again, for their societies were so very different.

But Evangeline's circumstances had thrust them together and was the sole cause for the manner in which she could hardly stay out of Kingsbridge's arms. Given this truth, therefore, she had but to see the adventure through to an end, and then she would be rid of him and his expert kissing and hugging and she could be easy again.

At least she hoped this much was true.

One way or another, however, she was so deeply into their journey north that there was precious little she could do to effect a change, even if she knew what change ought to be made.

With her thoughts settled, she at last made her way down the stairs and into the parlor where her breakfast awaited her.

A half hour later, however, Emily watched the curricle in front of her and sighed deeply.

Breakfast had been something of a trial, and now she and Kingsbridge were travelling apart today. He in the curricle, she in her town chariot, and their servants together in his travelling coach behind. She would have taken Gwendolyn up with her, but her maid was forced to travel the same stretch of road a great deal more slowly than herself. Dear Gwendolyn had not complained once of her carriage sickness and indeed, when Emily informed her abigail that she would be travelling with Kingsbridge's valet, her maid had not even flinched. In fact, for the barest moment Emily thought her maid would smile, for her lips had quivered ever so faintly. The truth of her feelings however were soon revealed when her cheeks became suffused with a pained blush of mortification at being forced to travel with a man who was a virtual stranger. Good, kind, dear Gwendolyn. So devoted was she to Emily's service that she had not uttered a single complaint against the arrangements.

As for Kingsbridge, Emily understood him, or thought she understood him. He was telling her through his conduct that she could have none of him.

Apparently, the night had given him counsel as well.

He had been uncommonly short with her during breakfast. At first she had supposed that he was playing out his brotherly role for the benefit of the maidservant who waited upon them. But when that round-cheeked young miss had curtsied herself from the parlor, leaving them to enjoy eggs, ham, and fresh peaches in private, his stiff manner did not leave him.

When she had eaten the last of her peach and was sipping her chocolate, she asked him quietly if she had in some manner offended him. He had been startled by her gentle query, she had seen as much in the blinking of his hazel eyes, but his answer had been less forthcoming, "No, of course you have not," he had responded sedately. "Merely, I should not—that is—"

"But how serious you are this morning, Kingsbridge. You don't need to be, I assure you. Or are you angry that—that I am teasing you by enjoying your kisses so much?"

His mouth had fallen agape and a remorseful, guilt-laden expression quickly overtook his features. She wanted to lift a hand to his brow to smooth away his concerns, but she stayed the impulse.

"I can find no fault in you," he stated. "The fault is all mine. But you must understand, that I have no intention of remaining here with you—"

"In Leek you mean?" she had offered teasingly.

She had coaxed a chuckle from him then.

"You know I don't mean Leek."

"Kingsbridge, pray don't make overly much of kissing me. Please. I have enjoyed it above all things and if anything, I should be begging you to forgive me, because I know it must be a sort of cruel torture to a man."

"Not as you suppose," he had offered kindly. "It is merely that I have nothing to give you."

"I don't want anything," she had returned with just such an edge that caused his brows to snap together into a frown.

"What do you mean?" he asked coldly. "You are a female. You want marriage and children, and I am unwilling to give you either."

"I don't want those things—I want the wind in the trees." Why had she said that? Where had such a thought come from? She had been so careful to arrange her mind earlier so that she could be comfortable with herself in company with Kingsbridge, and now she was saying things that were likely to increase their intimacy instead of decreasing it. Yet she could no more stop herself than she could stop the wind.

"Oh god," he breathed, rising from his chair at the same time. "You must stop saying such things to me."

"I don't say them to you," she responded, tears again in

her eyes as they had been more than once in his company. "But to the world in which I am forced to play a part I have come to despise."

He had looked at her hard at that moment. She knew he understood what she meant. Yet he still seemed incomprehensibly angry with her.

"I am having the horses put to," he said, giving his chin a determined lift. "I want you to travel in your own chariot with your maid. We will probably be journeying a long distance today as it happens, for I have discovered troublesome news. I didn't tell you earlier because I wanted you to enjoy your breakfast. But when I awoke this morning, I dressed quickly and hired a horse. I trotted over to the Swan and ferreted out the stable gossip. It would seem that *Mr. Smithe* let drop that he, his wife, and his wife's *sister* would be travelling to the Lake Country."

"The Lake Country?" Emily cried, astonished, settling her cup on her saucer with a loud clatter. "I was thinking Manchester, perhaps, or even Lancaster, but how will we find Evangeline if they have tucked her away in some cottage among the tors and lakes of Cumbria?" She had risen from her chair and stared at him. She was shocked by his news and at the same time aggrieved by his expression. He was so solemn, so serious, so agitated by the nature of their improper relationship that she felt compelled to say, "You've done enough already, Kingsbridge. Why don't you leave me to tend to this matter myself? I never meant to drag you halfway across the country. I promise you I never thought it would come to this. I thought all would be neatly settled in Derbyshire."

She had shocked him by her suggestion. "If we were on a picnic, I might not think it unwise to take leave of you now. But, by god, if you think I would desert you knowing full well you will chase the Glossips as far as Northumberland if you must, then you offend me, Miss Emily Longcliffe. You offend me very much."

This time, she lifted her chin. "I can see that I have wounded your masculine sensibilities, but I promise you I don't have need of you. I could hire a man to accompany me, perhaps a constable from Manchester. I just don't want you to feel obligated—"

"I don't," he snapped in return.

"Good. Then we ought to be going."

"Fine. We shall go."

"Fine."

But none of it was fine, Emily thought as she watched Kingsbridge through the front glass of her travelling chariot. His back was straight, and puffs of white dust roiled up from the wheels of his curricle as both vehicles moved tidily along the highway toward the county of Cheshire.

She didn't like brangling with him. But he had put up a wall so thick that she hardly knew where to begin in trying to tear down the heavy stones of his obstinance.

The truth was, she didn't quite understand him. Given his reputation, he should have been delighted that she fell so easily into his arms. But he didn't. Yes, of course, he enjoyed kissing her, but evidently the remorse he felt afterward was so painful as to have destroyed the joy of the moment. How very odd that she hardly felt remorseful at all. Well, a little, perhaps, but guilt was not what attended her, but an anxiety that her future was being penned in much the same manner that the Glossip's schemes, unbeknownst to them, were being undermined with each spin of her coach's wheels.

She sighed deeply as a dip in the road caused the curricle in front of her to disappear for a long moment. How oddly complicated their journey had become, unexpectedly so—and over a few harmless kisses at that!

But perhaps not so harmless, she thought, again with another sigh. For some reason, these brief, intimate exchanges served to set a fire in her soul and an equal fire to burning in Kingsbridge's conscience.

Where would it all end, she wondered.

In the Lake District, perhaps.

After an hour or so, the monotonous drone of the wheels on the macadamized road soon calmed her agitation and she gave herself to enjoying the passing beauty of the Cheshire landscape.

She glanced out at the countryside, noting that the land was gradually changing. The landscape was riddled with delightful little lakes that the local people called meres. Some of them were natural in origin, but many had been created by the great pits left after salt extraction for centuries prior.

The county of Cheshire was a pretty land of predominately rolling countryside; the Pennines dipped across the borders frequently to create a succession of charming valleys and hillocks. Many of the homes were of a local red sandstone, while others were of the ancient black timber frame design. The contrast was enchanting.

In Macclesfield, Emily left word for Gwendolyn that they would be proceeding to Knutsford. When she climbed back into her coach, Kingsbridge reported that an hour only separated them from Evangeline and her abductors.

Knutsford confirmed that they had not been misinformed.

When they reached Warrington, with the smell of the sea wondrously heavy in the air, Kingsbridge saw Emily settled in a comfortable parlor and a delightful nuncheon provided for her. He left her for a few minutes to confer with the stable boys to see if the Glossips and Evangeline had been seen in their pretty town. He returned to her, beaming. From everything that he gleaned from a lively discussion among three of the posting inn's stable hands, the Glossips could not be much above thirty minutes in front of them.

Emily was delighted and would have suggested that they postpone partaking of their midday meal in order to gain more ground in their pursuit, but the famished light in Kingsbridge's eye stopped her. He drew back a chair and, almost before his breeches touched the soft, red cushion of his chair, he had pierced a thick slice of Yorkshire ham with

his fork and began slicing it with his knife. Instead, therefore, she gave herself over to the enjoyment of the flavorful meal of ham, potatoes, asparagus, fish stew, and cherry tartlets.

They spoke of nothing, of everything, of his enjoyment of the simple country food, of her pleasure in the sight of the ever-changing architecture of each county, the weather, the fields ripening under the summer sun, the efficiency of the posting inns. Anything, everything. Any earlier contention between them had seemingly dissipated during the long hours that had separated them while travelling apart, and in its stead was a pleasant camaraderie that in many ways reminded her of her earliest times with Bertram in the apple orchards of Aldwark Manor.

"I must confess," he said, when they finally rose from the table and prepared to leave Warrington, "that you do not seem in the least fatigued, or are you merely pretending to keep up your spirits for the sake of your cousin?"

Emily lifted her brows. "Why would I be tired?" she asked. "We have travelled such a short distance after all. It cannot be much above fifty miles."

He stared at her for a long, unblinking moment. An expression she could not read entered his eye as he watched her. His lips twitched and a strange smile played at the corners of his mouth. She knew he was surprised, but she did not quite understand either why he was or what the odd, quirky smile on his lips meant.

"Are *you* tired, my lord?" she asked, wondering suddenly if perhaps he was no great traveller and was finding the journey difficult to bear. She would have been stunned to have learned he was, but she didn't want to assume any such thing.

He started slightly, then chuckled. "No, I am not tired. Not a bit."

"Good," she said. "Then we ought to be going."

"Yes, of course." He gestured for her to lead the way back to the inn yard.

He turned his curricle north toward Wigan, and as Emily

settled herself in the travelling coach once again, she couldn't help but sigh a little. How very much she would have enjoyed handling the ribbons at least for a few miles. Perhaps once they reached the next town he might relent a bit in his insistence they travel separately, that she might have a little pleasure in guiding his carriage for a few stages of the journey north.

At Wigan, where cotton mills had sprung up in recent years, their pursuit of her cousin hit a snag. No one, in any part of the town, had seen or heard of the trio.

"They must have travelled to Manchester from Warrington," Kingsbridge said, a frown pinching his brows. "The hostler said this was a route favored by many just to break up the journey a little."

"I suppose that is precisely what happened. But what do we do now? Do you think we ought to travel north anyway and hope that we meet up with them in Cumbria?"

He shook his head. "We can't take such a risk. For all we know Glossip might purposefully have let the Lake District notion drop merely to throw us off the scent."

"I hadn't thought of that," she said, chewing her lower lip, her gaze settling on his York tan gloves. He had his hand braced on the window frame of the coach, his hat in his hand, and a breeze blew his dark brown hair into a slight crown of tufts. She continued, "I suppose this means we must return to Warrington."

He nodded. "I'm sorry."

"What for?" she asked sharply, jerking her gaze to his face. "It's not your fault they chose to elude us somewhere after Wigan."

"I should have made a greater effort to determine which lane they chose."

"Stuff and nonsense," she replied. "I didn't think of it either, so why should you apologize to me? Besides, I am beginning to wonder—Evan, why don't we continue north anyway. The major highway leads through Wigan to Leyland

and Preston. Preston isn't terribly far, only twenty miles or so, and if we cannot find them there, then we can travel southeast through Blackburn back toward Manchester. These are the only two routes they could have taken without having gotten tangled up in a mess of country lanes that would undoubtedly have been difficult to traverse."

"How is it you know this country so well?" he asked, his brows lifted in faint surprise.

"Well, I have been to the Lake District before," she said. "And I have always had a fondness for maps and the like. I planned our route carefully from beginning to end, and except for the fact that Prudence was quite carriage sick and we could not travel as quickly as I would have liked, the entire expedition was without mishap."

"You enjoy travelling, then?" he queried.

Again she saw that odd smile at the edge of his lips and the quizzical expression in his hazel eyes. Whatever did he mean by it? "More than you will ever know," she responded quietly. Her gaze shifted from his face to the window in front of her. She sighed deeply. She recalled a moment to mind of her youth, a time with Bertram when they had set out all the old maps in the Aldwark library in front of them and began plotting their next adventure onto the Iberian Peninsula. Of course in this journey, she was a Lieutenant-Colonel with Lord Wellington's army in Spain and Bertram was in charge of the Congreve rockets in the rear. He was wounded that day, by the bayonet of a charging Frog who had somehow broken through all of his lordship's defenses and had somehow managed to lance the officer in charge of rocketry. She had bandaged him up a little too well that day, and had cut off the circulation in his left arm so that his fingers turned purple. What fun they had had!

Lord Kingsbridge watched Emily curiously, his senses stunned yet again by her. She was not anything like the woman he would have supposed her to be. As a fusty Longcliffe, he would have expected every manner of complaint from her about everything—the unsuitability of the food at their various lodgings, the dampness of the sheets, the long hours confined within a carriage, the ache of her bones, or the monotony of their journey. Yet, instead of any of these, she had exclaimed over the beauty of the countryside or the fine old buildings to be enjoyed in the next town or village, or what delight it was to be eating local fare instead of the usual fancy dishes to be found in the best drawing rooms of Mayfair.

But even more than this, he was surprised by how little the exigencies of travelling affected her. The only time she had grown tired was after the excessively long day she had spent earlier when calling upon Lord Trent, returning to Kegworth, and immediately climbing aboard his curricle and travelling northwest through to Leek. Even he had been nearly fagged to death. But right at this moment, when any other lady of his acquaintance would have been white-faced from fatigue, Emily had said she was not tired, and he believed her. In fact, she had a glow on her cheeks and in her eye that told him she did indeed love moving about the countryside hours on end. This circumstance alone was likely to be the undoing of *Mr. and Mrs. Smithe!*

He thought of his ship in Falmouth and for the barest second pictured her in his berth on the fine sailing vessel, asleep, her long light brown hair swept over the pillows, as the ship rose and fell among the waves. He would kiss her a hundred times a day, they would stand side by side at the bow, facing into the wind, daring the ocean to mar their happiness for even a second, and when the inevitable storms would come, they would ride them out, if not with an entire absence of fear, then at least with the knowledge that—but what was he thinking? His mind had begun rambling in an idiotish fashion, more in keeping with the workings of a schoolgirl than a man bent on seeing some of the most backward cities in the world.

"What are you thinking?" he asked, trying to divert the silly nature of his thoughts.

She giggled. "Of nothing. Merely of campaigning with Wellington."

"What?" he asked, chuckling with her.

She shook her head and felt a warmth grow on her cheeks. She turned to eye him shyly. "I was recalling another of my childhood adventures."

"With my brother-in-law again?"

"Yes."

How very much he wished she had not told him that. Now his mind was full all over again of Emily Longcliffe beside him at the prow of the ship, his arm about her waist, sea spray dousing them over and over.

"Why do you look so serious of a sudden, Kingsbridge?" she asked quietly.

He blinked, trying to dispel the image from his mind. But he could not do so entirely. Instead, he heard the creaking of the ship as it forced its way through the ocean's waves. He could smell the salt air. He could feel the hot sun on his neck. Emily would wear her hair in a long cascade about her shoulders and sit on deck in the sunshine and become as brown as a berry. "Are you bewitching me, Miss Longcliffe?" he queried.

"I—I don't know what you mean?" she asked.

How breathless she sounded. Damn! Her lips were parting again. She was so very pretty in her white bonnet, her large blue eyes staring at him as though she was seeing deeply into his soul.

Damn and blast!

He drew himself up firmly and slapped his hand on the window frame. "You are far too pretty," he said, drawing away from the door. "Let's go on, then. Just as you've said, Preston is scarcely little more than twenty miles."

Thirteen

On the following morning, after spending an uneventful night at an inn in Preston, Emily watched Lord Kingsbridge pay the shot. He was groomed to perfection, as always, in buckskin breeches, a blue coat, and pale yellow waistcoat. Over his shoulders he wore a loose cape against the darkening aspect of the sky. His top boots gleamed even in the gray light of the cloudy morning, the efforts of his valet's late night ministrations evident on the shiny black leather. His dark brown hair was brushed *à la Brutus* and ready to receive his fine tall hat of beaver felt.

As he settled his hat on his head and pulled on his gloves of York tan, he turned to face her with a serious expression. She knew in part why his brows were pinched together—their journey, it would seem, was destined to take them just as Glossip had said, into the Lake District, and such a trek would by its nature become increasingly more difficult to manage.

When they had arrived in Preston on the night before, Kingsbridge's usual, discreet inquiries, revealed that the Glossips had passed through two hours earlier, a measure of time that unfortunately forestalled any further travel. Night had already fallen and the dangers involved in travelling on a rutted dirt highway in the dark, with only two or three weak carriage lamps to light the way, were too risk-laden to be entertained with much serious intent.

Therefore, they had stayed in Preston in order to continue the journey on the morrow.

Now, as she met his concerned gaze, she knew that something more was troubling him than just the fact that they had lost an advantage over their quarry by being forced to stay the night in Preston.

She would have asked him the meaning of his grimly pinched lips but the innkeeper, quite *aux anges* at having a nobleman frequent his poor inn, kept bowing to him. Only as he pushed open the door and gestured for her to pass through was she able to broach the subject.

"What is it?" she whispered.

"I'll tell you in a moment," he murmured. "But not until we are entirely out of earshot of the innkeeper. He is a brutally nosy person who made mention of my previous conversation with the hostler. The nature of his remarks told me he had sought out his information with great determination."

"Ah," Emily responded. Her curiosity would have to wait it would seem, which was just as well since her attention, once she took several steps into the gravel drive of the inn, was caught by the surrounding vicinity.

The air struck her first, smelling wholly unpropitious. She glanced about the yard and beyond to the elms on a hillock behind the inn, and comprehended the source of the odor since a gray dust was settled on everything. "My goodness," she murmured, turning a full circle about her. "It must be the cotton mills," she said.

Kingsbridge's troubled face was forgotten for a long moment as she took in the results of the industrialized town.

Preston was one of the first northern cities to harness coal power to fire up the spinning mills that were quickly turning the county into a vibrant center of modern industry. But the effects on the land were disastrous, in strong contrast to the prosperity the factories brought to the mill owners. The streams near the mills were bereft of trout, and the air was thick with dust and debris from the numerous chimneys marring the skyline.

"I will not be sorry to leave here," she murmured.

"Nor I," Kingsbridge agreed, his gaze also drawn to the injured town and land.

He guided her toward her travelling chariot, but she stayed him with a hand on his arm. She was entirely disinclined to ride another day within the close confines of the vehicle. Fresh air was what she wanted of the moment.

"Please let me ride with you today," she said. "I promise to be very good and not to speak of the wind or anything of the like, then you may be at leisure to tell me why you are so solemn this morning."

He glanced up at the cloud-laden sky. "It will likely rain," he said.

"I have an umbrella," she returned. "And a woolen pelisse. The latter is already stowed in the curricle."

"You brought an umbrella with you?" he asked, a smile lighting his hazel eyes.

She chuckled. "Whyever do you look at me as though I've corn growing out of my ears? For heaven's sake, Kingsbridge, you begin to offend me. Why wouldn't I have taken an umbrella? The truth is I always carry one, no matter where I go. I am not in the least content to have my bonnets ruined all because of a stupid belief that it couldn't possibly rain on one or the other of my excursions."

"I don't mean to give offense," he responded. "It is merely that, in general, your sex does not prepare for every eventuality."

"Now you have offended me," she responded with a lift of her chin.

It was his turn to chuckle. "I can see that I have," he returned facetiously.

"Well, all right, I am not offended, but I am amused by your obvious choice of female companions. Have you ever tumbled in love with a lady of at least moderate sense?"

At that, he laughed outright. "I am beginning to comprehend my former obtuseness," he said. "Oh, very well, you may accompany me, but please keep your conversation somewhat dull, for I am beginning to like you more than is good for either of us. Only, where is your umbrella?"

Emily felt breathless suddenly and gestured toward her own travelling chariot, which was being brought forward by the hostler. "On the seat," she murmured. She was grateful he instantly moved toward her coach, because she knew that her cheeks were warm with a deep blush. She did not know if she could explain the origin of her embarrassment, except that his words had pleased her beyond anything else he could have said to her.

I am beginning to like you more than is good for either of us.

She turned her back to her chariot and looked up at the inn of gray stone. She swallowed hard and tried to still the strange butterflies that had begun turning cartwheels in her stomach. She had never felt so strange before, so simply moved by a few words, so dizzy.

She liked him, too.

Oh, dear. Could this be? Was it possible?

She shook her head. Her bonnet of green silk felt suddenly heavy on her light brown locks. She swallowed again.

"Come, Em!" he called to her in his sharp, *brotherly* manner. "We cannot keep the horses standing about. They are ready to be going, and so am I!"

She drew in a deep breath and schooled her face to one of a petulant grimace. Whirling about on her toe, she retorted, "I was merely enjoying the beauty of our delightful inn, Evan. But it is just like you to ruin everything."

She walked boldly and hotly toward the waiting curricle. She saw Kingsbridge's narrowed eyes which she knew purposely disguised the twinkle she would find in them once they had tooled out of the inn yard. His arms were crossed over his chest and the umbrella dangled from his left hand.

When she reached the curricle he thrust the sturdy, black silk umbrella at her. She took it with a whip of her hand and threw it on the seat in front of her, landing on her gray wool pelisse. She lifted up her skirts of forest green silk and with his hand hooked beneath her arm, climbed aboard the fast, light conveyance. He followed quickly after, gestured for the hostler to release the horse's heads, and set the pair briskly in motion.

Once the inn had been left behind, Emily returned to their former subject. "And now, if you please, pray tell me why you were so somber this morning when I descended the stairs."

He pursed his lips, then began, "I spoke for some time with the landlord and he gave me to understand that Kendal—which is where we are headed—is the main gateway to the Lake District as well as to the northern route to Gretna—"

"Are you proposing an elopement?" she suggested playfully. He was uncommonly grave and she wanted to dispel some of his air of doom.

He smiled, but only halfheartedly. "You know I am suggesting no such thing. But do attend to me—"

"You needn't explain. I believe I know exactly what the landlord told you—that Kendal is like a wheel with many spokes radiating out from the center. Therefore you are sure we are going to have great difficulty in discovering which spoke the Glossips took—"

"Yes, and that is assuming they are taking Evangeline to Cumbria."

She nodded. "There is a westerly route to Newcastle-Upon-Tyne on the east coast which, though so far north, is actually not that far from here. But I still think they intend to sequester her on one of the pretty lakes near Ambleside—Grasmere, perhaps or Rydal Water, Windermere, or even Conistan. There are more lakes of course, but they are much father north and in far more rugged country then the nearer lakes. I don't see what they would have to gain by doing so."

"You may be right," he murmured, giving the horses a slap of the reins. The wind picked up quite suddenly. "Those clouds have turned quite black. If I don't miss my guess, we're in for—"

His words were drowned in a sudden flash of lightning, followed abruptly by a loud crack of thunder. Emily started to giggle as she quickly grabbed her umbrella and popped it open just in time for the deluge to commence.

Lightning and thunder, bright and loud against the rise of the beautiful green fells to the east, again rattled the curricle. The horses never skipped stride, which led Emily to believe that the pair was used to the harsher northern climate that in any season tended to be far more lively than the weather in the south.

She held her umbrella tightly against her bonnet with one hand and gripped the edge of the curricle with the other. Kingsbridge glanced over at her and smiled quite wickedly. Her pelisse was quickly becoming soaked. She merely lifted a brow to his impertinent expression that apparently meant to say, *I defy you not to complain.*

She turned her face away from him and smiled so that he couldn't see her. She watched the heavy raindrops bounce off the low, gray drystone walls that lined parts of the highway. Rabbits and mice bounded for cover beneath thick hedgerows. Lightning flashed, thunder boomed, rolling down the fell toward their carriage and sending a vibration flowing through Emily.

The grassy hillside was swept first one way then another and another, as the wind-driven rain slanted and swirled over the land. A tall elm, tucked into the hedgerow and shading part of the highway, gave a moment's respite from the onslaught, but the very second the horses pulled the carriage from beneath the safety of the foliage, a wall of rain pelted Emily.

She felt as she had earlier, when Kingsbridge had told her he was beginning to like her. She felt dizzy and excited.

Undoubtedly her cheeks were suffused with a bright flush of pleasure. The masquerade ball came suddenly to mind, along with the exhilaration she had experienced while being pursued by the mysterious Turk and later while being held in his arms.

This is no different, she thought, startled. The storm was having the very same effect on her, of brilliant light, of thunder, of strange vibrations through her heart.

Goodness! What was happening to her?

Before very long, the wind and rain began to abate. The brief summer onslaught had passed, but the horses began to kick up a great deal of mud. After her pelisse became dotted with the watery mud, Emily did the only sensible thing and placed her umbrella in front of her to serve as a screen.

Kingsbridge noted her improvisation and let out a crack of laughter. "Are you always so undaunted?" he asked.

She laughed as well. "And are you always so impressed with so little?"

His cape was soaked and splattered as well. He swiped water off his forehead, nose, and cheeks. His nicely starched shirtpoints looked like two wilted rose petals, petals that were soon flecked with mud, as was his face. By the time they reached the next village, a small hamlet by the name of Newsham, even his eyebrows wore a layer of dark, wet dirt. The roads so far north had not yet seen the happier effects of macadamization.

There was nothing for it. They could not continue in such a muddy condition. A change must ensue.

They waited for the slower travelling coaches to arrive at Newsham and afterward Emily saw her wet clothing exchanged for a much more comfortable dry ensemble of white summery muslin, a matching poke bonnet decorated with wild roses of pink silk and dark green leaves, lace gloves, and pink leather slippers.

She emerged from her bedchamber and descended the stairs wondering if Kingsbridge would now laugh at her for having arrayed herself in such a pretty costume, but instead he took on his brotherly manners. "I suppose now you will expect me to carry you to your waiting chariot so that you do not dampen your slippers!" he stated curtly, scowling all the while.

She turned her shoulder impatiently. "Well, of course!"

He now wore a riding coat of brown twill, fresh buff pantaloons, a clean, white neckcloth and a shirt which bore finely starched points that touched his cheeks handsomely. All signs of the mud were gone. His hair however was still damp, but arranged attractively. He exchanged a quiet word with the landlord, placed a sovereign in his hand for the brief use of his inn, and turned toward Emily.

He crossed to her in a quick, angry step, picked her up bodily, and swept her from the inn. Emily again felt a little dizzy, as one arm slid about his neck and her opposite hand came to rest on the lapel of his coat.

Puddles littered the yard of the cobbled inn, and he carefully began a slow progress toward the waiting travelling chariot. She watched him from the confines of her bonnet, the sides of the white muslin confection obscuring her lateral view. His skin was a fine olive complexion, and because the hour was still early his morning shave was still fresh. She could even smell just the hint of soap. A jerk, a small leap, a sidestep, and he picked his way through the maze of small lakes.

When he reached the coach, however, instead of immediately throwing the door open and tossing her inside, he paused and met her gaze. "You've been watching me rather intently," he said, still holding her in his arms.

She nodded. "Indeed. I wanted to see whether or not your valet had cut you shaving this morning."

His lips twitched. "What an undecorous thing to say," he murmured.

"I felt you would not want me to say something flirtatious or otherwise *wind-laden*," she hinted.

He shook his head, his gaze drifting to her lips. "I am glad you are wearing that ridiculous bonnet," he said, trying for a rise.

"Why?" she asked, ignoring his taunting comment.

"Because your bonnet prevents me from kissing you."

"You shouldn't say such things," she breathed.

"And your eyes should not speak to me with such fire."

"Am I so obvious?" she asked, lifting her hand off the lapel of his coat and scandalously untying the pink ribbons of her bonnet.

He shook his head. "What am I going to do with you? A little rain, a little mud, and it's all hallow with me."

"Kingsbridge," she began, a bubble of devilment in her throat. "You had best put me in the carriage else the landlord will begin to wonder why you stand on the cobbles holding your *sister* forever in your arms."

He nodded. "You are right, of course." But he set her down on the cobbles, then astonished Emily by drawing apart the ribbons of her bonnet and pushing the brim back just sufficiently so that his lips were on hers before she knew what he was about.

Oh, what a devil, she thought with delight. *A wondrous, wretched, exciting devil! Always unexpected and teasing and exhilarating! Heaven could not be as sweet!*

The sunlight suddenly broke through the persistent layer of clouds and spread a blanket of heat over her back and shoulders. His tongue touched her lips. If a little mud and a little rain afflicted him, then the feel of so strong a man holding her in his arms and kissing her so sensually was *her* bane. Her knees quickly became buttery and useless. She parted her lips, the heavens opened, the angels sang.

After a long, long moment, after the tension of the kiss had risen to a sharp peak then subsided in a series of gentle waves that pummeled her heart into a shapeless mass, after the horses had been snorting and stamping their feet a dozen times, Emily drew back from Kingsbridge.

She met his gaze and saw in his eyes a question, and an odd constriction took the puddle of her heart, gathered it up, and quickly forced the treacherous organ back into its original form. She slid her arms from about his neck. She did not want him to ask the question so evident in his eyes. The subject frightened her, for she knew he was wondering about the future.

"Emily," he whispered. "We must talk."

"But not here, not now, not yet," she responded on a quiet, urgent whisper. Why did she suddenly feel so frightened, as though fate was closing tightly in upon her, threatening her, demanding something of her she was unwilling to give.

The thought rose sharply to mind—if she didn't take care, she would become as her sisters and bear a dozen children, no less than a dozen. For if the sequence was right, she was destined to give birth to at least as many. Prudence had out-birthed Meg. And in turn, Sophia had borne more babes than Pru. Why would she be exempt from such a clear, marked destiny?

"Why do you stare at me, Em, as though I've suddenly grown horns?" he queried, a half-smile on his lips.

She drew back from him abruptly. "I—I don't know," she lied. She couldn't tell him the nature of her thoughts. She didn't want to give voice to any of them, not now, not yet.

"Have my embraces frightened you?" he asked, taking a small step forward and taking a gentle hold of her arm. "Please tell me it is no such thing."

Emily felt her heart twist in anguish. "It is no such thing, I assure you. Your kisses don't distress me—but the look in your eye just then—Evan, please, please, don't ever kiss me again. I couldn't bear—that is—please try not to."

She turned to open the door to the carriage, but he caught her arm. "I have only kissed you," he murmured. She glanced at him and saw that his eyes were heavy with desire. He held her in a grip that was tight and needful.

"There can be only one end to this, Kingsbridge. You know as much. Are you truly willing to consign yourself to such a future? The worst of it is, I find I can hardly resist you, especially when your lips touch mine, and then you—" She broke off, but placed her fingers on his lips, feeling that she was refusing a glass of water even though she was parched with thirst.

He caught her fingers with his hand and kissed her palm passionately. Through the lace of her gloves, she felt the softness of his lips and the passion in his kiss. As though having taken a little too much laudanum, she again turned toward the carriage, fumbled with the steps, and stumbled her way inside.

If only the roads weren't muddy, then she might be safe, for he could drive his curricle. He had hired a postillion to see his carriage farther north until the roads grew more manageable. Therefore, he could do nothing more but follow her inside.

Once within, she pressed a hand to her chest, trying to still her heart. She had never known such agitation before. The postillion started the horses forward and the movement of the coach helped the tensions of the moment to subside a little.

"I'm sorry, Em," he murmured. "I can see that I have caused you terrible distress."

"No," she cried, turning to face him. Oh, why was he so handsome? Why was she drawn to him as she was? "You have not caused me distress, but great happiness and joy. Yet it is so wrong—because, because, what would the end be? Would either of us truly be happy?"

He frowned at her, his thoughts drawing inward. He covered her hand with his own, but turned his gaze away from her, directing it to the backs of the horses. A faint drizzle had commenced that quickly gathered on the front window glass, obscuring the view.

"Yes," he murmured on a low, somber voice. "What would the end be?"

Fourteen

The ancient town of Kendal, situated in the valley of the River Kent, was a welcome sight to Emily. If the Glossips had spoken truthfully about their intentions to visit the Lake District, then Evangeline would be very close at hand once more.

The market town was a sparkling diamond under the July sunshine, set as it was in the rich green valley. It was known by a quaint appellation—the "auld grey town"—which referred to the gray limestone used to construct most of its buildings.

Upon crossing one of the six bridges in the town, Emily chanced to turn to view the shops along the High Street to her right. At the same time, so did a young lady in a travelling coach briskly crossing traffic from the east. Emily blinked and started as she met the gaze of the lady in the opposing coach.

The beautiful young woman had dark brown hair worn in ringlets beside each cheek, and her eyes were as rich and dark as her hair. She possessed thickly arched brows, a small, retroussé nose, a slightly pointed chin, and pretty bowed lips.

Evangeline!

Her mouth dropped agape. "My cousin!" she exclaimed.

"Where?" Kingsbridge cried, turning in her direction.

Evangeline, however, had immediately averted her face, and Emily could only point to her equipage as the yellow bounder swept by. She was not alone and had appeared as though she shared cramped quarters with her abductors.

"We must follow after them!" Emily cried, preparing to lower her window in order to shout her orders to the postillion.

Kingsbridge, however, stayed her with a gloved hand on her arm. "We cannot," he said seriously. "The horses have already pulled the coach ten miles. We must change soon. They are in no condition for a hearty chase across the moors."

Emily felt her heart sink. "You are right, of course. But we must do something. Evangeline was so close, and I know she recognized me. I know she did, for she appeared as astonished as I was."

Kingsbridge glanced up the intersecting street, then down again. "I wonder," he murmured. A moment later, he opened the door and before the postillion could respond to his order and bring the horses to a halt, he had leapt from the slowly moving coach, rounded the corner of the street opposite their coach, and was gone.

My goodness, Emily thought. He's chasing after Evangeline on foot. She was utterly astonished. Of course Kingsbridge had shown great fortitude in accompanying her so far north and in such a short time, but never would she have believed that he would exert himself so much as to actually pursue a briskly rolling town coach across the gray stone cobbles of Kendal in his glossy Hessians!

How odd to think of the Marquess of Kingsbridge doing so.

She found herself wondering what she ought to do. They must have fresh horses, but would it behoove her to take a few minutes and pursue Kingsbridge? She decided on the former and leaned her head out to instruct the postboy accordingly.

Once the horses were being attended to at the Fish Posting Inn, Kingsbridge returned, his brow dotted with perspiration, his stride long and purposeful. She descended the coach and met him halfway across the cobbles. "What did you discover?" she asked, glancing furtively from side to side making certain their conversation could not be overheard.

"They are gone northwest, just as I thought they would."

"To Birthwaite near Windermere Lake?"

He nodded. "I believe so. But Ambleside is not far beyond Birthwaite and might just as easily be their object. Grasmere is not far from there."

"We must follow them," she stated. She turned back to look at the horses now being led to the coach.

"Of course you are right, but I have been thinking—a good friend of mine, Lord Winsford, owns a property on Windermere, a fine cottage called Winsford Ketel. He has been in the habit for years of retiring to the lakes during the summer months. I believe we ought to pay him a call and see if we might not stay the night at his house. Birthwaite and Ambleside are both such small hamlets that our presence would become quickly known were we to spend the night in either village."

"What an excellent notion," Emily said. "I am most strongly in agreement with you."

His hazel eyes shifted away from her slightly, and she could tell that for some reason he had grown uncomfortable.

"What is it?" she queried.

He drew her even farther away from the coach where the hostler was busily harnessing two strong beasts to the travelling chariot. In a low voice, he murmured, "Winsford will know you are not my sister."

His expression was so dark and full of meaning that Emily could only smile. "Is that what concerns you?" she queried.

"As well it should, miss!" he retorted sharply. "It is bad enough that we are travelling in this infamous fashion—were any one of either of our acquaintances to recognize us, your reputation would be in shambles—"

"And you would be forced to offer for me," she said, staring up at him in a teasing manner. "And that wouldn't do at all. I should dislike it above all things."

"Here, I say," he whispered, his smile crooked. "You've already told me you don't wish for a marriage with me, but I promise you I would be a good husband."

At that, Emily met his gaze and laughed outright. "You would be a hateful husband, for your passions are far too strong to be bound to a house and a brood of children. You love to gamble, and what of your membership in the Four-in-Hand Club? And twice on this journey you have told me of swimming feats I am convinced must be more an invention of your imagination than any true act. Tell me I am wrong?"

He narrowed his eyes as though angry with her, but she knew better, especially because his lips twitched. "I could school myself," he replied.

"Oh, indeed, you could!" she retorted facetiously. "I should like to see that. I should enjoy very much watching you wait upon a wife like a devoted dog and pet your children while they say nasty things and get into all manner of mischief."

He placed a hand over his heart. "Madam," he cried playfully. "You strike fear into the very center of my being."

"Stuff and nonsense," she returned on a murmur. "There, the horses are ready. Pay the man and let's be on our way. We shall deal with Lord Winsford when we arrive." She then left word for her maid and for Kingsbridge's valet of their intentions to travel north toward Ambleside as well as the location of Winsford Ketel.

Lord Winsford was two years Kingsbridge's junior and received Emily's hand with brows lifted so high in astonishment that a dozen wrinkles rose to flow into his blond hair.

"How do you do, my lord?" she queried, her heart beating with the thrill of playing off yet another trick. "We have not met for some time, but then I have been a happily married matron in Devonshire until Evan persuaded me to join him for a brief holiday in the Lake District."

"Well met, er, *Mrs. Matford,*" he said, bowing over her fingers, his cheeks pink with consternation.

When the footsteps of the butler had disappeared down the hall, he turned to Kingsbridge and queried a very succinct, "What the devil are you doing? And that," here he turned toward Emily, "with a Longcliffe?"

Emily was not in the least offended but merely glanced up at Kingsbridge and said, "Yes, what are you doing with a Longcliffe?"

He chuckled. "Winsford, though I don't mean to cast even a mite of disparagement on your staff, wouldn't it be best if we left your entrance hall and concluded the remainder of this conversation *in private?* "

"Oh, yes, indeed, yes!" Winsford cried. He turned to the left and gestured awkwardly to the library, then turned to the right and waved toward the drawing room. "Oh, the devil," he murmured. "You are right about my servants. If I sneeze it is well known within an hour that I have contracted an inflammation of the lungs."

"I, for one, my lord, have been exceedingly wishful of viewing the lake," Emily suggested. "My *brother* has told me what a delightful prospect you enjoy."

Lord Winsford's brow lightened considerably. "Yes, of course, and it is truly a marvelous sight though I must warn you that the weather here is wholly inconstant. So if I tell you we must race back to the house, you will know why." He gestured for them to follow him, and he began moving toward the back of the manor down a darkened hallway where several amateurish landscapes hung.

"The hills to the south can be glowing with sunlight," he said, further expounding on Lakeland weather, "when the lake suddenly whips to a froth and a thunderstorm appears at the northern end with such violence that the whole manor shakes. An hour later, the lake is sparkling beneath an expanse of sunshine brighter than before."

The hall opened up to a charming sitting room which had a beautiful view of Windermere. The wall facing west was made up exclusively of windows, and the afternoon sun poured in like a pathway to heaven. The warmth of the chamber was a delight, and the overstuffed furniture, not in the least in the current Grecian mode, was more inviting than anything Emily had seen in a long time. The fabrics were of a pretty chintz, the bright yellow, red, and blues a cheerful contrast to the nature of their arrival at the manor.

"But how lovely," Emily cried, gesturing with a sweep of her hand over the charm of the chamber. Her gaze then moved in the direction of the lake. "And Windermere! Truly, I have never seen anything so magnificent. You are quite fortunate, Lord Winsford."

"I am indeed," he murmured, glancing at Emily with a smile of deep appreciation on his strong features, his gaze fixed firmly on her and not on the lake. She lifted her brows in surprise. She could not mistake the flirtatious nature of his retort.

He was not precisely a handsome man, she thought, but there was an easiness in his manners and in his expression that she found quite appealing. His eyes were a lustrous brown, his brows well arched, but his nose was large and his jawline too firm to be sculpted with anything but affectionate tolerance. Yet, still, she was drawn to him.

"Come," he continued, extending his arm toward a door to the right. "Let me take you on a walk to the lake, or are you greatly fatigued, *Mrs. Matford?* I would suppose you have been travelling for some time, now, and would not consider myself a proper host were I not to offer you an opportunity to retire to a bedchamber for a much-needed respite, if I do not mistake the matter."

His eyes twinkled. He was enjoying his role and delighting in pretending she was Kingsbridge's sister.

"I am not in the least fatigued," she said, lifting her chin slightly. "Your suggestion of a walk is precisely what I need to restore my limbs to a place of contentment."

He smiled suddenly and looked at her with a question in his eye. Emily had a very strange sensation as she watched him, as though he had slipped into her mind for a moment and liked what he saw. After a few seconds, she realized that for some reason he was intrigued by her.

Kingsbridge cleared his throat and, in a voice a little deeper than he was used to employ, begged his host to lead the way to the lake.

"Just so," Lord Winsford murmured and opened the door for Emily to pass through.

A few minutes more saw them walking three-abreast down a well-kept graveled path, stair-stepped with thick boards in numerous places. The grasses about the lake were strewn with pungent ferns. Red squirrels scampered across the path in the distance and scurried up the trunks of ancient conifers to the far left and right of the manor lands. In many places, the edge of the lake was crowded with trees which both enhanced the beauty of the vista, but also obscured the view of the lake from the roadside.

Once out of earshot of the manor, and after sweeping the surrounding woods, gardens, and paths for any signs of one of his servants, Lord Winsford said quietly, "I have never suffered such a shock as being introduced to Horatia Matford only to receive the hand of Miss Emily Longcliffe." He turned to eye them both, his expression kind but insistent on an explanation.

Emily smiled, and Lord Kingsbridge quickly detailed the nature of their expedition. The moment he spoke of a kidnapping, Lord Winsford halted in his tracks and went no further, but rather listened intently. Kingsbridge's speech was interjected several times by his lordship muttering a sympathetic, "Good god."

"So you see," Emily finished on a subdued tone, "though

it would seem we are conducting ourselves in an entirely scandalous fashion, we had no choice but to set out in pursuit once we saw that clearly something had transpired to change the Glossips' intentions of travelling to Tewkesbury. I have sent word to my uncle in Derbyshire, but because I can only assume he would have been *en route* to Gloucestershire before my missive could reach him, I would not expect him to come north for several days at the very least."

Lord Winsford was now completely taken aback, one arm cradling the other and two fingers tapping his chin thoughtfully. "You must stay here," he said at last. "The pair of you. We live in such seclusion that no one would ever discover that you've been here—well, at least not for a long time, and then I doubt that there would be serious repercussions. No, you must stay here."

"I will confess," Kingsbridge said, "that I was hoping very much that you would offer your hospitality."

"Whatever you need I will place at your disposal," he said urgently. "I have a small sailing craft and a rowboat, horses of course, and a nice light gig. Anything I can do!" His brown eyes began to shine with a sensation so familiar to Emily that she giggled.

He glanced at her and queried, "Why do you laugh?"

"Your enthusiasm," she murmured. "I would have to suppose then that your life here during the summer months is perhaps not quite so exciting as might please you?"

"Is it obvious then?"

"Only a little."

He turned more fully toward her and said, "So, how is it that a Longcliffe would engage in such a journey as this? I know your sisters well, especially Lady Chaddeley. To my recollection—"

"Yes, yes, I know," Emily returned, "but you must realize that I am the youngest and I have always been something of an oddity, as well as the frequent despair of my sisters' kind intentions to make me what I am coming so plainly to comprehend that which I am not."

She was not certain he was aware of doing so, but he took a small step toward her, his attention fully engaged. "But how refreshing to meet with such candor and, dare I say it, *enthusiasm?"*

Again Emily giggled. She would have said more, she would have elaborated on the nature of her sisters' despair where she was concerned, but at that moment Kingsbridge again cleared his throat—as he had most curiously done earlier—and took a broad step toward Lord Winsford, effectively placing himself between his friend and Emily.

"I knew I could rely on you," he said, narrowing his eyes at Winsford in a meaningful manner, before continuing, "in every possible sense."

Emily looked up at him, wondering what he meant, especially since his gaze as he stared at his friend was rather piercing.

Lord Winsford glanced at Emily, then back to Kingsbridge. The men exchanged a silent understanding which merely made their host smile broadly and laugh outright. "So that is the way of it, then?" he asked.

Kingsbridge nodded. "Let us just say that while Miss Longcliffe is in my care, I shall do all that is necessary to protect her." Emily was astonished, and began to understand that her travelling companion saw Winsford as some manner of threat.

Winsford, however, was not cowed in the least. "I am always a gentleman," he responded. "And if you wish to infer more you will have to name your seconds!"

Ignoring Kingsbridge's astonished visage, he turned on a bright step toward Emily and offered his arm to her, "My dear *Mrs. Matford,* I daresay you are in need of a fine meal after a long journey. I am myself fully acquainted with the frequently indifferent fare to be found along our best highways and assure you that my kitchen gardens are well stocked. We are able to bring all manner of delightful lobster, clams, and fish from the coast."

"I will not deny that I am hungry," she said, taking up his arm and walking beside him. She again heard Kingsbridge growl, and smiled inwardly. Could it be that the marquess was experiencing one or two twinges of protective jealousy? She couldn't help but be flattered, just a little. She turned her attention fully, however, to her host and continued, "Travelling as we have, always heightens my appetite. But I promise you, I can have no reason to complain of the food on our journey, for I have found most of it quite delightful, though I will not deny that I have been wanting my supper ever since we last supped at Milnthorpe."

"You could not have arrived at a better moment," he said brightly, "for I was out on the lake angling all morning and brought home a fine array of trout which Cook has kept iced for dinner."

"How sublime," she responded truthfully.

"And how pleasant to have good company as well."

Emily heard Lord Kingsbridge mutter an inaudible scoffing remark. She bit her lip and again smiled to herself. There could be no two opinions on the fact that her travelling companion was not happy with Winsford's flirtations, a fact that pleased her much more than it should have.

Fifteen

The dining room overlooked the ten-mile-long lake and the low hills in which Windermere was situated. Winsford Ketel Manor had been built three centuries prior by a poetic baronet, later to become the first Lord Winsford, who had become deeply attached to the Cumberland lakes. He had built the manor to make the very best use of the beautiful vista, and consequently every principal chamber of the graystone house enjoyed a view of the lake.

Emily sat at the dining table, along with the gentlemen, having enjoyed a delightful repast. She sipped a glass of Madeira contentedly, at the same time staring out at the fading sunlight. She held her glass in her right hand, her left settled comfortably on her stomach. Earlier, the housekeeper had seen her to her bedchamber, one of her portmanteaux had been unpacked and the wrinkles of her muslin gown ironed out. Though her maid had not yet arrived, one of the undermaids had proved quite clever and had helped her with her toilette before supper. She was gowned therefore in a simple muslin round gown, designed high at the waist and adorned with billowy puffed sleeves. A single strand of small garnets was draped elegantly about her neck. Her hair was caught up in a loose chignon, with a spray of curls trailing from the back and a thin frill just touching her forehead.

Sunset glowed in orange streaks on the lake and the bright green leaves of scattered elm trees glittered in the long slanted rays. She had fallen silent, along with her companions, lost in her own thoughts as the waters performed their mesmerizing magic.

Nothing more would be attempted tonight, that much had been agreed upon. But tomorrow, Lord Winsford had offered to drive to Ambleside in order to make a few careful inquiries and determine, if possible, where exactly Evangeline was being held captive.

How odd it seemed to Emily that she should be enjoying her wine and the beauty of the lake while her cousin was suffering the fear and agitation of being held against her will by ruthless strangers bent on using her, as well as her father and Mr. Buxton, so ill. Whether or not the Glossips' schemes extended beyond the extraction of largess, she could not begin to guess. Besides, she absolutely refused to ponder the hideous nature of the question.

The beauty of the lake dimmed with each passing moment that she kept her thoughts fixed to Evangeline. She took another sip of Madeira and sighed, letting her gaze rise heavenward. No stars as yet had appeared to presage the night. Where was Evangeline even at this moment? Was she, too, staring out a window and wondering what next might happen?

Another sip.

Another sigh.

"Come," Lord Winsford called to her.

Emily gave herself a shake and glanced up to find that her host was standing beside her chair and had extended a hand down to her. She lifted her brows in surprise.

"You are blue-devilled, Mrs. Matford," he said with a half-smile. He wore a coat of blue superfine fitted snugly to a pair of broad shoulders. He seemed equally as athletic as Lord Kingsbridge, and during supper had professed his love of hiking about the Lakeland fells. His blond hair gleamed with Macassar Oil and was curled attractively at the temples as well as in a gentle roll below his collar. His neckcloth was fresh and his shirtpoints touched his cheeks at a moderate height. It was no wonder he was a friend to Kings-bridge—they were very much alike.

He continued, "I can see by your woeful expression that very soon you are like to fall into a fit of the sullens and that *will not do.* Of course, you've every right to be distressed, but I simply can't allow it. Come to the drawing room and we'll sing a few duets. After all, I'm sure you don't want to set the servants gossiping because of your unhappiness. They will be expecting a little music after dinner. You do play and sing, don't you?"

Emily rose to her feet, knowing he was right in addressing her sorrowful countenance. "Yes, tolerably well," she said, summoning a smile that felt a little wooden on her lips.

"Tolerably well?" he chided her, then burst out laughing. "You are a Longcliffe and if you don't play like an angel, I shall be stunned."

A new smile touched her lips, this one not so stiff. Lord Winsford's playful manners were infectious. "You are right. My sisters forced me to practice until I was sick to death of Bach, Handel, Haydn, and poor Mozart. I had to turn the hourglass at least twice each day and see all the sand through to the end, before I was permitted to rise from our rosewood pianoforte."

"Just as I thought." He glanced over his shoulder at Kingsbridge and winked at him.

But as they stepped into an antechamber that connected the dining room to both the entrance hall and the receiving room, the sound of carriages was heard in the drive.

Emily gasped, realizing that her maid, Gwendolyn, would have just then arrived. "We did not tell them of our subterfuge," she whispered urgently to Lord Winsford. "Your household will be set in an uproar if the truth comes out!"

"Good god!" he murmured. Turning to her, he asked, "Can your maid be trusted to withstand the prying efforts of a most determined housekeeper?"

Emily pursed her lips as she quickly evaluated her maid's

character and smiled. She knew Gwendolyn well, for she had been her abigail for nearly eight years. Though her countenance was as sweet as honey, her outer appearance of gentleness belied a will of iron. "I believe she would find it a challenge of the most delightful."

He nodded, seemingly satisfied. He glanced at Kingsbridge, who was now standing beside Emily on her left. "And I know your valet. He would consider even the smallest question an offense to your dignity, would he not?"

"That he would."

"Let me tend to this then," Winsford said. He directed them both to the drawing room and on a quick step returned to the entrance hall, where Emily was certain he would not hesitate to arrange the stories of both their servants suitably.

Emily preceded Kingsbridge into the drawing room. The chamber had two views, the primary vista employing a long expanse of windows that fronted the lake. The second view looked north, from which vantage point Emily could see a few scattered lights through the falling dusk as candles, oil lamps, and lanterns were lit to replace the failing sunbeams.

She crossed the room to the windows overlooking the lake and took up a winged chair of a soft blue velvet nearby. Her gaze was drawn to Windermere as though the darkening waters held some message for her. She wondered again where Evangeline was. She might even be nearby, or perhaps the Glossips had taken her across the fells to Penrith, even beyond to Scotland.

She held her hands together tightly on her lap, the thin white muslin of her gown soft against her fingers.

Kingsbridge drew near and leaned over the back of her chair. "I have not seen you so quiet in the whole of my acquaintance with you," Kingsbridge said, his words spoken lightly into her ear.

The warmth of his breath sent a shiver rippling down her neck and back. The sensation was so sudden and so pleasing that her pulse quickened. She turned slightly to meet his gaze. "Forgive me," she said. "I have been caught up with thoughts of Evangeline."

He smiled, touched her chin with his fingers in an affectionate gesture that served to comfort her. He moved past her and took up a seat opposite her in a matching blue velvet chair.

His gaze drifted to the lake and she took a moment to glance about the chamber. The room was low-ceilinged and as cozy as the flowered sitting room. The chamber was long and rectangular, cottagelike in arrangement and decor. The same overstuffed comfortable sofas and chairs littered the room, accompanied by tables of a gleaming mahogany. A large, friendly fireplace, opposite the windows and empty at present, promised to provide a pervading warmth for the chamber in the midst of the chilling, northern winters. The windows were covered in a single valance of a pale yellow silk. Several branches of candles held the room in a pretty glow, reflected more and more in the windows as the sun slipped behind the hills to the west and darkness descended over the lake.

"You are worried for her," he said, bringing her gaze back to his face. "That would only be natural."

"Yes," she murmured. "It seems so odd to me that while we were travelling I could be somewhat free of my cares for her safety. But now that we are so tidily settled in a place of such beauty, I feel as though I have forsaken her."

"But you haven't."

"I know. It is wholly irrational, but I begin to think that I cannot be content unless I am in motion."

He smiled faintly as he watched her, holding her gaze and looking deeply into her eyes. "You are so unlike your sisters," he murmured softly. "I would never have thought to have found someone who so nearly shares my own peculiarities in a Longcliffe. For instance, if I hadn't seen your agitation, I would not have been aware of the reasons for my own restlessness since we have arrived here."

"You feel it, too, then?" she asked, leaning forward slightly. "A sense that we ought to be doing and not just sitting?"

He nodded.

"It is strange, though, isn't it?"

"Yes, it's as though we're doing nothing, yet there is nothing we can do except wait—"

Lord Winsford appeared in the doorway. "And sing duets!" he called out. "For heaven's sake, the pair of you are as mournful as owls. Come! A little music will dispel the megrims. You must trust me in this, *Mrs. Matford.*"

Emily responded by rising from her chair. "You do enjoy calling me that, don't you?"

He chuckled. "What I am enjoying is that you have come to brighten my summer sojourn, to dispel a little of my boredom, and even to bring a spot of adventure into this poor house."

"You are too much alone here," Emily said, moving to the pianoforte near the north windows. Seating herself, she added, "You ought to have a wife to keep you company in the evenings."

"What a teasing expression you wear, as though you are daring me. But the nearest thing to a wife I might ever want to join in a pair of hefty leg-shackles has only just arrived, and seems destined to trip as quickly from my life as she came."

"You flirt so prettily, my lord. Now let me sing you a song." She placed her fingers carefully over the appropriate keys and plunged into the lyrical ballad entitled, "Captivity." Marie Antoinette supposedly sang the song during her imprisonment.

"Oh-ho!" he cried, laughing outright, the tones of the slightly out-of-tune instrument dancing across the low ceilings and flooding the chamber. "You are a minx. I am liking you more and more. Now, why have I not met you before in London?"

"The Longcliffes?" she returned playfully. "To attend the soirees of such a roguish set of creatures! Never!" Then she began to sing.

Kingsbridge moved to stand by the pianoforte as well. His lips twitched as he watched her perform the pretty melody for their host. Occasionally she would glance at him, her eyes dancing, but mostly she played her song for Winsford.

When she was done, she bade the gentlemen sing a duet together, a ballad called, "Her Hair is Like a Golden Clue." They didn't know half the words and poor Winsford had an ear like solid banging against a tin pan, but joy pervaded the drawing room even with such a small circle and even when her cousin's fate was uncertain.

Emily had never been around men of their stamp before, but what little she had thusly experienced was both surprising and pleasant, much more pleasing than she would ever have imagined. As she played and laughed and coached the men by repeating the lyrics before each line, she thought never had she been so at ease in company before. Always, within the circle of the High Sticklers to which she and her sisters belonged, an air of constant improving criticism and judgment prevailed, whether with regard to fashion, or to the placement of food on a sideboard, or to musical performance. But here, in the presence of two men reputed to be such horrific rogues with whom no lady of moral conviction would dare align herself for a moment, she felt entirely at home.

The thought caused her to sigh. So, she was only comfortable when surrounded by rakes and rogues. How poor Meg would perish if she knew what she was doing right now!

Of course, this thought served only to lighten her spirits and her fingers flew even more quickly over the ivory-topped keys.

* * *

On the following morning, Emily paced the dining room where Kingsbridge was making a good breakfast and where she had been able to do little more than sip a now lukewarm cup of chocolate. She wore a travelling gown of dark blue silk, made high to the neck with a pretty white ruff of lace beneath her chin. The sleeves were full and puffed and enjoyed a delicate point lace, trimming just the lower edge. Her gloves, in a matching shade, rested on the white linen of the tablecloth.

"You should eat," Kingsbridge pressed her. "If we find we must leave the moment Winsford returns, you will want to have taken some nourishment."

Emily turned back to glare at her plate over her shoulder. "You are right, but my stomach is doing such acrobatics, you can have no idea! Oh, Evan!" Here she looked at him. "I am amazingly discontent to be so idle, to wait, to wonder, to speculate. I feel as though I am going mad!"

"Well, *Horatia*," he said pointedly, "as I see it—"

"Did I call you Evan!" she cried, a hand flying to her cheek. "And that so easily!" She was a little embarrassed at having addressed him by his Christian name without even a moment's hesitation. She had done so previously, but only by arrangement as a matter of upholding their pretense to a brotherly and sisterly relationship. "I do beg your pardon most sincerely."

"You needn't," he said softly. There was an expression in his eye that made her look at him closely. "I admire you very much, Miss Longcliffe," he continued. "You've a warm, open, generous spirit. I am very glad to have made your acquaintance, and truthfully would not be adverse to hearing my name on your lips as often as pleased you."

"And my name on yours," she returned sincerely, realizing suddenly that she had come to feel a great deal of affection for her travelling companion. He wore a brown coat, buff breeches, and top boots. His necklcloth was arranged to perfection and his hair was brushed as always *à la Brutus*. She searched his face, wondering at the ease of her friendship with him. "You are all so composed and so easy in your addresses and manners—you, Winsford, Byron. I must confess I've never felt so little scrutinized in my entire existence, and for that I thank you, for you can't imagine what it is to be a Longcliffe, the responsibility of it all, the heights of the expectations weighing on one's shoulders as though the universe would most certainly fly apart if one does not behave appropriately at every turn."

He cocked his head. "Have you been behaving inappropriately then, with me? I certainly have found no fault with your manners." He seemed genuinely bemused.

At that, she trilled her laughter. "Behaving inappropriately?" she cried. "My lord, I have been travelling alone in your company for several days now and posing as your sister all the while. I've allowed you several kisses which I should not have. I have addressed you by your Christian name. Good heavens, Kingsbridge, how can you say any of this was *appropriate?*"

"Because there is not a particle of self-interest in you."

She felt the air in the chamber begin to vibrate and then to crackle as his gaze held hers in a tight embrace. She felt her breath escape her and at the same time she couldn't seem to draw in a new breath.

"Oh," she murmured.

"Just so," he responded quietly.

She could read his thoughts, for they were her own. Was love blossoming between them? A true love, a lasting love? Or was their ease with one another only the result of the strange and exhilarating journey on which they had embarked together?

The question floated in the air, yet she could not bring herself to speak it aloud, nor did he.

She couldn't be tumbling in love! She couldn't. Yet she liked Kingsbridge ever so much.

He rose to his feet and crossed the room to join her. He

took up both of her hands in his and his hazel eyes searched hers as though demanding an answer. She returned his gaze, questioning her own heart, wondering about his, and finding that a terrible uncertainty rose in her breast.

"What is it?" he murmured.

She gave her head a shake, the curls dangling beside each cheek tossing about prettily. "I cannot say," she whispered. "I—I don't know what to say, or to think, or even to feel."

"But you are *feeling* something, aren't you?"

"A lovely warmth, a concern, and even a fear."

"That I would hurt you?" he asked, appearing cast down by the mere suggestion of it.

"Oh, never," she breathed, assuring him that she did not hold him in such low esteem. "I know you would not, at least, not intentionally."

"By accident then?"

She smiled faintly. "By dint of the fact you're a man, and one who is used to living as he wills."

"Why do I begin to suspect that next you will say you want the wind in the trees?"

She swallowed hard. She felt as though she was rejecting a proposal of marriage, yet he had proposed no such thing. "Yes," she responded.

"I am not wind enough?" he queried.

"How could any man be," she responded warmly. "I don't mean to disparage you personally, Kingsbridge, only the nature of the average relationship between man and woman. Once a lady is wed, she is burdened with a constant bearing of babes. A man then does as he wishes, or as his labors direct him."

"Lady Harley would disagree with you," he said, holding her soul captive with his eyes. "She commands her life entirely."

Emily wondered at his reference, since Lady Harley was a beautiful young woman who had taken many lovers over the years and whose children were generally known as the

Harleian Miscellany because of the dubious parentage of each. Even Lord Byron had been linked with her in recent years, and it was even suspected that one of her brood was his offspring.

"I would not belittle Lady Harley," she said softly, "but I fear in this I would be more a Longcliffe than you would have me be. I should like to think that were I ever to marry, fidelity would be the chiefest of its bonds."

He frowned a little. She knew such a strictly moral dictum would not be pleasing to him. She saw his hazel eyes become cloaked, and he pressed her fingers more firmly than he had been.

She tossed her head. "There, you see!" she cried. "Now I have disappointed you. I can see as much in your eyes."

"You don't know what you see," he retorted evenly. "Perhaps only what you wish to see. But I will tell you what I think of your observations."

She felt uneasy suddenly and wished that she could withdraw her hand from his.

He continued, "You live in a sort of dread that were you ever to marry you would end up like your sisters, outshining one another as fruit-bearers. I have often wondered why you never tumbled in love and married. Certainly you've had offers?"

"Yes."

"Several?"

She nodded her head.

"You are afraid to fall in love?"

"I am," she admitted, the warmth of his hands about hers and the intimate nature of the conversation causing her to feel breathless.

He smiled suddenly. "How alike we are, for until this moment I've never understood myself. You are a mirror to me, you know."

She tilted her head slightly. "You've known the same sentiments then?"

He nodded. "And the worst of it is, I feel wretchedly in danger of having my fears tested as they have never been tested before."

She could not mistake his meaning, nor did she want to. Instead, when he released her hands, she leaned into him as he tenderly drew her into his arms and kissed her. She slid an arm up about his neck and another about his back. He embraced her fully and warmly, kissing her hard upon the lips as though not to do so would cause him to lose his courage in assaulting her at all.

She felt her heart slip in that moment. A little piece of her soul slid from her breast and entered his, a piece that she believed would now never return to her. The gentleness of his queries and the simplicity of his speech had done as much to her. Was he purposely coaxing her heart toward him?

He only released her when hurried footsteps were heard in the hall.

Sixteen

"I saw her!" Lord Winsford cried, entering the dining room on a brisk tread. "At least I believe the young lady I saw was Miss Matford. She was quite pretty with dark hair and large, dark eyes and was in the company of a female sporting a red wig and a tall man with black hair."

"That would be my cousin and the Glossips!" Emily cried, taking a step forward and wringing her hands together. "Where did you see them? Did Evangeline seem well? Were you able to learn anything of her location?"

He lifted a hand and patted the air in front of her as though to gentle the flow of her questions. "I've ordered my travelling coach brought round, the one that is coachman driven." He turned to look at Kingsbridge. "We'll enjoy a deal more privacy that way, though I would suggest that we have one of my stable boys bring your curricle along. I have already taken the liberty of ordering your servants to follow in our wake." He returned his gaze to Emily. "By the way, the Glossips are travelling under the name of Smithe—though I do think their choice of appellation reveals a distinct lack of imagination—and the young lady is purportedly sister to the woman with the red hair. You say she was an actress at Drury Lane?" he queried with a slight grimace, glancing toward the marquess.

Lord Kingsbridge, who had been staring out the window since Winsford's arrival, turned back to him. "Yes," he said.

"Adequate in her way, I suppose. Small parts, mostly. Her husband as well."

Lord Winsford pursed his lips.

"What is it?" Emily asked, wanting to know why he appeared so curious and speculative of a sudden.

"Well, nothing to signify. I would suppose then that it was Mrs. Smithe's vanity that made her decide to be sister to Miss Matford. She looked more of an age to be her mother."

Emily groaned. "You are right on one score, m'lord. It does not signify in the least. Only what did you learn? Which direction were they headed? The north? Northeast? Northwest?"

He grunted. "Northwest—toward Grasmere, though I was not able to ascertain if they meant to stop permanently in the village there."

Emily dropped into the chair beside her, her spirits downcast suddenly. "I was so hoping that they were going to sequester her on Windermere, for you know the lake and its environs so well."

He nodded. "Yes, and Grasmere is in wilder country—steeper fells and the like. But never fear. I know of a cottage we can hire until we discover where your cousin is. I frequently walk the distance to Grasmere and the landlord of The Swan knows me quite well."

Emily's spirits brightened. "Indeed!" she cried. "Then we are saved."

Lord Winsford looked down at her, his brown eyes softening in quick stages. "How much I enjoy hearing you say as much, for I am actually beginning to feel of some use to you. So, tell me, Mrs. Matford, when this whole nasty affair is brought to a happy conclusion, would you allow me to call on you?"

Emily heard a strange grumbling sound from Kingsbridge, who was still standing by the window a few feet behind her. She blinked at Lord Winsford and wondered what he was about? She replied carefully, "I would always be gratified to count you among my friends."

"Ah," he responded. "Not precisely the response I was looking for, but sufficient to give me hope. But dare I hope or am I wishing at unreachable stars?"

Emily offered him a half-smile of disbelief. "Lord Winsford, I shan't tell you to hope or not to hope, especially when I believe you are only funning."

He placed a hand on his chest. "Funning!" he cried. "You wound me. I am most serious, I promise you. It has been some time since a lady has captured my fancy as thoroughly as you have."

But there was too much laughter in his eyes to take him seriously. Emily smiled and shook her finger at him. She would have rebuked him for teasing her, but at that moment he turned his head sharply to the left. "There is the coach now," he cried. "Come!"

The journey by coach to Grasmere took several hours, for the country became more difficult to navigate the farther north and northwest the coach rolled. At every hilltop, the lumbering conveyance—nearly as bulky as the Royal Mail Coaches—had to come to a complete halt, at which time the skids were placed in front of the rear wheels for the descent in order to keep the coach from bounding out of control down the hill.

At the bottom of the hill the skids had to be removed, a process that considerably added to the time spent in the coach.

For Emily, however, the incomparable beauty of the landscape made up for the intermittent pauses. From either side of the coach the view was extraordinary. The massive, wide-based fells dipped and rose in seemingly unending majesty.

Descending into Grasmere, Winsford named the surrounding mountainous terrain—Helm Crag to the northwest, Rydal Fell and Nab Scar to the east, Yew Crag and Silver Howe to the west, Red Bank to the southwest. Whatever the names—and Emily found them all charming—the small, deep blue lake, cradled by the protective scars and crags, was pleasing in the extreme.

A forest of what appeared to be oak and fir trees swept up one side of the valley wall, while most of the land about the remainder of the lake was grassy and riddled with undulating drystone walls of gray granite. A scattering of whitewashed farmhouses and outbuildings could be seen about the valley and Emily couldn't help but wonder if it was to one of these that Evangeline had been taken.

On the lake was a pleasant little island dotted with trees.

"Where do you intend for us to begin?" she queried, directing her question to Lord Winsford.

"At the Swan Hotel of course," he replied, glancing out the window and scrutinizing the valley below. "Let us only hope the Glossips have not gone past Grasmere to Keswick. The highway passes through the village, on to Dunmail Raise, past Thirlemere, and eventually beyond Derwentwater, ending in Keswick."

Emily sighed deeply. "Indeed." Keswick was a village situated farther northwest near the lake called Derwentwater, but not so far as Bassenthwaite.

Sometime later, Winsford's coach drew before the Swan Hotel. By parting the carefully drawn shade from the window ever so slightly, Emily had a clear view from her side of the equipage of the side of the inn and a portion of the front. She was curious to see if the hotel had changed at all since her last visit of so many years ago, but seemingly it had not. It was still the cozy whitewashed building she remembered, framed by neat rows of windows and bearing several serviceable chimneys.

The inn had been constructed in the mid-seventeenth century and was presently owned by a jovial man by the name of Anthony Wilson. She was able to see the inn's sign, which utilized words from one of William Wordsworth's poems which topped a depiction of Grasmere Lake and the surrounding fells.

Who does not know the famous swan, the sign read.

In the foreground was a beautiful swan with two cygnets swimming nearby. In the background a brief show of sky rose above distant fells, while a fir and oak woodland climbed a closer hillock. A miniscule sailboat drifted in the distance, giving an appearance of quietude and peace.

How odd, she thought, that the lake could hold both such serenity and yet such wickedness as the abduction of her cousin at one and the same time. She felt Kingsbridge's hand cover her own and she glanced at him, curious as to his meaning.

"Don't worry," he said softly. "We'll find her. The Glossips cannot be so stupid as to think of doing her harm. There have been too many witnesses on this journey of their having travelled together."

"You are right, of course," Emily responded, releasing a sigh. "Was my agitation so obvious?"

"You were chewing on your lip again."

Emily chuckled, but was relieved when Winsford emerged from the doorway of the hotel with a confident smile on his lips. After giving a string of instructions to his coachman, he opened the door of the coach and climbed aboard to take up his previous seat on the forward squabs.

Once the coach was in motion, he revealed what he had discovered. "You will be happy to know that I was able to secure a cottage not far from here where we can conduct our search of the lakeside. I did not feel it at all wise to inquire about the Glossips just yet, but I did hear some gossip about the pretty young lady who'd arrived not two hours prior in the company of her elder sister and brother-in-law."

He then could not restrain a smile. "It would seem I was not alone in my opinion of Mrs. Glossip's vanity, for the comment that I heard made was that the speaker pitied the *mother* of the siblings for it was clear some twenty years must have separated the births of those two."

Emily could not keep from laughing nor could Kingsbridge, and the very air within the coach grew lighter. One thing for certain, she thought, as the coach worked its way up and down the natural undulations of the road and across creek beds that occasionally parted the highway—Evangeline had been described as *pretty.* She could only conclude therefore that her cousin was as yet in good health and in reasonable spirits.

She felt her heart pick up its cadence as the coach climbed another rise and began yet again another quick, brief descent. They were near to their prey and surely a matter of days, if not hours, would see Evangeline wrested from the hands of her captors.

The cottage Winsford had hired for a sennight was situated on the edge of a wood with a slight view of the lake visible between large, ancient fir trees. Behind the cottage was a four-foot-high drystone wall, covered in patches of green moss and yellowish lichen. The keeper of the cottage, who also served as Cook, was a woman of advancing years whose eyes were misty in appearance. Clearly, she could not see entirely well.

Well enough, however, Emily noted as she scrutinized the well-tended house and a few moments later the kitchen garden. She moved into the sunshine, enjoying the neat and bountiful rows—the beans staked on high arched trellises, the artichoke clumps healthy and littered with young green fruit. The tomatoes were a brilliant red against the green of their stalks, each plant bearing the fruit in a gradation of stages that promised enjoyment for several months in succession. Cauliflower and cabbage faced each other as though competing, carrots and beets, both hidden beneath the ground, presented contrasting headdresses—the carrots in frilly green bonnets, the beets in elegant, purple-veined plumes.

The air was cool and pleasant, for even though the July

sunshine beat down on the garden with a summery intensity,
Cumbria was too far north to know anything of the heat of
the southern counties. On a sudden impulse, she removed
her bonnet of dark blue silk and loosened her hair. Of the
moment, she was alone at the cottage save for the presence
of the cottage-keeper, therefore there was no one to see her
long tresses or to rebuke her for appearing in a state bordering on *undress*.

Kingsbridge and Winsford had deserted her to perform
the role of advance guard, though in secret, of course, by
visiting the Swan by themselves. The gentlemen had forbidden her to attend them since her presence, should her true
identity become known—or even her false one as Mrs. Matford—would alert the kidnappers to their presence in Grasmere. She had been unable to argue with their reasoning, but
of course she was unhappy about having been left behind to
kick her heels at the cottage.

Ostensibly the gentlemen meant to enjoy a glass of whisky
together and to while away a few hours in the taproom, but
with the darker purpose of listening to as much countrified
gossip as could be enjoyed in a few hours at a local inn.
They also intended to intercept the servants' coaches in order
to direct Gwendolyn and Kingsbridge's valet to the cottage.

She moved to the drystone wall and leaned against the
warm stones gathering the reflected heat into her back and
legs. She tied the ribbons of her bonnet together at the ends
and slid the loop over her arm. She sighed deeply. Her sur-
roundings were magical, and the only sound to be heard was
the soft wind of the midday sky soughing through the tops
of the nearby fir trees. The fragrance of the conifers, min-
gling with the variety of vegetable foliage, was proving a
pleasure unimaginable.

Regardless of her wish to be going and doing, Emily let
the rich bouquet of the land flow into her spirit. The sunshine
doused her with warmth, and the view of the lake, blue and
sparkling in the distance, eased the agitation of her soul. She

felt suddenly as though the lake and the round of fells in which the deep blue green pool was situated began to speak to her, of peace, of joy, of refreshment, yet of an urgency she couldn't explain.

The sight of the lake simply called to her. She could not resist the quiet sirens whispering her name and without so much as forming the thought, she picked up the skirts of her dark blue carriage gown and began moving in the direction of the lake.

She left the garden by way of an iron gate that snapped shut briskly behind her in protection against all manner of four-legged intruders, and followed a stone-edged gravel path toward the lakeside. Her half-boots crunched noisily, a sound that pleased her.

On her left was a narrow stable and carriage house, empty for the present. It would house Kingsbridge's curricle and a pair of horses hired from the inn at the village of Grasmere.

The grasses leading to the lake were scattered with bunches of parsley ferns as well as the taller plume ferns. Red squirrels skittered up and down the silver gray tree trunks, the bases of which were littered with dark green needles and small brown buds scattered throughout the thinning grasses. The trees were very old and the bark scaly.

Beyond these trees, was a group of younger fir trees on the left, while on the right, the small forest flowed unrelieved to the lake's edge. Yew trees, alder, and oak were mixed in with the first, giving a delightfully mottled green appearance to the whole.

The path met suddenly with a stream that she could now see flowed into the lake. The clear water revealed a rocky stream bed and even the banks of the gill were more rock than grass. A small stone bridge, charming in configuration, crossed the gill. The sound of her footsteps echoed off the stone.

Once past the bridge, the gravel path widened a trifle, the tough northern grasses uninterested in penetrating the neatly and probably deeply laid path. Several stair steps led to the rocky water's edge at a final steep grade. Larger rocks were cast about on the shore as though the lake had spewed them out at random. Smaller rocks and a coarse sand packed the remainder of the shore. She stopped, unwilling to go farther since her skirts would soon become soiled by the damp, muddy shoreline were she to venture down the steps to the water's edge.

She lifted her gaze and noted that the island was not far away. She could see alder and fir trees as well as a small stone hut. She wondered what manner of adventures had been enjoyed in such a pretty and somewhat isolated place.

From the corner of her eye, Emily caught sight of a rowboat appearing at the bend in the shoreline, the prow of the boat emerging from just beneath an overhanging oak branch. There were two people in the boat, a young lady and an older man, the latter tall with black hair.

She started as the young lady turned to look in her direction. She was some distance away, but even then she recognized Evangeline's peculiar manner of lifting her chin rather high, as though her neck hurt to do otherwise, when she turned her head. Emily was not close enough to see her eyes or even to ponder the expression of her face, but she could not have mistaken her cousin.

Afraid of being recognized, she turned around abruptly and began a slow progress up the path, hoping to appear nonchalant.

What foolishness, she thought, knowing that her cheeks burned with self-blame and consternation. If Evangeline recognized her and in her recognition gave warning to Mr. Glossip that a relative of hers was in Grasmere, all would be lost before it had even begun.

Since her hair was tumbled down her back and she still dangled her blue silk bonnet from her arm, she hoped that somehow Evangeline had not guessed who she was. She doubted as well, that she would look in any manner familiar

to her cousin from behind, particularly since her gown bore
a small bustle at the waistline which lent a pretty, if un-
formed, flow to the silk of the gown. She trusted that she
gave the appearance of a countrified girl wishful of a little
sunshine and air before afternoon tea.

She ambled back up the path, striving for an indifference
she did not in the least feel. She longed to whirl around, to
wave her hands at the small rowboat, to call out her cousin's
name, to do anything but while her way back up the path.
Yet she knew, despite these impulses, that to do anything
else would only harm her cousin's precarious position.

When she drew near the cottage, she found that the servants had arrived and poor Gwendolyn, emerging from her
travelling coach in a lethargic manner, was ashen in appearance from the undulating journey through the hilly Lakeland.
To her surprise, Kingsbridge's valet followed afterward, from
the same coach. He caught up her elbow, his brow furrowed
as he whispered something to her. Clearly he was concerned
for her health.

How nice of the marquess's valet to be so attentive to poor,
suffering Gwendolyn!

Her abigail nodded briefly to the valet, but quickly brought
a kerchief to her lips. He guided her gently toward the front
door of the cottage.

The cottage facilities could only care for two horses at a
time and only one carriage. Therefore the coaches—once the
postillions, under the supervision of Kingsbridge's valet, un-
loaded them—would be returned to the village of Grasmere
where they were to be stowed and boarded near the hotel.

On the heels of the servants' arrivals, Winsford and Kingsbridge returned in the latter's curricle, driving a pair hired from
the inn. In addition, a young lad—apparently employed to
care for the horses—was perched up behind the body of the
carriage, his face aglow with what she could see was his
sense of adventure. She thought he might as well have been

standing at the prow of a sailing vessel and taking the salty sea spray straight in the face, so alive were his features.

As soon as Kingsbridge drew rein, the lad leaped off the back of the curricle and began immediately tending with quick, light, considerate hands, to the brown horses and curricle given into his care.

Emily greeted the gentlemen, anxious to learn word of Evangeline's location as well as to impart her own earlier experience. She could see, as she eyed both men, that Winsford was pleased with their eavesdropping efforts and Kingsbridge not less so.

Winsford began whipping off his gloves as he turned toward the north and scanned the length of forest directly behind the cottage. Kingsbridge, also drawing off his gloves, approached her from the near side of his curricle, which was even then being drawn toward the stables and the coach house.

"We sat for nearly three hours," he said in a low voice, his eyes noticeably reddened, "sipping small glasses of whisky, waiting for the Glossips to come to the inn or to hear word of them. Several times your cousin was mentioned because of her beauty, but nothing of her location or her abductors until only a half hour past. You will be glad to know—they are not far—in a cottage on the other side of the forest, a quarter mile only, in a dwelling similar to our own."

"I thought as much," she said, keeping her tone low as well so that their new stable hand would not be able to hear their discussion. "I saw her—not a few minutes ago—on the lake!"

Seventeen

Kingsbridge instantly turned around. "Winsford!" he cried. "Come here at once."

He then hooked Emily's arm and drew her toward the front of the cottage, gesturing at the same time for Winsford to join them. Winsford, who had been pacing the path next to the kitchen garden and scrutinizing the woods to the north, retraced his steps. When he had joined them, Emily quickly explained to both men precisely what she had seen and in what direction the little boat bearing Evangeline had been headed. She also explained that she hadn't been able to remain on the banks since her cousin was near enough to her that she would have risked discovery had she stayed watching the lake. She then confessed to hoping that because her hair had been dangling about her shoulders, Evangeline and Mr. Glossip would have taken her for a country miss.

Kingsbridge, as though noticing her curls for the first time, ran his gaze over the windswept mass and lifted his brows as though a little stunned. "Oh, I say," he murmured, "how very charming."

"Very," Winsford added, with an amused smile on his lips as he regarded his good friend from Eton days, "but hardly the appropriate subject of the moment."

Kingsbridge, however, did not seem to hear him, but instead took a curl from off her shoulder and wrapped it around his finger. He seemed dumbfounded and a little lost. Emily felt a blush rise on her cheeks. He appeared—dare she think it?—utterly besotted!

Winsford, upon seeing that his friend had not heard him, burst out laughing, a circumstance which prompted Kingsbridge to glance at him with a frown creasing his brow. "What the devil are you chortling about?" he queried.

Lord Winsford could scarcely contain himself in light of his friend's obvious distraction. "Nothing," he whispered, holding back another chuckle. "Only that I have observed a mooncalf, pierced so perfectly by Cupid, that I vow he isn't even aware of it."

Kingsbridge appeared indignant. "I'll say it again, Winsford, what the devil are you talking about?" he cried, lifting his hands in an impatient gesture. But because at that moment he forgot he had a light brown curl wrapped about his finger, Emily gave a cry.

"Good God, Em!" he cried, horrified. "Why didn't you say something?"

Emily merely blinked at him, wondering if her cheeks were as red as they felt. "It—it doesn't signify," she responded quietly. "Only, do release my locks—yes, that's better, thank you—and let me return to the cottage. I've—I've been out-of-doors far too long and I believe the sun has rather touched my senses in an unhappy manner." She placed the back of one lace-gloved hand against each cheek in turn, then gestured toward the lake. "Perhaps you ought to see if Evangeline is still in the rowboat. I promise you it hasn't been but a few minutes since I saw her." She hoped her speech would disarm the situation.

Kingsbridge nodded briskly. "Yes, of course," he said, following her lead. "I can see now that you are a little sunburnt. Do go inside. Winsford and I shall tend to everything."

With that he brushed awkwardly past her, barking a quick command at his friend, urging him not to dawdle and flirt with Mrs. Matford.

Emily watched them go, noting the long strides Kingsbridge was taking. He was clearly overset by his own conduct and Winsford helped none at all by turning around and winking at her. She took a deep breath and placed a hand at her bosom. Good heavens, she thought, what if he *is* tumbling in love with me?

She felt herself divide into two parts at that very moment. One part took wing and began to soar toward the heavens as though propelled by a force unearthly in origin. The other part set her knees to trembling as a well of tears sprang to her eyes and constricted her throat. Never had she known such a division of sentiment before. Never. And the sensation was proving excruciating in the extreme.

She retired to her bedchamber, grateful to find that Gwendolyn had lit a small coal fire in the grate and had set her curling tongs to heating. "Excellent," she breathed as she tossed her dark blue bonnet on the bed and took up a seat in the chair near the tongs.

"I thought you might be wishful of having me dress your hair. Though it looks pretty in its way, you can't be at all comfortable."

I am too comfortable, Emily thought despairingly. *I am too comfortable being with Kingsbridge, being kissed by him and having him lose himself so thoroughly while wrapping my hair about his finger.*

To her maid, she said, "You are right. I am not in the least at ease. Can you have the white cambric and the olive green overdress ready in half an hour? This travelling gown is wholly unsuited to walking about the fells."

"The flatirons are heating in the kitchen even as we speak. Cook was very helpful. What a dear, she is—a lovely, sweet-tempered old woman, though she's not the look of it which reminds me about that saying not to judge a book by its cover. She said she'd be of what help she could to me and thought you was a nice-enough lady, though she did have some worries about your travelling about the countryside as you were—with two gentlemen. It seems she's not at all convinced that you're Kingsbridge's sister."

Emily glanced over her shoulder at her maid, who had begun brushing out her hair in long gliding strokes. "Did she say why?" she asked.

"Nay," she responded, a troubled light entering her eye. "But gossip being what it always is, if that is wat she's thinkin', t'won't matter at all—she'll say wat she thinks, then wat she thinks will become wat is true. 'Tis always the way. I've seen it times out of mind."

"I wonder what I ought to do then."

"Might I make a suggestion, miss?" she queried.

"Yes, of course."

"Well," she began slowly. "I've taken her measure, so to speak, and I think she ought to be trusted. I'd like permission to tell her the truth. After all, if in trying to find your cousin, one or the other of you disappear in the middle of t'night, Mrs. Thwaite will think it odd, will she not?"

Emily giggled. "She will begin to wish us away. Let me speak with Kingsbridge and see what he advises. For myself, if you believe her to be trustworthy, I cannot help but agree with your opinion that we ought to confide in her."

An hour later, with her hair caught up in a swirling chignon and a proper fringe of curls settled elegantly on her forehead, she greeted the gentlemen in the small parlor. They rose to bow politely to her, each holding a glass of sherry in hand. She was offered one as well, accepted, then took a seat on the gold velvet sofa which was situated adjacent to a darkened, well-used fireplace, but opposite an expanse of small-paned windows. Winsford poured her a small glass and brought it to her. She thanked him and began sipping the light wine.

Heavy dark blue velvet draperies flanked the windows and were hung on rings so that during inclement weather they might be drawn over the cold glass. For the present, the drapes were open, allowing the hillside, a portion of the oak, fir, and alder wood, as well as a sliver of lake to be visible from the parlor.

The chamber had simple, whitewashed walls, bore small coaching prints and one watercolor of a view of Grasmere from the top of one of the fells. Beside the wall nearest the doorway sat a scarred wooden writing desk, paper, a tray of pens, and an inkpot.

Kingsbridge seated himself in a winged chair covered in a plaid wool of dark blue, red, and gold, situated near the fireplace. The floor creaked as Winsford crossed in front of the sofa and moved to stand to the side of the windows. He continued to sip his sherry and scrutinize the forest to the north.

Emily addressed Lord Kingsbridge. "Did you chance to see my cousin?" she asked. "Or were you too late?"

"We arrived near the lake's edge only just in time to watch a rowboat slip about the opposite side of the island."

"Do you suppose Glossip has taken her there?" she asked. "To the island?"

Kingsbridge shook his head. "I don't think so. There is nothing on the island except a small hut, and the whole of it is accessible to anyone from the surrounding lakeside, so that I can't imagine he would be foolish enough to keep her imprisoned there. She would undoubtedly be discovered in a trice."

"Where do you suppose he has taken her then?"

Lord Winsford turned away from the windows, took a sip of sherry, and cleared his throat. "There are one or two isolated cottages, inaccessible by carriage, across the lake."

"I noticed a rowboat overturned in back of our stables," she offered hopefully. "Perhaps we could cross the lake together and discover if either of the cottages are inhabited. I could disguise my face with a half-veil." She looked from one man to the other and back, her heart beating strongly at the thought of rowing across the lake, vanquishing Evangeline's captor, and whisking her cousin back to safety. She added, "It is not yet four o'clock. We certainly have ample time to make a crossing and return before nightfall."

Winsford looked back at the window and scowled. His gaze rose to scrutinize the fells and the sky beyond, particularly to the north. He shook his head. "Though we have sufficient light, I promise you we'll have a delightful squall before the covers are removed following dinner, and you do not wish to be upon the lake during a brisk summer storm."

As though confirming his opinion, a soft rumble was heard in the distance and a stiff breeze suddenly ruffled the tops of the fir trees.

Emily looked out at the whispering trees and the brilliant blue sky beyond. She tried to comprehend what Evangeline was feeling in this moment, whether she feared for her life or, more likely, was irritated because she could not enjoy the conveniences of her own bedchamber. Evangeline was in every respect a petted, spoiled beauty, if not by her stepmama and papa, then by the servants of Aldwark, who had doted on her since she was a babe. A journey into the wilds of Cumberland, even resting frequently at posting inns, would have proved a sore trial for her.

In this respect, she was so very different from her cousin. Travelling as she had been over the past several days seemed to have heightened Emily's every sense—the sky seemed not just blue, but a vivid blue. The sherry on her lips didn't taste of wine, but of burnt nuts and fire. The feel of her cambric gown was not just of a fine fabric, but the silky fur of a cat. Euphoria, she realized, had characterized the whole of her response to the journey thus far.

But not so for Evangeline, she had little doubt.

She glanced at Kingsbridge, who she found was watching her over the rim of his sherry glass which he held pressed lightly to his lips. No, Evangeline would be utterly miserable in her current circumstances and probably waiting passively for her father to pay the ransom, while she . . .

Emily let her gaze drift away from Kingsbridge, back to

the window and to the gently swaying treetops beyond. No, *she* would not wait passively; she would plot and scheme until she could steal away from her captors and do some mischief before she made her escape. If they dared try to stop her, she would kick and scream and tear at them with her bare hands if need be. She would devise means of leaving word at their various inns by surreptitious means. She would . . .

Her happy thoughts were interrupted quite abruptly by Mrs. Thwaite's announcement that dinner was served.

Adjourning to the dining room, Emily remembered her earlier conversation with her abigail and, after Mrs. Thwaite had served them all, then left the room, she explained her maid's perceptive ideas. The gentlemen listened carefully, all the while taking rather large bites of a fine, fresh, grilled trout. She paused mid-sentence, however, as the aroma of the trout suddenly reached her senses.

"Oh, dear," she murmured. "And the faintest bouquet of lemon." She lost the thread of her discourse, picked up her knife and fork, and cut a square of the delectable fish. She placed the trout on her tongue and sighed with complete pleasure. "Is there anything finer?" she breathed. She took a sip of Madeira, then another bite of trout. "Why am I so hungry of a sudden?"

Lord Kingsbridge smiled, but said nothing. He, too, was busily engaged eating the flavorful fish. Winsford offered his opinion. "I daresay it is the lake that has given you an excellent appetite. After residing in Cumbria for so many summers, I have concluded that each mere has a spirit of its own, and will make itself known to one and all in due course. Clearly Grasmere's spirit tends to the fattening of trout!"

Emily laughed outright, but wondered about his jest. "I am beginning to think it is the lake that drew me toward Evangeline earlier today. I remember being in the kitchen garden, and suddenly having the strongest impulse to go to the lake's edge." She then smiled. "Oh, but I am being ridiculous, aren't I? It is all fancy, of course . . ."

"But of the most delightful," he responded. He held a speared bite of trout up for her inspection. But the delightfully large fillet was so tender that it broke on the tip of the tines and fell with a thud onto the plate below. "Oh, the deuce take it!" he muttered, wiping splattered lemon and butter sauce off his coat and the fine lace front of his shirt.

Emily giggled and Kingsbridge nearly choked on the Madeira he had been swallowing. All three of them then laughed together in warm camaraderie.

Once Winsford settled back to devouring his fish, Kingsbridge offered his opinion of the subject at hand where the cottage-keeper was concerned. "You may be right," he said, "in thinking we ought to inform her of the nature of our presence here in Grasmere. But what if she takes to gabble-mongering?"

"I've thought of that," she responded. "But I believe it would be worse if she began offering to her neighbors every manner of unhappy speculation of our peculiar relationships, especially since she already suspects I am not Mrs. Matford."

She watched Kingsbridge frown as his chewing motions slowed markedly. She wondered what his thoughts were, but suspected they were of too delicate a nature to broach. Instead, he took another sip of the fine wine and nodded slowly. "Your argument is irrefutable. Mrs. Thwaite should be told." Here he turned toward Lord Winsford. "Unless you have an objection?"

Winsford shook his head. "My only objection can be that Miss Longcliffe risks her reputation in being alone with us tonight—"

Emily waved a hand at him as though his concern was negligible. "According to my sister, I was all but ruined by attending the masquerade at Scarswell."

Lord Winsford lifted both his brows. *"You* attended the Scarswell masquerade ball?" he asked, astonished. He glanced at Kingsbridge, then back to Emily. "Well, no wonder you have turned my friend's head, for you are certainly a most remarkable female."

"Why do you say such a thing!" she cried, astonished and not a little embarrassed, as much for herself as for Kingsbridge. "It was only a masquerade."

"A masquerade among rogues," he countered, "and you a Longcliffe!"

"Oh, pooh!" she cried. "If you knew what a dreadful cross my surname is to bear, you wouldn't speak so!" Forgotten was her discomfiture. She attacked another part of her fillet and chewed angrily in response.

Both men, however, were not in the least impressed with her display of temper and merely laughed at her.

After a time, as the wind began to blow more briskly over the slate roof of the cottage, it was agreed that on the morrow—given that the lake proved calm and the skies clear of a single trace of clouds—they would row to the opposite shore and travel the footpaths with the appearance of being earnest and eager hikers.

"With a little luck," Kingsbridge said, "we shall discover the precise location of our quarry and proceed from there."

Emily nodded briskly, visions of wresting her cousin from the Glossips vividly enacted within the boundless scope of her fertile imagination.

Eighteen

On the following morning, Emily dressed carefully in a patterned calico Empire gown of tiny blue and yellow flowers with a matching summery overdress of dark blue cotton twill. Her half-boots of soft brown kid were excellent for marching about the lakeside and along the paths wending their way up the fells. Her hair was caught up in a tight chignon over which she settled a straw poke bonnet, trimmed with a spray of artificial bluebells. She tied the ribbon of blue silk beneath her left ear into a floppy bow.

As she stared into the mirror, she quickly pinched her cheeks, then fell to regarding her reflection as though she had never peered into a looking glass before.

What did Kingsbridge see, she wondered suddenly. The speculative thought was so at odds with the coming trek across the lake that she was surprised at the strange workings of her mind, yet she couldn't help but pose the question to herself again.

What did Kingsbridge see when he looked at her?

Her eyes were large and the prettiest of the four sisters, for she resembled her mother, who had been a great beauty in her day, while her sisters took after their father. Did Kingsbridge admire her eyes? He had said so, more than once, but was he paying the common flirtatious courtesies so habitual for a confirmed rogue? Or did he indeed admire her?

Her complexion was creamy white—did his lordship pre-

fer ladies of a more Mediterranean or even a French hue?
Was her skin lovely in his eyes or perhaps sallow and uninteresting?

She touched the bridge of her nose where a faint smatter-
ing of pinpoint freckles had long since made their home.
Was the marquess partial to freckles of this sort, or would
he consider them all a mar to her general beauty? Did he
think her passably pretty, very pretty, or beautiful, as many
of her beaux had proclaimed?

She wasn't certain why she was asking herself these questions, but somehow the answer to them suddenly seemed the
most important matter of the day.

Where had all these wonderings and supposings come
from? She recalled yesterday how his finger had become
trapped in one of her curls and that he had scarcely been
aware of what he had done. Was Winsford right? Was
Kingsbridge succumbing to the effects of Cupid's arrow?
What did all of it mean, and why was she suddenly so consumed with questions?

She felt an odd sort of anxiety wriggle through her chest.
What if she was nothing like the usual sort of female that
appealed most to Lord Kingsbridge?

But what did it matter?

Why was she pondering such foolish questions?

Yet, it did matter.

But why?

Her gaze shifted away from the small looking glass fixed
to the top of the chamber's chest of drawers, to a crack in
the wall. She sighed deeply, her thoughts drifting backward.
She thought about all the ladies who had undoubtedly pursued Kingsbridge over the course of his years among the
haut ton—dozens, nay, hundreds, and enough of them far
prettier than she, no doubt. Yet none had even come close to
mastering his affections.

Another wriggle of anxiety travelled snakelike through her
heart.

She blinked and blinked again.

What a novel sensation, she realized with a start. Never in her entire career as a reigning London belle had she been anxious about the good opinion of a man before. She had always taken every Mayfair drawing room by storm, with her head high, her spirits invincible, and with a determination to rule the hearts of as many silly beaux as she could collect about her in the space of an hour. And she had never failed in her object. Never!

But this morning, as she chewed on her lip, she knew very well that she could no more bring Kingsbridge to heel than she could snap her fingers and bring the sun from behind a cloud.

Even if she wanted to!

She stamped her foot lightly on the wood floor and gave her head a shake. What useless musings were these that had gotten trapped in her head? She was no schoolgirl to become fluttery and jittery at the sight of a man. Not for Emily Longcliffe to succumb to a fit of nerves over the affections of a beau!

Never!

She lifted her head and then her chin and peered into the looking glass once more. Besides, she reminded herself, nothing ought to come of a few delightful kisses with one of London's most notorious rakehells, except a number of pleasant memories to be enjoyed in her later years. Nothing more!

Indeed, Kingsbridge could be nothing to her, not now, not ever. And she was certainly nothing to him. An amusement perhaps on their northerly adventure, but nothing more!

She nodded to her reflection, her confidence returning in full force. She turned on her heel, and after brushing past her maid who stared at her in a rather wide-eyed manner, evidently astonished by her recent antics, she entered the hall.

Her timing however was unfortunate, for given her recent

determination to steel herself against Kingsbridge's musical hazel eyes and the promise of his lips when he would smile at her in just that manner, she collided with him at the very moment she closed the door shut with a snap.

He, too, it would seem, had just emerged from his bed-chamber.

She gasped, backed away, and extended her hand flatly toward him as though warding him off. "Oh, dear, I do beg your pardon!" she cried.

He seemed faintly amused. "I am uninjured," he said. "I assure you. You may feel my limbs if you are unpersuaded."

Emily blinked at him and felt an odd tingling sensation begin at the top of her head and travel in slow, languorous stages down her neck, into her shoulders, arms and hands, her chest, her hips, her legs. She lost all sensation in her feet and could not even feel the floor beneath her half-boots.

She blinked again as she watched him. He was ever so handsome. Oh, dear, his lips were twitching ominously and there was that familiar glint in his eye as though he had secrets to tell.

She smiled faintly and then an odd thing happened. He began to disappear, yet not disappear. His entire being became surrounded in that moment by a strange glowing mist and a faint halo of light. She could see that he was speaking, but she couldn't hear a word he was saying.

Touch his limbs. He had told her to do so in order to make certain he was uninjured. Now she felt she had to in order to keep him from disappearing!

She moved forward, dreamlike, and as though responding to some inner mischievous spirit, she placed her hands on his arms and felt first his shoulders, then his arms, his elbows, his forearms, and finally his hands and fingers. Every particle of his arms and hands were firm, strong, sinewy. "You are quite well," she whispered.

If there was some part of her that begged to know what on earth she was doing, she ignored that sensible voice. She released his hands and felt the oddest impulse to touch his cheek, but this impulse she stayed. Instead, she looked into his eyes and noted how the glow of light all about him seemed to enhance the greenish part of his hazel eyes.

He was groomed immaculately and wore a coat of dark blue superfine, a neatly folded neckcloth—*trone d'amour*—and moderate shirtpoints that touched the very place on his cheeks she wished to touch. His buckskin breeches fit his legs snugly and top boots molded his calves to perfection. His valet had seen all remnants of dust and dirt removed from his boots. They gleamed nearly as brightly as the light all around him.

A voice intruded.

"Here, Kingsbridge, I have found it!"

The glow quickly disappeared as Winsford emerged from his bedchamber and the tingling sensation throughout Emily's body faded quickly, returning her booted feet to the planks of the hallway floor at one and the same time.

In Winsford's hand was a small pistol. When he caught sight of Emily, a faint blush covered his cheeks. "Oh, I say—I hope I haven't alarmed you!"

Emily stared almost unseeingly at the pistol. Awareness dawned brightly and suddenly upon her. She felt as though for the past several days she had been living in a dream, ignoring the truth of the situation. She had been enjoying an adventure. She had been experiencing strange and forbidden romantical interludes with Kingsbridge. She had been travelling in safe pursuit of a coach-and-four, always just out of reach.

Good heavens! A pistol.

A pistol could be loaded, primed, and fired.

Someone could get hurt.

Someone could even get killed.

She glanced at Kingsbridge and, drawing in a deep breath, said, "How foolish of me to have brought you and your friend to Grasmere, when I have just now come to comprehend that either of you, or both of you, could get killed. I could not live with myself were that to happen."

Kingsbridge turned to scowl sharply at Winsford, who instantly withdrew into the bedchamber muttering that he fully intended to return the weapon to its case.

Emily raised a hand to stay him, for in truth she felt they ought to go across the lake armed, for there was no telling how desperate the Glossips would become once their plot was uncovered. But before she could protest, Kingsbridge had taken her arm firmly at the elbow and was guiding her down the steps. All the while he apologized for Winsford's stupidity in having brought the pistol along at all. There were a dozen ways in which to deal with the current situation, and he seriously doubted that the Glossips represented a threat to any of them.

"You think not?" she asked, doubtful. They reached the bottom of the stairs and she turned to look directly into his eyes.

His gaze shifted slightly to the left before replying, "I see no reason why they would be," he responded.

She knew he was telling a whisker, and that he was doing so for the silliest reason of all—to keep her from feeling frightened.

The truth was, she did not feel frightened. She was exhilarated, and not for the first time since becoming acquainted with Lord Kingsbridge.

Winsford stepped lightly and quickly down the stairs. He was dressed in a comfortable riding coat of brown twill and wore a burgundy waistcoat, buff pantaloons, and top boots which gleamed as brilliantly as Kingsbridge's, whose valet evidently had performed his services for both men. "I've had our lad see the rowboat to the lake's edge. He informed me earlier that it is lake-worthy and the oars, though peeling a bit, will see us wherever we wish to go. Shall we then?" He pulled on fine gloves of York tan, stretching each finger tautly into the soft leather.

Kingsbridge nodded, but Emily had a different notion.

"I do beg your pardon, my lords, but I have forgotten something. I shall join you presently at the boat. I shan't be above five minutes."

The men exchanged a knowing glance of mild irritation and bowed to her in acquiescence, neither appearing greatly surprised that at the very last moment she was delaying their departure. She knew they were supposing she had some vanity or other she felt compelled to attend to before she could cross the lake, and that never in a hundred years would they guess her true intentions.

She ran up the stairs and, without a second's hesitation, she entered the bedchamber the gentlemen had shared the night before. She glanced quickly about the room, recalling that Winsford had said his pistol was kept in a box. She immediately went to the chest of drawers backing the stairwell wall and opened and shut each drawer in quick succession.

She found the beautifully inlaid box she was seeking in the bottom drawer. She withdrew it and settled it on top of the bird's-eye maple chest, slid the small latch to the left, and popped the lid open. The small pistol, a canister of powder, and a canvas sack of pistol balls were all settled neatly within.

She blessed Bertram in that moment. How many hours had they spent firing his duelling pistols at targets deep within the home wood? How many rabbits, squirrels, and birds had they frightened with their incessant shooting? Too many to be numbered. Enough, she supposed, to make her an expert shot and also skilled at loading the intricate weapon.

She returned to her own chamber and seeing that Gwendolyn had already descended to the kitchens to enjoy a cup of tea with Mrs. Thwaite, she tied up four pistol balls and the small canister of powder in a kerchief. These, along with the pistol, she tucked deeply within the pocket of her gown and drew in a sharp breath, committing to memory the strong need for her to keep her skirts away from anything of solid construction or from either of the gentlemen, lest in her clumsiness she reveal the presence of the pistol.

She then opened the top drawer and withdrew a white muslin shawl. This she settled over her bonnet and let the sides drape down over her shoulders. She would appear as she hoped to appear—like a lady who was afraid of burning her complexion in the morning sunlight.

The looking glass again caught her eye, and she saw reflected in the mirror this time a lady whose eyes were so bright that she scarcely recognized herself. This time, as she met her own gaze, she understood a very real truth about herself more clearly—Kingsbridge would like her this way, full of fire, too much fire perhaps.

A few minutes later she was running lightly down the bank and saw that the men were only awaiting her arrival to be going. With her spirits soaring, she quickly took up a seat on the center of three planks, using her hand to keep the pistol from striking any part of the wooden boat.

An oar was settled in front and one in back. The men climbed quickly aboard, Kingsbridge first, taking up the position on the aft plank behind her, and Winsford at the bow of the serviceable if not elegant boating craft. Another moment and the swift, coordinated movements of the gentlemen set the vessel into deeper and deeper waters, all the while moving swiftly toward the far shore of the small lake.

The breeze picked up once they were a few yards from shore. With no hillocks, trees, or houses to mar the course of the wind, Emily had to hold the muslin shawl tightly in place or it would be blown like a sail into the sky. Conversation lagged, but the excitement among them was a tangible thing, shared and enjoyed. She knew that neither man feared what they were doing, nor did she. Confidence was what she felt and knew that to be true within each of her compatriots as well. Together they were sharing an adventure and, regardless of what might happen during the next hour or so, for the rest of their lives they would be united by the experience.

Passing the island, Emily could see that fir and alder grew in thick abundance on the geographical upstart. The small hut, appearing to be in good repair, had undoubtedly been placed on the island in the event the weather became unexpectedly violent and leaving the island an impossibility.

Birds suddenly flew low over the lake, and Emily darted a glance to the north. Just as she feared, clouds were seen to be piling up on the horizon. The old adage was true that when birds flew low, rain was near.

"A storm," she stated. Both men turned as one to look to the north, but neither commented on the fact.

In front of her, Emily could see that the reeds were quite thick on the opposite shore and tangled among them at the edge were dense stands of ferns. She drew her muslin closely over her bonnet so that her eyes were half-shaded by the gauzy fabric. The sides of the muslin she pulled close in at her chin.

Two cottages, about a half mile apart, were now visible from the lake. One had closed bright red shutters, the other had cheerful chintz curtains and a plume of gray smoke rising out of the kitchen chimney.

"Which do you think?" Winsford called back.

"The one which seems inhabited," Kingsbridge returned.

But Emily gazed from one to the other and frowned. "I beg to differ," she said. "The Glossips might want to conceal their presence on the lake as much as possible. I should think the one to the north."

"Kingsbridge?" Winsford asked, by way of insisting that he make the decision on which direction they should go.

Emily turned back to look at the viscount, wondering if he would be angry that she had dared to disagree with him. She met his gaze as he plied the waters, but there was nothing of pique in the expression which turned to her. If anything, he was taking her opinion seriously.

She was infinitely pleased.

"To the north," he said. "Miss Emily's mind works in a rather devious manner—as I know by experience—and so I will bow to her judgment in the matter."

Emily chuckled. She knew he was referring to their first meeting at her home in Upper Brook Street, when she was playing off her tricks with her sister, Meg.

Both men began dipping their oars in long strokes toward the north shore.

Winsford spoke over his shoulder. "What do you say? Shall we land a quarter of a mile above the cottage, in that stand of oak?"

"That will do to a nicety," Kingsbridge responded.

Emily slid her hand down the skirts of her gown and touched the pistol concealed in her pocket. She felt wholly and fully alive. Every romantic adventure she and Bertram had taken during their youth seemed to coalesce in the smell of the approaching storm, the sight of the birds wheeling riotously about in the freshening breeze, the way all the colors on the shore seemed brilliant because of her heightened senses—the rich green of the oak trees, the white of the cottage, the cherry red of the shutters.

A shutter opened as if by magic and framed in the open window was the forlorn profile of her cousin.

"Evangeline," she murmured. So her instincts had been right. The Glossips were inhabiting the cottage that appeared deserted.

She quickly averted her gaze and began gesturing toward the north and pretending to be engaging the men in a discussion of the beauties of the lake in order to avert suspicion. Evangeline couldn't hear her, of course, since the freshening wind would carry her voice in a southerly direction, so she was not in the least concerned that she would be recognized.

She did not again glance back at the cottage. By the time

they landed the rowboat at a small opening between reeds
and several large rocks, the clouds to the north had already
begun casting a shadow over Helm Crag to the northwest.

A downpour was imminent.

Nineteen

Emily disembarked carefully, keeping her right hand poised low on her skirts in order to keep the pistol from banging the edge of the rowboat. She stepped onto the rock-strewn shore, where the lake, the reeds, and nearby stand of oak trees were cast in ever-darkening shadows as the clouds moved steadily overhead.

Twice the muslin over her bonnet nearly blew away. A chill went through her as a cooling breeze swept over Helm Crag, a wind wet with raindrops that tugged and pulled at her blue-and-yellow-flowered skirts and her dark blue over-dress. She finally tied the muslin beneath her chin in exasperation.

Kingsbridge dragged the boat ashore completely out of the water. "We'll have rain soon," he said, popping his hat hard down about his ears. "We need shelter, and quickly."

Winsford spun about hard on his heels. "There," he cried, gesturing toward the southern edge of the wood. "A shed just beyond that drystone wall."

Emily glanced at the direction of his outstretched arm and caught sight of the barest edge of roof. "That should do!" she cried and stepped in behind Winsford as he began walking briskly toward the wall. A path soon appeared leading in the direction of the shed as well as toward the two cottages. She could hear Kingsbridge marching behind her.

When a distant roll of thunder crested at the top of Helm Crag, Winsford began to run. Just as Emily picked up her skirts to follow suit, the first of the fat raindrops struck her on the shoulder and another quickly thudded her bonnet. She squealed and raced toward the wall. Winsford found the gate, holding it open for her and Kingsbridge. She wasted no time, passing quickly through and running twenty feet more. She raced into what proved to be an abandoned shelter, the opening facing to the south.

She moved deeply within. The storm broke open in a sudden torrent of rain just as Winsford and Kingsbridge catapulted themselves inside at the very same moment. Winsford tripped and somersaulted over the hay that littered the floor of the shed. He came up laughing. Kingsbridge immediately swiped the hat from his head and began brushing the water from the brim and from his shoulders.

"We just made it!" Emily cried. Turning to Winsford, she exclaimed, "I know you told us that the weather could turn quickly, but this was really astonishing!"

Winsford regained his feet and began flicking straw off his pantaloons. "You can't say I didn't warn you at Windermere," he said. "Though I must add that the tumultuous changes in weather is part of the reason I'm drawn to this part of the country. Nothing ever so quixotic or wild happens in London."

He glanced at her, his eyes rather penetrating as he met her gaze.

"You are right about that," she responded cheerfully, ignoring his flirtatious expression. "I suppose that is one reason I frequently feel so bored during the Season. At least in the country, one has a chance of being caught in a summer storm while out riding. But the worst that can happen in London should it begin to rain, is that if you are enjoying the five o'clock parade in Hyde Park, for instance, you will be forced to open your umbrella until the postillion can raise the hood over one's landau."

Winsford laughed, then clucked his tongue and shook his head. "Abominably tame."

She smiled as she began to pluck hay from his now hatless head, his neckcloth, and the back of his coat. "Intolerably so," she responded. The hay was old and smelled musty.

"Here," Kingsbridge called. "Let me help you, Miss Longcliffe." Before Emily knew what was happening, he had jockeyed her away from Winsford, stepping between them, and began slapping in a rather forceful manner against Winsford's coat, head, and neck. She watched him in much astonishment and wondered at his strange conduct, until she saw the look on Winsford's face of deep amusement.

Emily bit her lip, then compressed them together to keep from smiling. How very protective Kingsbridge was being, not so much *of* her, but of some sort of primordial *claim* to her.

Winsford threw up an arm and turned around to ward off more of Kingsbridge's kind assistance. "Whoa!" he exclaimed. "Given the nature of our business here, I daresay I don't give a fig about a little hay on my coat."

By now he was nearly laughing and his brown eyes were lit with warm amusement, so much so that Kingsbridge understood full well he was being laughed at. He grunted and turned away from his friend.

Emily found she couldn't breathe very well as she watched Kingsbridge. The implications of his conduct began to settle deeply into layer upon layer of her heart. She liked that he kept her from touching Winsford, even though her efforts had been of a friendly and harmless nature. She was attracted, enormously so, to his most basic qualities, for they were manly, strong, and made her whole being quiver with something she could not precisely define.

She moved toward him, drawn as if by a magnet, and took up a place beside him pretending to do what he appeared to be doing, looking out at the rain-drenched countryside.

A gray drystone wall, not fifty feet in the distance, created the boundary of the small pasture which must have provided shelter and grazing land for at least one horse, possibly two in the not too distant past. The land was a little rocky, but thick grasses covered most of the ascending pasture. A few parsley ferns dotted the green expanse and grew in thickets next to the northernmost stone walls.

To her right near the path, the land was a little boggy and several carnivorous sundew plants could be seen with their fuzzy, hungry leaves waiting for an insect to chance by. The plants bore delightful yellow flowers, the enticement used to draw unsuspecting flies, gnats, and the like into its sticky clutches. Once caught, the insects were digested. She and Sophia, much to Meg's consternation, had brought one of the plants home on their return journey from Lakeland and kept it alive for some months by placing raw meat from the kitchens on its leaves.

She turned and glanced at Kingsbridge, who finally deigned to meet her gaze. He fairly glared at her. She looked away and smiled.

"You needn't appear so very pleased," he snapped.

"I like to see you make a cake of yourself, m'lord," she whispered. "Very becoming."

He grunted again, but refused to give her answer. Instead, he folded his arms across his chest and stared stoically out at the rain.

Fifteen minutes more, the downpour ceased as suddenly as it had started, and a quick-spreading path of sunlight followed, glinting enchantingly off the wet grass, trees, and foliage, sparkling so brightly that once or twice Emily had to avert her gaze. She felt as though a dozen mirrors were being reflected at her in quick jolts.

Winsford drew abreast Kingsbridge. "Shall we go?" he queried, low and purposefully.

Something in the tone of his voice caused Emily's heart to turn over sharply and the pulse at her neck began to thrum upward into her ears.

The moment had come to assault Evangeline's cottage.

Kingsbridge addressed Winsford. "The front door is

placed perpendicular to the lake, as our cottage is. We won't be seen until we are there, unless someone is about or happens to peer over the garden wall. I suggest we travel three abreast down the lane conducting ourselves as travellers and pretending only a modicum of interest in the cottage itself. At the last moment, Emily should remain in the lane and you and I shall make a run at the front door. Unless either of you object, I intend to walk straight in as though I've mistaken my cottage. The rest, well, we shall see what follows."

Emily stared at him in wonder. "Are you sure that would be wise? What if Glossip is armed?"

Kingsbridge shook his head. "Why would he be, in such a place of seclusion? I would rather expect him to be sipping his tea with Evangeline sequestered in a bedchamber at the other end of the dwelling."

Emily could think of no reason to argue with the logic of his opinions, nor could Winsford, therefore he gave a quick nod of his head. "Well, then, shall we?"

He held his hand wide in a gesturing motion for Emily to pass him by and to enter the path leading to the lane. She smiled at him in response, her nerves feeling pricklish and her head a little dizzy as she stepped beyond him and moved toward the drystone wall and the small iron gate that led to the lane.

Once there, she pushed the gate open, the water spraying fanlike in a quick, pretty movement across the already dripping gray rocks. The grass was wetter still and, before she had taken many more steps, her skirts were damp about the hem. She eyed the muddy lane with some misgiving and turned back to suggest to both men that she thought it wiser to cling to the higher elevations at the edges of the lane rather than walk in a line through so many dark puddles.

She felt Kingsbridge's hand on her back and his breath warm on her ear as he whispered over her shoulder. "You are right, of course. But no more speaking, lest Evangeline hears your voice and recognizes you in such a manner as to give away our presence here."

Emily drew in her breath sharply. He was right. Even though the cottage was still a quarter mile away they ought to take every precaution.

She began to walk quickly along the muddy edge of the ungravelled road. She held her hand against her weighted pocket.

She was breathing harder in a few minutes since her pace was brisk and steady. The cottage drew closer and closer. In the distance, thunder returned to them from the receding storm. The sun on her right shoulder however was a delightful warmth in contrast to her legs, which were cold and damp from her skirts which were now wet to the knees.

Winsford commented on the beauty of the fells and the several sundew plants he could see even from the roadside. Kingsbridge stated that he thought this side of the lake was even prettier than the other. Emily remained silent.

Only a hundred or more yards separated the party from the cottage. Emily's heart began to race, as much from the excitement of the moment as from the exertion. Their plan was simple—to walk in and take Evangeline home with them. The Glossips were to be ignored, unless of course they were stupid and became violent.

Fifty yards.

The smell of chicken stock and herbs lingered in the air and Emily lifted her gaze to note that smoke now darkened the air above the chimney. The Glossips were at home, certainly.

Twenty yards.

Her heart became a steady pounding against her chest wall. She wanted to walk faster still, to hurry the future toward her with good speed, to ease the tension mounting in her limbs, but to do so, if observed, would be to incite suspicion. Therefore, she kept her pace even and unremarkable. She heard the men chattering behind her. Her mouth was dry, her lips more so. She licked them and drew in a deep breath.

Five yards.

She picked her way carefully around three unjoined puddles. She could hear the men splashing their boots through the edges of the puddles with little concern. She reached the corner of the cottage where sword ferns fronted the whitewashed wall. She stopped and turned to look at Kingsbridge.

He was right behind her, met her gaze once quite firmly, nodded to her, and when he passed by her, gave her arm a reassuring squeeze. Winsford was close on his heels.

As soon as they were out of sight, she removed the pistol from her pocket, as well as the pistol balls and the powder. From long practice, though executed some years ago, she tipped the narrowed end of the container carefully, easing a little of the powder down the barrel. Resealing the powder container and returning it to her pocket, she then slipped a pistol ball inside. Forcing the ball down the barrel with the rod, she returned the rod to its sheath and then put more powder in the flintlock pan.

The pistol was ready—so was she.

She tied up the remaining balls and returned these to her pocket as well. She held the gun pointed away from her and upward into the air. She listened intently and heard a hard thumping noise, then silence. She began to count. When she got to twelve, she heard a woman shriek. She rounded the corner, expecting to see no one.

Instead, however, a sight met her eyes that filled her with dismay, for there on the lake was Evangeline, some two hundred yards away, in the same blue rowboat of the day before, and the Glossips paddling madly toward the opposite side.

The men emerged shortly afterward and glanced first at her then quickly toward the lake.

"What the deuce!" Winsford cried.

Kingsbridge groaned. "Damn and blast!"

"The devil take it!" His compatriot complained with a dip

of his knees and a grimace on his face that loudly bespoke his anguish.

Then, as though each realized something else was amiss, they turned slowly around to face her, their expressions nothing short of dumbfounded. Winsford's eyes were like saucers as he stared at her, and Kingsbridge's mouth fell unattractively agape. Each followed the line of her arm and the pistol she held aloft and ready.

Her heart was still beating hard.

"Emily!" Kingsbridge called to her. "What the devil do you think you are doing with a pistol?"

Winsford's comment was worse. "You took my pistol from our bedchamber?"

Emily felt a slight blush begin to creep up her cheeks. "I thought it might be best and, and, and you must agree that we didn't have time to brangle about it."

Winsford and Kingsbridge turned toward each other and exchanged curious yet disbelieving expressions.

Kingsbridge moved first, stepping quickly toward her. "But it isn't loaded and primed, now is it?"

Winsford laughed, following closely on Kingsbridge's heels. "Of course it's not. Just like a lady to think that all one must do is hold a gun and it will fire."

Both men began to laugh, a sensation Emily found irritating in the extreme.

On top of the stable nearby was a running rabbit weathervane pointed to the south, since a purposeful wind had followed in the wake of the storm. She levelled the pistol at the vane, held her sight steady, and pulled the trigger. The loud retort caused the wind to cease for a moment and was followed instantaneously by the clink and spin of the weathervane.

The men stopped, stared, and marvelled. They looked at the spinning vane, they glanced at her, they shook their heads, they were utterly nonplussed.

When they remained where they were for a few seconds

more, Emily cried, "If we hurry, we might just stop them before they get very far!"

These words set the men in motion. Once she saw their hesitations had ended, she turned back toward the lane and began to run. Within a few seconds both gentlemen reached her, drawing abreast. The puddles were still thick on the lane and none of them were minding where they stepped. Muddy water flew everywhere.

Winsford, upon coming up to her right side, reached for his pistol, whose barrel was steaming and still a little warm, and took it from her.

"I wouldn't want you to burn your fingers," he said. He held the gun in his hand and marvelled at it, as though wondering how it had come about to prime, load, and fire itself. Emily was pleased with his consternation.

Kingsbridge, however, did not even look at her, but took up her left elbow and began pulling her along. She began to run faster. He let go of her arm and began to run more quickly as well. She met his pace. He glanced askance at her and ran faster still. She picked up her skirts and again matched his long stride.

Winsford called after them. "Wait!"

Emily ignored him. She set her sights on the patch of reeds in which the boat had landed and did not let her gaze waver as she challenged Kingsbridge's abilities. She knew mud was flying everywhere from both sets of boots, but she didn't care. She had her skirts nearly up to her hips in order to stretch her legs as far as she might go.

Exhilaration poured through her. She could feel blood rushing to her face, tingling her cheeks as the cold, wet air flowed into her lungs and then was released as steam. She was gasping for air, but Kingsbridge could only outstrip her an inch for every five strides. Even by the time they reached the landing she knew she could push him on the shoulder if she wanted to, and she did. He stumbled in his running, but kept his balance and turned down the small path toward the boat.

In spite of their need to be hurrying, and the fact that Evangeline was so close at hand, he came up laughing. "What a madcap vixen you are!" he cried.

She eased up her pace, but still meant to hurl past him in order to reach the rowboat first, touch it, and claim a victory, but he caught her hard about the waist and swung her around in a circle.

"So you knew what I was about!" she cried.

"I'm beginning to understand you very well. But what the deuce were you doing with a loaded pistol? One misfire and you are maimed for life. You knew nothing about Winsford's weapon, having never discharged it before, and for all your skill, you might have inadvertently killed either Winsford or myself or the poor cottage-keeper we surprised in her kitchen."

"I am not so ham-handed!" she cried, instinctively reaching down to touch the container to see if the lid was still secured tightly on the powder. To her relief, it was. "There you see! I know how to manage myself."

Winsford was out of breath as he reached them. "Do stop brangling!" he cried. "The pair of you. Get in the boat and I'll shove off."

Kingsbridge took the forward position and readied himself with his oar. Emily sat behind him. Winsford shoved off and, after two steps in the water, hastily clambered aboard.

A minute more and the men were steadily pushing their way through the water, just as they had done not a half hour past.

Twenty

By the time the boat rounded the small island, the Glossips were nowhere to be seen.

"They could not have rowed back to their cottage so quickly!" Emily exclaimed. "Do you suppose they are secreted on the island?"

Kingsbridge continued to dip his oar deeply into the water and pull the boat ever forward. "I don't know," he said over his left shoulder. "But I wouldn't advise a search of the island. If the Glossips are there, Evangeline could be harmed."

"I agree," Winsford said.

"Back to our cottage then?" Emily asked.

"Yes," the men replied together.

When Emily stepped onto the bank, her spirits plummeted. To have come so close, to have seen her cousin, only to have the Glossips escape with her practically beneath their noses was disheartening in the extreme.

As she picked up her muddied, flowered skirts and began climbing the steep bank toward the path, Kingsbridge came up beside her and supported her arm. "Don't fret, Em," he said softly. "We'll find her. Glossip may have outwitted us by stealing from the cottage during the rainstorm, but he can hardly leave Grasmere without passing by The Swan. Winsford and I have decided to set up watch at the inn again."

Emily paused in her steps and turned to look at him. "I'm coming with you," she stated firmly. He started to take umbrage, but she cut him off abruptly. "I'll not stay here, kicking my heels as I did yesterday, never to know what is happening. Besides, even you must admit that the Glossips are unlikely to recross the lake, so pray don't tell me that I must set up a vigilant watch of Grasmere, for I tell you now I shall do no such thing!" Odd tears smarted her eyes.

Kingsbridge watched her through a veiled expression. She couldn't tell in the least by looking at him precisely what it was he might be thinking, though she guessed he was angry with her belligerence. After a moment, he released the hint of a sigh. "As you wish," he said quietly.

"Thank you," she said, also in a softer voice. "I'm grateful that you do not mean to brangle with me."

A crooked smile tipped his lips. "Of what use would it be to cross swords with you, when I can see that you are in a state? If there is one thing I have learned during these past several years regarding the females of my acquaintance, it is that once their passions are aroused, stubbornness must always rule the day."

She glared at him. "Spoken just like a man. Were Winsford to declare he meant to go to the inn whether it pleased you or not, you would think him strong of spirit, determined, even courageous. But let a woman force her way and she is a stubborn, willful, ungovernable termagant!" She shook his hand off her arm, turned more fully to face him, and dared him to give her answer with a flare of her nostrils.

He merely laughed and told her she rose so prettily to the fly that he vowed one day she might even become a most agreeable companion.

Though she could see that he had been teasing her, Emily was not appeased, since generally she had found the entire exchange to be an exact reflection of the way the gentlemen of her society thought and conducted themselves. Her uncle, only a few days earlier, had told her not to bother her pretty little head about Evangeline's kidnapping! Therefore, she growled at him in response, turned away with a flip of her skirts, and continued her hike up the hill to the cottage.

Once inside, she exchanged her gown for a light pink muslin confection rimmed at the hem with a narrow row of ruffles and topped with a dark green silk spencer embroidered with fanciful roses. Over her curls she settled a charming straw bonnet, dyed to match the spencer and folded back at the forehead. A spray of artificial pink roses pinned the brim securely in place. On her feet she wore green leather slippers, and in her hand she carried a pair of white lace gloves. The effect was summery and modest and entirely proper for the taproom of The Swan Inn.

When her toilette was complete, she descended the stairs slowly, drawing on her gloves at the same time. Her thoughts fell to her cousin's circumstances. Something nagged at her about the disappearance of the rowboat, but she couldn't quite determine what it was. If only she comprehended either of the Glossips' minds, then she might have some understanding of their intentions.

She stopped on the bottom step and, with quick, careful movements, settled the snug gloves to the base of each finger. She could hear the gentlemen chatting in quiet tones just beyond the door but out of sight, their words indistinct. A delightful breeze flowed through the cottage, cooling her cheeks and to some degree her anxious mind. She could hear the snorting of the horses and the stable boy's cheerful words as he spoke to his waiting pair.

She considered the routes that would have been open to the Glossips and wondered if it was possible that they had merely circled back to the cottage by keeping the island between themselves and her rowboat the entire time. But why would they risk returning? Surely they wouldn't have done so. Or was it possible that they had another dwelling in which to hide as well? That would make three in all.

She gave her head a shake. No. All these schemes were far too complicated. She was of the opinion that whatever had happened, the Glossips had had a very simple scheme in mind by which to thwart their pursuers, for it was now evident they believed themselves pursued.

Whatever the case, if the Glossips were intent on leaving, they would have to pass by the inn.

Later, when they reached The Swan, Emily again adopted her former relationship to Lord Kingsbridge, presenting herself as his sister, Mrs. Matford, a pretense which was nearly undone by the sudden arrival of a former acquaintance.

"Byron," she murmured as she settled herself at a table in the taproom, her gaze fixed to the door some ten feet away. Kingsbridge heard her and instantly turned in the direction of her gaze.

"Good god, so it is!" he cried. He pushed his chair back and bowed to his "sister" before leaving her with Winsford in order to welcome his friend to Grasmere.

"What has brought you to Lakeland," Kingsbridge cried, extending his hand to Byron and shaking the poet's proffered hand enthusiastically.

Byron handed his coat to the serving girl who slung it on a peg by the door. He took off his hat and handed it to her as well. Emily watched in some amusement as the young woman took a deep breath and bobbed a curtsy, her cheeks falling quickly into a hearty blush. He said something to her, pressed a coin into her hand, then offered her a warm smile. The young woman bobbed another curtsy, blinked several times, and held his hat to her bosom, her gaze transfixed by the handsome patron.

Emily understood precisely how the young lady felt in the presence of Byron. He was an extraordinary creature, whose most essential charm was centered on the simple fact that whoever was his object of the moment felt herself to be the only female in the universe. His attention, once fixed, was unwavering, and his smile was like the sun bestowing a magical warmth that could soften the heart of even the most indifferent feminine breast.

"Do come and greet my *sister*," Kingsbridge said pointedly. "I know you have made her acquaintance recently, for she attended the Scarswell masquerade a sennight past."

"I had thought your sibling was fixed in Devonshire, er, for the duration," he said, a frown between his brows.

"No, no, you are mistaken," he said meaningfully, drawing the poet toward their table.

Byron lifted his brows in surprise but turned toward Emily and paused only a fraction of a second in his halting limp as he caught sight of her. A glint in his warm, gray eyes, of amusement and appreciation, struck her and caused her to laugh.

"Well met, my lord," she said, inclining her head politely to him as he approached the table. "But I would never have supposed you were journeying to the Lake District, else I would have suggested you join our little party at the outset."

He stepped up to her and bent over her proffered hand, placing a gentle kiss on her lace glove. "Had I received such an invitation from you, Mrs. Matford, nothing would have kept me from drawing my carriage into your entourage."

"Gallantly spoken," she responded. Again she giggled, for he had fallen in with their little deception so easily and indeed, his eyes were glimmering with his enjoyment of it.

He took up a seat to her right, Winsford sat across from her, and Kingsbridge drew back his chair on her left. She ordered a glass of sherry as did Kingsbridge. Winsford barked for a whisky and Byron again directed his warm gaze toward the pretty serving girl, who nervously asked what he desired. Since he did not offer her an answer immediately, but instead held her gaze in something very near wickedness, the young lady took a deep breath and fluttered her lashes in a cross between embarrassment and excitement. "A cup of tea, if you please," he responded at long last.

"Yes, me lord," she answered on a deep sigh as she dropped another curtsy.

Emily wondered if she would be capable of bringing any beverage but Byron's. She marvelled, as did Winsford and

Kingsbridge, at the poet's singular abilities. She also wondered about his reputation or whether the exchange she had
just witnessed formed the whole of it—that a mere look from
Byron was enough to set a lady's heart fluttering wildly.

Once the sway of the maid's brown skirts had disappeared
into the nether regions, Kingsbridge asked Byron why he
had come north.

The poet looked at each one of them in turn and said in
a low voice, "I spoke with Marcus Peveril three days past.
It would seem Mrs. Browne used her influence after all and
obtained a release for him from prison. He asked if I had
any news of Miss Longcliffe and her search for her cousin.
I suppose you could say I determined at that moment to forge
my way north, first to Derbyshire and later to Cumbria, to
see for myself just which way the wind was blowing. So, tell
me, Mrs. Matford, is your sister-in-law found?"

Both Kingsbridge and Winsford turned to Emily in silent
acknowledgement that only she could reveal all that had transpired where Evangeline was concerned, since hers was the
primary relationship to Miss Matford.

Aware that Byron had had an interest in the matter early
on, having provided Kingsbridge with some information regarding the Glossips, she did not hesitate to commence a
quiet retelling of their adventures since leaving London. Besides, she trusted Byron implicitly, for there was something
in his manners and attentiveness that inspired confidence.
He listened intently, his gaze never once wavering from hers,
his expression keenly intelligent.

"And so," he offered at the end of her recital, "you are
here to see if their coach should happen by?"

She nodded. "Their cottage is situated in such a place that
they can only leave by passing The Swan."

He frowned slightly. "Are you aware that Glossip was used
to reside near here, not far from Rydal Mount, I believe,
when he was young?"

Emily shook her head. "I did not know of it."

"Nor did I," Kingsbridge added.

"Not that it would have the smallest bearing on their next move," he said, "but perhaps the information will be of use to you."

At that moment, the serving maid arrived bearing a steaming cup of tea. Emily couldn't help but smile, wondering where her sherry was, or Kingsbridge's, or Winsford's whisky.

When Byron again placed another coin in the palm of her hand, his fingers lingering longer than necessary on her wrist before releasing her, the serving maid glanced about the table and noticed that Byron's was the only drink present. She gasped slightly, a sudden blush suffusing her cheeks and returned to fetch the spirits.

The table at which they sat was situated near a window and what little traffic ambled by was visible to them all. Now and then a lone conveyance, such as a cart, drawn by a single, sturdy, swaybacked hack, would appear and slowly disappear. Once a pretty phaeton driven by an elderly man with a gray-haired matron beside him clip-clopped over the cobbles. Even a rider in a blue coat and mounted on a lovely chestnut rode straight-backed down the lane.

But not a single travelling coach or post chaise happened by.

The sun began to set, and supper was ordered in a private parlor that also faced the lane. The fare was hearty if not fancy; roast beef, duck, oysters in a fish sauce, peas, potatoes, and a broccoli soup. Byron requested a little vinegar as well, and Emily noted with some surprise that he ate very little during the course of the meal except a few potatoes sprinkled with vinegar, and some of the soup.

He was thin and appeared quite fit, but it would seem that the rumors she had heard of him were true, that he had once been a rather plump child and that he was in the habit of tending to his figure assiduously.

"So tell me," Kingsbridge said, addressing the poet.

"While you are in Grasmere, do you intend to call upon Wordsworth?" Emily knew Byron had no great opinion of the Lakeland poet who was known to reside not far from the inn.

He shook his head, however, and responded that he had had only one intent in coming north—to discover their whereabouts and determine for himself how successful *Mrs. Matford's* efforts had been in helping Miss Matford. He smiled as if to say, "See, the road led me here."

"But what of your trip?" he queried, still addressing Kingsbridge. "I thought you would have left Falmouth by now. Won't your crew and scientific gentlemen be anxious to be going?"

Emily glanced at Kingsbridge, a little surprised. "You were scheduled to leave England?" she cried. "Oh, Evan, do not tell me I have delayed your plans? Why didn't you say something?"

Kingsbridge wore an odd expression as he looked at her, almost of chagrin. Emily felt strange, suddenly, as though she had stumbled upon a secret, something not meant for her to know. A curious sensation of hurt took hold of her heart and refused to let go even when she told herself she was being silly.

"Your, er, *sister-in-law's* dilemma," he said quietly, "will in no manner affect the success of my venture, I assure you. So, you needn't repine. My ship won't be ready to disembark for another fortnight, perhaps even longer."

Such a formal answer. She could not be easy. Her mind was full of questions—questions she knew she could not ask. She wanted to know where it was he was going. And who were these *scientific* men of whom Byron spoke? Falmouth could only mean a sailing ship. Had he indeed hired a vessel, or purchased one? He was known to be a considerably wealthy man. Had he commandeered a yacht or a larger vessel?

She watched him. He was saying something to Winsford,

but she couldn't hear his words. Was her own silence notice-able? Could any of the gentlemen discern her thoughts? Would Kingsbridge notice how hurt she felt by his having withheld so momentous a scheme as a journey that for all appearances meant an adventure of no mean order? Why had he not felt he could tell her about something so important to him?

The grip on her heart increased. In a blinding moment, she came to see just how entangled she was with Kingsbridge and how the events of their northerly trek had caused her to feel more nearly connected to the marquess than she truly was. He was of course under no obligation to reveal every facet of his existence to her, but why had he not told her about his trip?

But at the very same moment that these painful sentiments were rumbling about her chest, an even stronger feeling rose up to consume the rest—she desperately envied the fact that he could conjure up such a scheme, then order a ship refur-bished in order to bring his scheme to fruition!

"Kingsbridge," she said quietly, laying a hand on his sleeve and interrupting the conversation of the gentlemen. "I beg your pardon, but you have distressed me sorely by this news. I am convinced you must have intended to journey to Falmouth from the time you left London. You should have told me such momentous plans were in the offing. I am sick with guilt."

He shifted toward her and said firmly, "Do not bother your head about it a moment longer. My schemes are not nearly as *momentous* as you suggest, I assure you." He was agitated, she could see as much by the faint scowl on his forehead. "It is nothing to signify."

Emily would have let the subject drop, but Byron broke in. "Nothing to signify?" he demanded, a crooked smile on his lips, his gray eyes wide with astonishment. "When you have spoken of little else for that past three months! Nay, the past year!"

She turned to look at the poet and saw a strange daring light in his eye, as though he were challenging Kingsbridge. In a flash of insight, she knew that he wanted her to know of the importance of the journey even if Kingsbridge did not. Byron spoke for her benefit.

The poet settled his soup spoon on the plate beneath the white china bowl and sat back in his seat. He turned his gaze toward Emily. "I can't imagine how it has come about that Kingsbridge has failed to tell you of his proposed journey, and I cannot explain in the least why he would say it does not signify, for it does, very much so." He turned back to Kingsbridge. "You must at least tell her the scope of your plans. For even if you cannot see that *your sister* possesses a kindred spirit to yours and to mine, I can."

Kingsbridge looked back at Emily and met her gaze fully. She thought she understood him, that in this moment he was utterly undecided about whether he should reveal more or not. To tell her would be to bind her more fully to him, and he was uncertain as to whether he ought to do so or not.

"It is a three-year journey around the world," he said at last, holding her gaze, willing her to read the deeper thoughts of his mind.

Emily was shocked. "Around the world?" she queried in what even to her own ears was a very small voice. She felt a wind begin to blow through her mind. A trip round the world! She could not conceive of anything grander or more full of purpose and wonder. Even Byron's love of adventuring had taken him no farther than the Levant, though his friends said he had always wanted to go to South America.

"Yes," Kingsbridge said, a faint scowl fixed to his face.

The hurt within Emily's breast took another hard twist.

"Oh, to be a man," she breathed, unaware she had spoken aloud. She let her gaze drop away from Kingsbridge. She could see him no longer in any case, for her vision had grown cloudy with unspoken longings. A trip round the world. Images of the Colonies, the West Indies, of Mexico, Peru, of

Africa, India, the Spice Islands, China, the Japannes, and what of Russian America?

A faint clattering on the cobbles intruded into her hazy reveries. She sensed a ripple of excitement course through the men at the table. Winsford rose suddenly, nearly slamming his chair to the floor as he pushed away from the table. He bolted to the nearest window and peered through the shutters. "A travelling coach," he whispered. Kingsbridge moved to stand next to him.

Emily watched them both, her mind clearing quickly. Forgotten were her daydreams and in their stead was the purpose of their present vigil. She rose from her seat, setting her napkin on the table, then moving to stand beside Kingsbridge.

Only a dim light from the hotel cast faint yellow shadows on the cobbled road. Black horses moved steadily by. The window of the maroon coach drew within the path of the light.

Emily's shoulders slumped. Only one figure was within, an old man, with long graying hair and a thick nose. She returned to the table, took up her seat, and smoothed her napkin across her lap once more. She dipped her spoon into the broccoli soup and sipped it slowly, savoring the rich flavor of the creamy broth. She glanced at Byron, who had not left his chair, and smiled as the two men took up their seats as well.

Emily watched the poet for a moment, who had ceased eating altogether. His gaze was upon her, his expression calculating. She knew he was pondering the recent interchange between herself and Kingsbridge. His manners were gracious, his conversation never above his company, and save for what she now believed to be his purposeful indiscretion in causing Lord Kingsbridge to reveal his plans, he was an agreeable companion.

"Do you intend to embark on another excursion yourself?" she asked, directing her question to the poet.

His smile was slow and warm. "I never stop thinking about returning to Europe," he said. "Though of the present I have too many distractions in England to permit of my leaving just yet."

"You enjoy flirting far too much," she said brightly.

His smile broadened. "Then you understand me far too well," he responded.

She took another sip of soup and eyed him speculatively. "I wouldn't think you could remain here in Albion and be content," she commented. "Though I do not know you well and can only infer a great deal from your poetry, I would suppose that a man caught up in a perpetual state of passion could not long remain in any one place."

He chuckled. "Nor could he shave with any degree of comfort or safety."

Emily was taken aback, then burst out laughing as did both Kingsbridge and Winsford.

"Do I take it to mean, sir, that you are not in a constantly *excited* state?"

"I am not. My health, nor the health of any normal man or woman, could not sustain such a condition for any length of time. But what of you, *Mrs. Matford?* Are you content to remain in England? I saw much that I believe would appeal to you in my travels."

She sighed deeply. "I will give you answer by saying that I should have been born a man."

He appeared as though he wanted to say something, but Winsford, who was overly content from having imbibed nearly a bottle of Madeira all by himself, suddenly drew his pistol from his pocket and set it squarely on the table in front of Emily.

"You must show Byron how you handle a firearm," he cried. "He wouldn't believe me if I told him, so load the weapon and then we'll have him select a target." Winsford turned to Byron, "She can do it—I swear it! 'Pon my soul, I swear it. I saw her prick the end of a weathervane with one shot this very afternoon. It spun faster than the wind blows, her aim was so true!"

"Indeed?" Byron queried, his brows lifted in surprise and not a little approval as he turned to meet her gaze.

Emily felt a blush grow on her cheeks. She was embarrassed that Winsford was putting her forward as he was, especially when he searched his pockets and afterward settled the container of powder and a small canvas sack of pistol balls on the table in front of him.

"Lord Winsford," she cried. "I will do no such thing. We are at dinner, not in the middle of a stable yard!"

"Byron won't mind and Kingsbridge is in his cups!"

Emily glanced at Kingsbridge, but saw at once that he was no such thing, but rather that Winsford himself was half-foxed.

Byron smiled. "I should like to see you run through your paces, if you wouldn't mind," he said, his gaze challenging her.

Emily glanced at the pistol and knew an impulse to oblige him. What would it matter, she thought. Besides, she was feeling blue-devilled because of the fact that her deepest longings would probably remain unsatisfied throughout the duration of her life. She straightened her shoulders and took up the pistol. Within less than a minute, the weapon was loaded and ready to be fired. She held it carefully, the barrel pointed aloft, and met Byron's gaze with a bold stare.

He applauded her, but when Winsford reached across the table to take the pistol from her, the poet quickly caught up Winsford's arms with his hands to prevent him from reaching the firearm. Emily reacted quickly, as well, jumping from her seat and retreating from the table, the pistol still pointed toward the ceiling. She snatched the powder from the table and quit the parlor. She knew that because Winsford was in his altitudes, he was wholly unreliable. She ran outside where she quickly primed the pan and discharged the pistol into the night sky before he reached her.

When she turned around to face the inn, she saw that he had succeeded in breaking from Byron's grasp and was heading straight for her. She had not erred in her judgment of the situation after all.

Kingsbridge was close on his heels and Emily did not hesitate to skirt Winsford and place the pistol in his hands. "I'm sorry," she whispered.

"What the devil made you load it in the first place?" he returned in a low voice, turning her back into the inn with a firm grasp on her elbow.

"Where are you going!" Winsford cried, following behind them. "Damme! It's my pistol! I want a turn!"

"You'll not have a turn tonight!" Kingsbridge cried, addressing Winsford sharply over his shoulder. "You'll awaken the entire village."

"Good god," Winsford cried remorsefully. "Damme, if I don't think you're right."

To Emily, Kingsbridge continued coming the crab, "As for you, I should like to see you exercise better judgment in the future. You're like to get us all killed in your attempts to impress my friends."

Emily felt her neck burn with irritation. "I've apologized, Kingsbridge. What more do you wish from me than that?"

"A great deal more. For one thing, you might consider behaving more like a lady—"

"Like a lady!" Emily cried with a gasp. She wanted to say more, but they had entered the taproom and she was forced by discretion to clamp her lips together tightly. She was in a towering passion and felt that were she to be pricked by an embroidery needle, so much steam would escape her and that so quickly that she would simply fly apart into a million raging pieces.

Like a lady!

The very thought of it fired the nerves along her spine until she was fairly itching with rage. At the same time, the thought of having to enter the parlor and engage either Byron or Winsford in any manner of quiet, rational speech seemed so much beyond her capabilities of the moment that she determined to take a new course. Turning abruptly on her heel, she brushed past Kingsbridge and headed back to the door leading to the High Street.

"I'm returning to the cottage," she said coldly.

"As you wish," he responded.

But when she stepped into the starry night sky, she was met by the housekeeper of their cottage astride a horse. "There ye be, Mrs. Matford," she said, guiding her mount nearer to the inn. Mrs. Thwaite had agreed to sustain their subterfuge for Evangeline's sake. "I've word fer ye that will be none too pleasin', I'm 'fraid."

Emily approached the pretty bay mare and looked up into the older woman's face. "What is it?" she queried, her heart picking up its cadence.

"They've gone," she said simply.

"What? Who?"

"The Glossips. I've had it from their housekeeper not a half hour past. They've quit Grasmere—and some time past if I'm not much mistaken."

Twenty-one

"What do you mean, they've gone?"

Emily stared down at Kingsbridge, still slightly bemused by the news Mrs. Thwaite had related to her just a few moments earlier.

"Just as I said," she murmured. "They've gone. Our housekeeper told me they left shortly after we arrived back at the cottage from our trek across the lake."

"But that's impossible," he said, rising from his chair and staring at her in utter disbelief. "All three of us have been here for hours, watching the lane, listening, waiting. Granted we were not entirely attentive for every second of that time, but surely we would have noticed the departure of a travelling coach and three passengers, even if they wore disguises."

"According to Mrs. Thwaite, who had her information from the woman who cares for the cottage the Glossips hired, they did not take their coach. It is still sitting in the carriage house."

A stunned silence settled heavily on the small, cozy parlor.

"My god," he breathed.

"We've been humbugged," Winsford said. He appeared more sober than previously, but still blinked at Emily in rapid succession as though attempting to clear his blurred, wine-laden vision.

Byron whistled. "So they walked out, eh?"

Emily stared at him, dumbfounded, the truth of the situation striking her in blinding clarity. "So it would seem," she breathed, sinking down into her chair. "I still can't credit it's true, though I must admit it never occurred to me, even once, that they might do such a desperate thing."

Kingsbridge tapped his fingers on the table. "They've committed a desperate crime which, if caught, could send them to Tyburn Tree—so why wouldn't their conduct border on the extreme?"

"Indeed," Winsford said, nodding his head, his brow furrowed deeply.

"They would be near Ambleside by now," Byron said, "if they left so many hours past."

"I would think, then," Emily said, "that this was why the rowboat disappeared. They simply rounded the island, waited until we were gone up the hill, and rowed toward the nearest footpath that would take them south."

"Undoubtedly you are right," Kingsbridge said.

"What do we do now?" Winsford queried.

"Perhaps we ought to harness the horses and leave immediately," Emily suggested. But at that very moment, in the distance, a low rumbling could be heard coming from the north. She glanced toward the window, laughed, and shook her head. "Will the weather never be still?"

Winsford chuckled, dropped his chin in his hand, settled his elbow on the table, and closed his eyes. Emily glanced at him and realized he was unfit to travel anyway. Besides, an approaching storm would be the very worst climate in which to journey across the Lakeland fells in the middle of the night.

She turned toward Kingsbridge. "We ought to put Winsford to bed and begin our journey in the morning."

Kingsbridge, whose expression was dark with concern, nodded in agreement.

"I cannot remember being more dispirited," she added.

"I feel like a fool," he responded. "To have been duped by such a fellow is more than I can bear of the moment." He rose and began taking his leave of Byron, who said he would be accompanying them in the morning, since he intended to sojourn at Winsford Ketel for a few days.

On the following morning, at the village Ambleside, Emily had her conjectures confirmed—the Glossips had hired a post chaise and headed southeast toward Kendal, retracing their earlier steps. After bidding the warmest of goodbyes to both Byron and Winsford, Emily climbed aboard Kingsbridge's curricle, her heart despondent. Part of her was genuinely regretful at having to leave two companions she had found wonderfully agreeable, and the other part of her was despondent that they had failed in recapturing Evangeline at Grasmere.

A stiff breeze pummeled the back of her dark blue velvet bonnet. Absently, she untied the ribbons and retied them more firmly beneath her chin. She held to the side of the carriage as Kingsbridge lifted the reins and gave them a hearty slap across the horses' flanks. A moment more and the equipage, followed by both their travelling chariots, was pressing on to Kendal.

Puffed clouds thickened the sky, rising miles into the deep blue beyond and casting shadows on the exquisite rise and fall of the Lakeland fells. But the beauty of the environs could not dispel the blue-devils that had greeted Emily when she awoke that morning and which had seeped thoroughly into despair since. She wondered if she would ever succeed in rescuing Evangeline.

Kingsbridge, too, was quiet and, glancing at him once or twice, she noticed that he was given to releasing huffs of sighs. He drove the horses at a brisk pace and their coaches were soon left behind. She wondered if he knew that he had outstripped their servants or whether he was aware that more clouds had begun piling up behind them. She doubted as much. His hazel eyes were directed steadfastly on the rise and fall of the lane in front of him, and she could see that his thoughts were drawn inward. She supposed that he was unhappy about the wretched progress of their northerly adventure, but she also intuited that he was still angry with her conduct of the night before.

The lane was not mended as carefully as the southern counties, and given the quick roll of the wheels, she kept a hand pressed to the side of the curricle in order to keep her balance. Kendal was a journey of at least two hours since the route was circuitous, two hours in which not to converse, but to think. Perhaps she should have ridden with her maid in her town chariot, especially given the quixotic nature of the weather, but she found she had been unable to bear the thought, given her present uneasy state of mind, of being confined within the town coach for any length of time.

No, far better to breathe the fresh air and let the wind buffet her bonnet, her warm woolen cape, and her cheeks. She glanced down at her side and realized with a start that she had forgotten her umbrella. She groaned inwardly, at the same time she wasn't sure she even cared if the storm spent its fury on her unprotected head.

She was about to ask Kingsbridge what he thought the Glossips might do next, but refrained, given the next sigh that issued past his lips.

Understanding that Kingsbridge wished for conversation as little as she did, she gave her mind over to considering her future. She recalled the events of the day before, in particular the thrilling sensation of hiding in the abandoned stables until the storm passed, then afterward preparing to assault the cottage in which her cousin was being held captive. She had not been in the least frightened, she realized, but rather quite exhilarated.

She took in a deep breath, savoring the very feel of that particular moment, how much the danger of their situation had set her pulse to beating rapidly and forcefully. Her entire being had been awash with the sweetest sensation, something bordering on ecstasy.

The same sensation washed over her now as she closed her eyes, straightened her back, and gave herself to remembering how green the fells had been, how musty the odor of the old hay in the stable, how humid the feel of the air. She remembered holding the pistol in her hand, the weight of it, the way the pistol ball slid into the barrel, the pleasure of pulling the trigger and seeing the weathervane spin helplessly at the command of her shot.

She opened her eyes as the curricle began another descent. Behind her a sudden clap of thunder struck the surrounding fells. The horses lagged in their strides, then bolted ahead. Kingsbridge called to them, flicked the reins on their backs, and encouraged them forward. She turned around and saw what the thunder had promised—the onset of yet another quick, violent storm.

When Kingsbridge also turned around, he quickly began drawing rein.

"What are you doing?" Emily called out.

"You ought to be in your coach," he stated.

"I don't like to mention it, but we left my coach and yours quite far behind, at least two miles back. They might arrive in due course, but I doubt we shall see them before this storm has come and gone. Besides, I don't give a fig if it rains a little, or even a lot, and we can hardly stop now for the horses' sakes. Keep going."

He frowned at her in disbelief.

"I promise you," she said. "The rain will not bother me, even if it drives down on us in a sheet of purposeful mayhem. I want only one thing of the moment, to get to Kendal as quickly as possible."

"We'll seek shelter beneath that tree," he murmured, commanding the horses to resume their former pace. Ahead of the curricle, in the dip of the fells, was a large spreading oak that shaded part of the lane.

When the rain hit, the drops were as fat as eggs. Lightning flashed and thunder rolled about the hills, over and over, until the horses were nearly mad with fright. Once at the bottom of the hill, Kingsbridge drew the equipage under the cover of the great oak. The surrounding crags and fells would suffer the brunt of the lightning were it to strike, but the tree at least gave the poor beasts the sense that they were protected, and they settled down to wait out the onslaught.

"You aren't even shivering," Kingsbridge stated.

"What?" Emily said, glancing at him.

"You aren't even shivering," he repeated.

"No," she said. "I'm not cold."

"Yet your cheeks are pink," he said, scrutinizing her face. He drew off a glove, even while the rain pelted them through the leaves of the tree, and touched her cheek. "By god, you're warm!"

Emily chuckled. "Why do you seem so shocked?"

"Because even I am cold. The temperature can't be much above fifty, even though it's July!"

Emily shrugged and let her gaze rove the rain-drenched landscape. Droplets bounced off a nearby drystone wall in pretty starts that took the form of small bursts of fireworks. "I can't explain it," she said. "The weather rarely afflicts me as it does my sisters. But then Bertram never would permit me even the smallest semblance of feminine weaknesses. Perhaps he trained me to it—I don't know."

"Whatever am I going to do with you, Em?"

She glanced back at Kingsbridge and saw a strange look was on his face. She felt her heart wheel about suddenly and turn to come racing toward her at breakneck speed. Before she knew what was happening, she was in his arms and he was kissing her as hard as the rain struck her bonnet. Lightning lit up the countryside, thunder rolled, her whole body became one with the violence of the weather and the incredible feel of being held tightly in Kingsbridge's arms. She forgot that he had been angry with her last night, she let him kiss her and go on kissing her, wildly and completely, his tongue taking possession of her as never before. She wrapped her arms tightly about him.

Again lightning penetrated through her closed lids and a mountain of thunder shook the curricle. The horses threw back their heads and stamped their feet. Cumbria seemed ready to rise up and throw itself back on its Pennine spine.

Kingsbridge was kissing her and gave not the smallest hint that he meant to stop. She reveled in the forbidden closeness of that moment, of the shared embrace, of shared danger, of shared purpose.

He drew back slightly. "Marry me," he whispered, his words as startling as they were unexpected . . . as they were sudden.

"What?" she asked, disbelieving she had heard him correctly.

"I said, Emily, put me out of misery and marry me, become my wife. I was half in love with you in the orangery at the masquerade, and the rest of this journey has sent me the remainder of the way and beyond. I don't want to live without you, I refuse to go another step on this island with you unless I know we shall be joined forever. I want you to bear my children and I promise I'll make the best of husbands."

Emily felt peculiar, as though her soul was being cut in half by the sharp edge of a heavy, thick, determined broadsword. "But Evan," she began, aware only faintly that she had addressed him by his Christian name, "what of your ship waiting for you in Falmouth?"

"I'll sell it off, my love. I'll suffer a loss, but nothing to compare with living without you the rest of my life."

"Do you want a lot of children?"

She saw his expression grow a little distressed. "I don't know—I suppose like most men I have not given the matter a great deal of thought—an heir, of course—yes," he responded uneasily.

Emily searched his face for a long moment; she could see

that he was sincere. She also understood that because of his rank as the Marquess of Kingsbridge, one of his first considerations to his title and to his family would be to produce an heir.

"Evan," she whispered. "I—I don't know what to say. I didn't expect, that is, I didn't think you had marriage in mind. You aren't feeling compelled to offer for me, are you, out of some sense of misplaced chivalry, for I promise you—"

"It is no such thing," he said forcefully, cutting her off. "I would never offer out of chivalry—"

She smiled and touched his cheek with her gloved fingers. Droplets from her soaked bonnet had seeped through the crown and were now trickling down her cheeks. "I wouldn't have thought so." The rain began to lessen with each passing second.

He kissed her again, but this time not so forcefully.

"Then you'll marry me?" he asked, nuzzling her cheek with his nose and kissing her lightly beside her lips.

"I don't know what to say, Evan," she responded truthfully. "There is a part of me that wants to, that wants to go on being held in your arms and assaulted in this most delightful manner until I disappear into the earth." She paused.

"However . . . ?" he suggested, slipping his hand beneath her chin and forcing her to look into his eyes.

"However," she responded, "I'd rather perish than be married to you."

She could see by the way he blinked and frowned and gasped that her words had struck him like a blow across the cheek.

"No, no!" she cried. "You misunderstand me."

"I understand enough," he returned quietly. "You do not love me, you do not hold me in sufficient esteem."

She dropped her mouth open to speak, but words failed her. His own response in an attempt to approximate her thoughts had caught her off guard. Did she love him? Did she esteem him?

He took his left arm from around her and slid it between them in order to again take up the reins. The rain had stopped. His jaw worked strongly as he set the pair in motion.

"No, you still misunderstand me," she said, laying a hand on his arm. She felt him flinch beneath her touch. "The truth is, I honestly don't know whether I love you or not, for I have known you but a short time—and, and I've never been in love before."

"Yet you fall so easily into my arms," he returned brusquely.

"What woman could resist your embraces, my lord!" she exclaimed ingenuously. "You are by far one of the handsomest creatures I have ever encountered, and there is something more, something indefinable about the way you carry yourself when you but cross a room, as though you are taking command of a ship. You know, you lead with your chest and your chin like a man who is used to braving thunderstorms everyday of your life. What woman could not feel dizzy in just watching you?" She took a breath, watching him, considering her feelings toward him. Finally, she continued, "There is so much strength in you, Kingsbridge, and I have wished for that strength to become part of me again and again. Each time you would kiss me, just for that moment, I would feel as strong and as proud as you. I know I must sound like the silliest schoolgirl."

He pressed the horses to increase their speed in order to take the next ascent as neatly as possible.

"No, not like a schoolgirl," he responded kindly.

She felt emboldened to continue. "As for esteeming you, I'm not sure what to say, for my sisters have so imbued me with the certitude that your manner of living cannot command respect, that to say I esteem you is to spit on their teachings—but so I shall. You are at ease wherever you go and that to me is the hallmark of a gentleman. I've never heard you once raise your voice to a servant and if you heard Meg's husband—who is everything that propriety dictates— you would be disgusted. Your friendships among your sex I envy, more than you will ever know, for I have seen a camaraderie that does not exist in my world. Affection, trust, loyalty—these are the attributes I have seen in you. So do I esteem you—yes! Oh, yes, very much so!"

He looked at her, hurt in his eyes, and cried, "Then why do you refuse me? Why do you say you would rather die than be married to me?"

"I should not have said *to you*. I would rather die than be married, even if it is possible that I am indeed tumbling in love with you, which I think might be true, or even if I do esteem you as I do. I don't want to be any man's wife. I didn't understand that until we, until I, undertook this journey. Evan! I've never known such happiness as these past few days flying in the face of every acceptable convention—you've no idea. I promise you, now that I understand myself, I wouldn't make you or any man a suitable wife. I am too much addicted to excitement and, once our journey is concluded and Evangeline is brought safely home, I intend to leave England. I have been considering going to the Colonies. I now intend to do so. I—I doubt that I shall ever come back."

Kingsbridge looked at her sharply as the curricle crested the hill. Once the conveyance was a few paces beyond the rise, he drew the horses to the side of the road and let them catch their breath. "You don't know what you're saying," he said quietly. In the distance, to the south, the storm flashed over the fells and thunder slowly returned to greet their ears.

Emily folded her hands on her lap. "You are mistaken, Kingsbridge. I know precisely what I'm saying. I've learned a great deal about myself ever since, well, ever since you kissed me in the orangery. I now know that I shall never be content to live as my sisters live. I had thought that I simply hadn't found a man worthy of my affections, or some such nonsense, but now I know that I received the proposals of several gentlemen who were beyond worthy. *They* were not inadequate—I was. No, Evan, I'll not marry you. Not now, not ever, even though—" She paused, unable to complete her thought.

"What?" he pressed her.

She lifted her chin. "Even though, dash-it-all, I think I do love you." She felt tears sting her eyes before she knew she was becoming a watering pot.

She watched his smile grow crooked, and he slipped his arm about her shoulder again and gave her a squeeze, then turned to take up the reins once more. His smile broadened.

"I don't know why you must seem so pleased in this moment," she cried, indignant.

He chuckled and again slapped the reins over the horses' flanks. "Because," he stated confidently, "one day we will marry, and you will be more than an adequate wife, for you shall be my wife."

Emily grimaced at him, irritated. "Weren't you listening? Didn't you hear me? Or are you one of those wretched men that will always insist that a woman is speaking flummery when she insists she is not?"

"I am no such addlepated half-wit, I assure you. But we will marry, Emily, make no mistake."

When he tried to take her hand in his, she tossed his arm away from her. "If that is what you think, m'lord, then I promise you, you are destined for a hard fall!"

He only laughed at her and bade the horses pick up their hooves and get on with it.

Twenty-two

Kendal.
Lancaster.
Garstang.
Preston.
Leyland.
Wigan.
Night fell at Warrington in Cheshire.

There was nothing for it. They had to stop, to rest, to partake of a good supper, to sleep well. At least they were only half a day behind the Glossips and Evangeline, who were clearly heading south—perhaps to Tewkesbury in Gloucestershire as originally planned.

The second day took them flying through Knutsford, Sandbach, Stoke-on-Trent, Stafford, and Stourbridge, where they finally stopped for the night to rest at the Talbot Inn.

By nuncheon on the third day, Emily's heart began to skip beat after beat. The curricle progressed steadily down the Vale of Gloucester, the Malvern Hills to the west, Bredon Hill on the east, the magnificent Cotswolds rolling in gentle green folds to the southeast, and the Welsh Mountains a distant rise of purple in the southwest.

The western artery that connected many of the northern and western counties to the burgeoning docks at Bristol experienced a steady traffic that increased as the highway neared Tewkesbury. The ancient town was positioned on the confluence of the Severn and Avon rivers and provided five

major inns for weary travelers—The Bell Inn, The Royal
Hop Pole, The Swan Inn, The Tudor House, and The Black
Bear, the latter of which boasted origins dating from the four-
teenth century.

Emily had visited the town once before, some eight years
previous, and felt all the nostalgia attendant at recognizing
so many familiar sights, in particular the majestic abbey and
its tower reaching over one hundred and thirty feet in height.
She had been at the very top of the tower on that journey,
where a view of the entire vale and the surrounding mountains and hills could be enjoyed from every vantage point.

Kingsbridge drew in his reins slightly to keep an adequate
distance from a lumbering wagon. "Do you recall the inn at
which the exchange of funds was to take place?" he asked.

"The Black Bear," she said firmly.

When the half-timbered building came into view at the
top of High Street near King John's Bridge, the marquess
urged the horses past at a steady trot. His gaze was locked
to the front of the old building, as was Emily's. She scrutinized every window, every bystander, every coach entering
or leaving the stable yard, but nothing struck even the smallest note of familiarity.

"What do we do now?" she asked.

He was silent apace as he clicked his tongue and kept the
horses moving steadily onward. "I want to make inquiries
at the other inns. I doubt that the Glossips would be so bold
as to actually take rooms at The Black Bear."

"You are right," she responded.

One by one, Kingsbridge drew opposite each of the other
major inns. Leaving Emily to hold the horses, he would enter
the stable yards and pose his discreet questions. By now, she
thought him expert at getting the stable boys to talk. Of
course he never once entered a yard without his pockets jin-
gling with shillings.

Just as he entered The Royal Hop Pole, however, Emily
noticed a dusty travelling chariot driving at a steady clip-clop

from the opposite direction. There were two within, a tall man and a woman whose hair showed red beneath a half-veiled bonnet of dark blue silk.

She drew in her breath sharply.

The Glossips!

As the coach passed by, she immediately set the team in motion. Without a great deal of concern for the amount of traffic on the street, she veered Kingsbridge's curricle sharply to the right, coming round to face the opposite direction. If she received any number of invectives from outraged citizens, cart-drivers, and horsemen, she ignored them all.

Once near the door of The Royal Hop Pole, she called for Kingsbridge. "Evan!" she shouted. "Evan! Come at once!"

The marquess came running out, his face a mask of white as he saw where the curricle was now positioned.

"Good god!" he cried.

"Come!" she called to him. "Hurry! Leap up here and crawl over me! I don't give a fig for decorum at such a time."

"You've found them," he murmured as he leaped up on her side of the carriage and, just as she suggested, slid over her legs. At almost the same time he took the reins from her, slapping them hard against the horses's flanks.

"Yes!" she called in a hushed cry. "The Glossips were here, not three minutes past. There! The yellow bounder!"

"I see it!" he returned.

His efforts to guide his curricle through the maze of coaches, gigs, men on horseback, and dozens of citizens on foot, were met with as little appreciation as Emily's had with earlier. He seemed as little concerned with their heated disapproval as she had been and, within another few minutes, they were nearly upon the post chaise.

"They must be heading for The Tudor House," Emily whispered as though afraid that some passerby would overhear her and warn the wicked couple of their presence in Tewkesbury. "That is the only inn we have not visited."

Fifteen minutes later, the yellow bounder drew into the inn yard of The Tudor House.

Kingsbridge did not immediately follow, but drew his equipage to the side of the highway—again to the protests of several nearby personages—to wait. He counted beneath his breath, his gaze fixed steadfastly on the inn as though willing the Glossips to dare to leave.

"That will do," he said suddenly. He glanced left and right and, seeing that the highway was sufficiently clear, crossed the street and drew into the yard.

The post chaise was being drawn to the carriage house. The Glossips were not in sight.

"Excellent," he murmured.

Emily laid her hand on his arm. Her heart was a loud drumming in her ear and she could hardly breathe. He drew the curricle to a stop, tossed the reins to a waiting hostler, and jumped lightly down on his side of the carriage.

Emily did not wait for him to round the curricle and modestly hand her down, but backed out quickly, lifting her rose silk skirts in one hand and setting her booted feet on the narrow steps. Just as she was about to plant a foot on the cobbles, she felt Kingsbridge grip her beneath the elbow and support her the rest of the way.

She did not speak, nor did he.

Together, they hurriedly entered the inn.

Kingsbridge drew her toward the inn's registry. A tall woman, wearing a neatly starched mobcap, smiled pleasantly and asked if she could be of service. Were they wishful of hiring rooms fer t' night?

Kingsbridge smiled pleasantly. "No, I thank you," he said in a quiet voice. "As it happens, we are meeting friends of ours—the Smithes. Could you tell me if they have arrived or not? He is rather tall with black hair and his wife is quite pretty. They are travelling with a younger sister who is accounted something of a beauty."

Emily glanced quickly behind her, but the entrance was

empty and of no threat. The smell of cinnamon and cloves drifted from the direction of the kitchens. Voices could be heard in what she supposed was an adjoining taproom, as laughter rose to the rafters time and again. The noise of the street was never far away.

"Does the young lady have pretty brown eyes and dark brown hair?" she queried.

"That would be her," he responded.

"Aye, they're here. In t'parlor. Would ye like me to announce ye?"

"No," Kingsbridge responded. "If you'll direct me, I believe we would prefer to surprise them."

Emily glanced at Kingsbridge and met his gaze with a wondering stare. Was this to be the end, then, so simple, so easy?

A moment more and Emily crossed the threshold of a parlor that was rather dark because of its small, ancient windows, but neatly furnished with a square table, a chair covered in shiney horsehair by a stone-lined fireplace, and a sideboard laden with a half-dozen dishes from which a lady with red hair was currently serving herself.

"Emily!" her cousin called out to her.

"Evangeline!" Emily cried, immediately rushing forward to embrace her cousin who was seated at the square table, a knife in one hand and a fork in the other. To all evidence it would seem that her cousin had not been suffering overly much, at least not by her appearance at the table, except that when Emily drew back from her, she noted the bluish circles under her eyes and the strained appearance of her features.

Kingsbridge joined them, ignoring the tall man completely. "Come, Miss Matford. We have a curricle waiting in the yard and are prepared to take you home this instant."

She glanced at Kingsbridge and blinked several times. She seemed dumbfounded and slightly disoriented. She glanced toward Mr. Glossip, who had been standing by the window and who was now turned fully toward the marquess.

Emily still had hold of Evangeline's arm and noticed for the first time the bruise on her cousin's neck. She felt the sudden tension in Vangie's body and heard a faint murmuring sound issue from her throat. Her limbs began to tremble.

Instinctively, Emily helped support her cousin in rising from her chair. She turned around, shifting Evangeline in front of her, as she began guiding her protectively toward the door, using Kingsbridge's body as a shield. But Mrs. Glossip chose at the moment to race for the door and close it with a loud bang.

"You'll not be leaving, not today, not with our charge," she cried. "We are in the service of Lord Trent, who hired us to care for his daughter. He gave us strict instructions not to let her out of our sight for even a moment."

"You're lying," Emily said. Again, she shifted Evangeline so that her cousin was between her and her adversary. She faced Mrs. Glossip squarely. "Let us pass or I shall gladly set up a caterwaul that will bring the town constable down on this building before the cat can lick her ear."

A smug, self-satisfied expression came over the actress's face. "You wouldn't dare," she murmured. "You're a Long-cliffe, aren't you? I should like to see the day that a Long-cliffe would risk her precious reputation in a horrible scandal. Do scream, but know that if we are harmed in any manner I shall not hesitate to make it known that you were travelling, unchaperoned, in the company of three of London's most notorious rogues for days on end. I have several friends at The Swan in Grasmere, for instance, or did you think you could arrive with such an entourage and not escape our notice?"

Emily scarcely heard more than one word out of every three that the actress spoke. Mrs. Glossip had lost her full attention the moment she said, *I should like to see the day that a Longcliffe would risk her precious reputation.*

Emily was sick to death of being a Longcliffe and if her journey north and now south had revealed anything to her it was that she no longer intended to hold so strictly to the conventions of her sisters. She opened her mouth and let out a piercing scream—part in frustration and part just for the delight of seeing Mrs. Glossip's eyes bulge in her pretty though aging face. She did not however, expect the stunning facer the actress planted on her cheek that effectively sent her slamming against the wall and sliding to the floor. Evangeline fell with her, then drew very close and wrapped her arm, cowering in a pitiful manner against her.

The blow must have stunned Emily, since she couldn't see anything for a few seconds.

When some of the shock of the attack left her, she heard Kingsbridge's voice.

"Put it away!" he called out sharply.

Emily heard his voice and tried to ascertain to what the marquess might possibly be referring. A loud buzzing had taken hold of her mind and a ringing sounded loudly in her ears. Her right cheekbone was stinging. Evangeline whimpered beside her.

"Don't be a fool, Glossip, put the pistol away. You don't want to hurt anyone."

Emily looked up and saw that Kingsbridge was but a few feet in front of her and moving slowly toward Glossip, who was rounding the table toward the door. As Glossip came into sight, she saw a pistol leveled at Kingsbridge and her heart nearly jumped out of her chest.

"Dear god," she murmured.

She felt Evangeline's sobs and understood that her cousin had suffered terribly in the *care* of her abductors. She was trembling and clung to Emily as though her life depended on it.

Emily looked up at Mrs. Glossip and saw that her gaze was fixed triumphantly on her husband. The actress then quickly stepped over Emily's legs and took Evangeline by her right arm and gave her a hard jerk.

Evangeline whimpered as her captor began dragging her

to her feet. In her fright, her legs became useless and her body's weight kept her pinned to the floor.

"Get up, you bird-witted ninnyhammer. Get up at once!"

Emily leaned forward and grabbed suddenly at Mrs. Glossip's skirts. She threw herself into the actress's legs and knew by the loud thud that followed that Mrs. Glossip had tumbled to the floor as well.

Confusion followed next as Mrs. Glossip let out a cry of frustration and leapt on Emily's back. She began slapping her and hitting her. Emily protected herself as best she could, then scrambled to her knees, at the same time rising up and throwing the woman backward.

A burst of cool air from the hallway flowed over her face and she looked up, startled, to see Major Buxton in the doorway. "I heard a scream!" he cried. "Good god, what's happening here!"

She saw movement to her right and then a loud retort as Glossip fired his pistol. She watched Major Buxton slip past her toward Kingsbridge, who had launched himself on Glossip.

She watched the actor struggle for a few seconds, Buxton's arm rise over his head, then drive down upon Glossip's head. The kidnapper slumped to the floor, unconscious. Major Buxton had hit him with the butt of his own pistol.

She felt a knee on her back as Mrs. Glossip scrambled over her trying to escape. She shot a hand out, caught the actress by her ankle and brought her again tumbling to the floor, this time through the doorway and into the hall beyond where she remained inert having struck her head when she fell.

A complete silence ensued. Emily glanced at her cousin who was hunched near the wall, breathing hard, her complexion white, her features drawn up into a knot of fear. She lifted herself off the floor and sat back on her heels and looked in the direction of Kingsbridge. The marquess was drawing himself up off the floor as well. He moved backward to drop into a seat by the table, his complexion pale.

He looked at her, his face a grimace of concern. "Are you all right?" he asked, his hazel eyes scanning each of her features in turn. When he saw her cheek, he winced visibly.

She nodded. "I'm perfectly well. Are you hurt? I heard a shot? Did the pistol ball strike anyone?"

But before he could answer, the landlord appeared in the doorway demanding to know what was going forward. Emily could see that a crowd was gathering around Mrs. Glossip in the hallway beyond. Major Buxton drew him aside, explained the essentials, and begged him to summon the constable as quickly as possible.

Emily helped Evangeline to her feet and embraced her. Evangline began to cry.

"You saved me," she mumbled through her tears. "Oh, Em, I used to think you were so silly to play at your games with Bertram, but now look what has come of it—you saved me."

"What nonsense," Emily returned, stroking Evangeline's hair and back.

"It is not at all nonsense," she responded. "When I saw you at the lake—"

Emily drew back and met her gaze. "You knew me then?"

Evangeline nodded and sniffed loudly. "There was only one lady I could ever imagine who would take off her bonnet and let her hair down—my Cousin Emily."

Emily smiled. "And I thought I was being so clever by just turning around and sauntering back up the hill."

"Unfortunately, Mr. Glossip recognized you at once as well."

"He did?" she asked, stunned. "But how could he know me? I've never seen him before in my life."

Evangeline shook her head and wiped the tears from her cheeks with the back of her hand. "Why, you're a Longcliffe," she responded, as though such an answer was utterly sufficient. "Who in London does not know you or your famous sisters?"

Emily rolled her eyes.

"Vangie," a resonant, masculine voice intruded.

Emily turned to see that Major Buxton had drawn near. He scrutinized Evangeline's face, which once more crumpled up as fresh tears sprang to her eyes.

"Teddy," her cousin murmured. Then, much to Emily's astonishment, Evangeline released her entirely and slid onto the broad chest of one of Wellington's finest officers. Major Buxton did not hesitate in sliding his arms firmly around his beloved and placing several heartfelt kisses in her hair.

Emily recalled that Lord Trent had insisted Evangeline was in love with the major, but until this moment she had not believed him.

A loud groaning came from the hall. Emily turned to see that Mrs. Glossip was now sitting up. Blood seeped from a wound on her forehead and she grimaced as she brought her hand to her head. Behind her, two men lifted her to her feet and though she begged to be taken to her bedchamber, the landlord made certain she was ushered back into the parlor instead. He then took charge of the situation by bringing three of his stable hands forward bearing sufficient rope to bind the kidnappers securely. Once the Glossips were bound, the unforgiving landlord withdrew them from the parlor.

With the Glossips disposed of, Emily turned her attention to Kingsbridge. His complexion was still pale, and where he had struggled with Glossip a bruise was forming on his chin, and his right eye was swelling slightly. He met her gaze and smiled. She smiled in return.

"Are you sure you're all right?" he murmured. "Your cheek is already purple."

She moved past Major Buxton, who was now fully involved in consoling Evangeline, and took up a seat next to Kingsbridge. Only as she was about to ask him again if he was certain he was uninjured did she notice the dark red stain on his neckcloth near the collar of his coat.

"Evan!" she cried. "You've been hit."

He shook his head. "The merest scratch," he retorted on a whisper, inclining his head toward Evangeline who was weeping into Buxton's shoulder as the major moved her toward the fireplace. "I assure you."

Emily understood him. He did not want her cousin further distressed by his own suffering.

"I'll get help," she whispered.

She rose from her chair and quietly left the chamber. She went in search of the landlord and found him in the vestibule where she could see the Glossips being shepherded down the hall in the direction of the kitchens. He informed her that he would keep them in the buttery until the constable should arrive to set everything to rights.

She explained about the marquess's wound, a circumstance that rippled his brow. He patted her shoulder and immediately bustled down the hall heading toward the stable yard and shouting out an order to summon the surgeon. "At once!" he cried. "At once!"

Twenty-three

While they waited for the doctor to arrive, Emily ordered a glass of brandy for Kingsbridge, then carefully helped him off with his coat. Afterward, she peered intently at the stain on his neckcloth, which was surrounded by dark powder burns, wondering how deeply the pistol ball had cut into his flesh. She was unwilling to disturb his cravat until his brandy arrived.

Major Buxton called to her from the fireplace, asking if she needed his assistance, but Emily, glancing at her distraught cousin, suggested that Evangeline, for the present, had the greater need of him. Her cousin continued to weep, suffering acutely from the shock of her recent captivity. The major settled her into a chair beside the stone fireplace and drew forward a chair for himself, which served to block her view of Kingsbridge and his wound.

Once the brandy arrived, Kingsbridge took the snifter gratefully. He sipped the rich wine after which Emily began to gingerly unwind the fine linen swath. He lifted his face to her and smiled.

"You are looking very pleased of the moment," she murmured, unwrapping yet another turn of the neckcloth. With each pass, the white fabric showed a broader red stain.

He chuckled faintly. "It is not everyday I am tended to by a Longcliffe."

"A Longcliffe," she muttered. "I vow I am sick to death of my surname. Not that I don't love my family, but you've no idea what a torment it is to be obliged to behave *just so* at every moment of the day. But what is worse is that everyone you meet will also be comparing you to a long line of forbears." She removed the neckcloth entirely. "Oh, dear."

"What is it?"

"The flesh is burnt away in parts, your skin smells quite odd, and part of the wound is blackened." The pistol ball had grazed the low part of his neck and was probably lodged in the wall of the parlor somewhere. The injury would indeed be termed by most gentlemen as a mere scratch just as Kingsbridge had said. Still the sight of it was unsettling.

"Powder burns," he remarked nonchalantly.

"So it would seem." She began to fold the linen into a square and settled it gently on top of the wound. "Most of the bleeding has stopped, but I think it best I keep the cloth pressed to your neck. Does it hurt overly much?"

"Really, it's not too bad."

She nodded and he looked up at her a quizzical expression in his hazel eyes. The afternoon light slipped through the windows and settled a golden glow on his face, brightening the blue, green, and gray flecks of his iris.

"What are you thinking?" she asked, smiling faintly as she held the cloth to his neck.

"Do you not feel even a twinge of nausea or even the mildest dizziness?"

As she looked into his eyes she rather thought she *was* feeling slightly dizzy, but not because of his wound as he was suggesting.

She shook her head. "Not a bit."

He chuckled faintly again and once more took a sip of brandy.

"Why do you ask?" she queried, curious.

He shook his head and settled the snifter back on the table. "You amaze me, Miss Longcliffe."

"Now, pray do not offend me by saying that you would never have expected *a Longcliffe* to be able to endure the sight of blood. The truth is, when I said Bertram and I played in the orchards about Aldwark so many years ago, I do not exaggerate when I say that some of our wounds were real. Although, I only broke a bone once, while Bertram suffered a break twice."

"Good god! How is it that your parents permitted such play to continue after so many mishaps?"

Emily looked into the past and smiled more fully. "Do you know I have always suspected that my father rather approved of my unladylike conduct. Perhaps it was because he had no sons, I don't know, or it might have been because my sisters were all so dull and decorous."

"Like your mother?"

"Would I be disloyal to her if I said yes?" She looked into his eyes again and saw an answering gleam of mischief in his eyes.

"A little," he said, an odd expression entering his eye. "I have a confession to make."

When he did not immediately continue, she lifted her brows. "Yes?" she queried, smiling. She couldn't imagine what it was he would next say to her.

"Your father once approached me at White's, a year past I believe it was, and recommended I seek you out, that he rather suspected we might be well suited."

Emily opened her eyes very wide. "He did not!" she retorted, stunned.

"He most certainly did, and for at least a fortnight I considered the prospect, but I must admit in the end I was daunted by the prospect of becoming acquainted with—"

"No, don't say it!" she cried. She knew he meant to speak her surname again and she didn't think she could bear it repeated one more time without screaming. She then added, "Papa must have been quite out of his senses to have approached you in such a manner, though I'm certain he never revealed he had done so to my mother."

Kingsbridge chuckled. "No, I don't suppose he did."

Emily felt her heart constrict. "I wonder . . ." she murmured, but could not immediately continue.

"What?" he pressed her.

"I—I can't help but wonder what possessed Papa to address you as he did?"

Kingsbridge took hold of her hand. "Perhaps he had seen into the future and knew we were destined to be together." He then lifted her fingers to his lips and placed a kiss on each of them in turn.

Emily felt dizzy as she looked down on his bowed head, his kisses warm against her skin. Tears touched her eyes, of affection, of fear, of wonder. Had her father truly looked into the future?

Her musings and Kingsbridge's sweet assault were disrupted by a scratching at the door. Kingsbridge called out, "Come," and a moment later, the surgeon crossed the threshold.

He wore a black frock coat, black pantaloons, a white shirt, neatly starched shirtpoints, and a black cravat. His sidewhiskers were gray, his smile crooked, his teeth not less so, and his blue eyes friendly. Emily liked him at once.

"So, what do we have here?" he asked, crossing the room in three quick strides. He was a tall man with very long legs. He glanced at the table as well as the sideboard and his smile broadened. "Was the fish not to your liking, m'lord?" he asked jokingly.

Emily couldn't help but smile. The table still bore Evangeline's unfinished dinner, and the sideboard was cluttered with the remains of the untouched repast.

Kingsbridge chuckled. "As you can see I always kick up a dust when my roast beef has turned on the spit too long!"

The surgeon smiled in response, though his gaze soon dropped to the wound on Kingsbridge's neck.

Emily lifted the pad of cloth for his inspection. He regarded it carefully, then slipped his hat from his head, settling it on the table. Afterward, he placed long, gentle fingers on the unburnt skin surrounding the wound. "I'll sew up the cut, but nothing more. I've found that the less I do, the better my patients heal. Don't know why, precisely. Served in the British Army in 1800 and discovered that for some reason the wounds caused by pistol balls or cannon shot and surrounded by powder, if left to themselves, would heal almost as if by magic."

He opened his bag and brought forward needle and thread. "A little darning should put you to rights."

He then glanced at Emily. "You'll not be swooning or anything of that sort, will you now, Miss?"

"No, sir," she responded firmly.

He eyed her speculatively. "I'll be needing to remove his waistcoat and shirt. Will your sensibilities be offended?"

Emily shook her head. Perhaps she ought to have fallen into a fit of the blushes, but she wasn't in the least disturbed by what needed to be done next.

"Good. Then you can help me, for of anything that I might do of the moment, removing these articles is likely to do more damage than any further ministrations. If you'll support his left arm, I'll slide the vest off first. Yes, that's good. Very good. Now the shirt. I know this must hurt, m'lord, but think of your lady's pretty blue eyes and you'll find the pain diminishes rapidly. There. Excellent. Now the other sleeve." Emily had no difficulty in following his instructions or in assisting him. She found she was enjoying the process enormously and, though she was a little startled by the sight of Kingsbridge's broad chest covered with a mat of coarse black hair, the forthcoming operation soon diverted her thoughts entirely.

"Excellent," the doctor murmured once the clothes were removed. "And the wound didn't start bleeding again." He lifted his smiling gaze to Emily. "Should you ever need employment I don't hesitate to say I should value your steady, responsive hands as an assistant."

"Thank you," Emily responded, also smiling. She was

pleased that he had complimented her. "Should I ever be in need of employment, I shall seek you out!"

"And now," he said, "why don't you come round on the other side of his lordship, and sit next to him. He seems a sturdy enough fellow, but you would be surprised how many soldiers can face a cannon full of grapeshot, yet swoon at the sight of a little needle. I suggest you hold his hand in a firm clasp and I'll be done with him in a trice."

Emily did as she was bid, circling behind Kingsbridge and drawing a chair forward to sit beside him. She took up his hand and, much to her pleasure, he gripped it tightly. She looked into his eyes and for the first time began to formulate the daunting thought that had Glossip's aim been a few inches lower, Kingsbridge would now be dead. Once or twice he winced, but otherwise he did not seem in the least bothered by the doctor's efforts.

"That should do," he said kindly at last. "But I would advise carrying your arm in a sling for a day or two, until the skin closes tightly. If you wave your arm about you'll soon find the wound opening anew, the stitches breaking, more required, and then you'll risk the fever I am hoping to avoid."

"I understand," Kingsbridge said. Infection was always the bane of any surgery.

"Excellent." He then withdrew a roll of muslin from his bag and after placing a clean pad on the wound, wrapped a length of muslin around Kingsbridge's chest, then tightly pinned a strip over the wound to meet the piece encircling his chest, back, and front. The doctor helped him on with his shirt and his vest and with another length of muslin made a simple sling for his arm.

When he was satisfied with his work, he looked down at the marquess. "Change the dressing twice a day for a sennight, or until you can see that the wound is closed up properly. If it becomes red or swells, you must confer with your physician immediately, or will you be staying in Tewkesbury where I can call on you?"

Kingsbridge shook his head. "My home is in Devonshire. We'll be leaving Gloucestershire on the morrow."

The doctor nodded. "If you need my services, the landlord will know where to find me. I'll let your lady restore your neckcloth and I'll leave my bill with the innkeeper. Right now, however, you will have to excuse me, for I've a list of patients today nearly as long as my legs." He smiled, bid farewell to them both, then was gone.

Emily did not immediately release Kingsbridge's hand, nor would he have permitted her to, she realized as she glanced down at her fingers and saw that they had somehow become tangled quite thoroughly among his. With his free hand, he overlaid their joined fingers and stroked her wrist and her arm.

She lifted her gaze to meet his and saw in his eyes a mountain of love and affection. Her heart immediately began to beat strongly, as though trying to match the steady thrum of his own. "I love you, Em," he whispered. His lips were on hers before she knew what was happening.

The parlor disappeared, as Emily closed her eyes and gave herself to the touch of his kisses. How gently he saluted her, over and over, each kiss an expression of gratitude, a reflection of his love and a promise for the future. She could hardly breathe, her heart was so full of affection for him. She didn't want the moment to end. She wanted him to go on kissing her forever.

The past slid away, as each gentle pressure on her lips beckoned her toward the future. Was she perhaps destined to be with Kingsbridge after all?

After a long moment, he drew back from her, his face warm with his love for her.

She caught her breath. Tears stung her eyes as some of the reality of the day's events tumbled down upon her "You might have been killed, Evan," she said, her throat painfully tight.

"But I wasn't," he said reasonably.

"I know."

"Would you have been sad had I stuck my spoon in the wall?"

She couldn't help but giggle at the silly expression, but her amusement faded as quickly as it sprang to her throat. More tears filled her eyes to finally roll down her cheeks. She swallowed convulsively. "Yes," she whispered. "Ever so much."

He smiled, lifting his hand to smooth away the tears on her cheeks. "I'm glad."

Her throat pained her with unreleased tears, and she felt as though the hands of a giant had her chest in a tight grip. She didn't understand why she felt as though she could flop over on the table and cry her heart out.

"My darling," he said, his expression growing oddly sympathetic. "Come to me."

Be released her hand only to throw his arm wide in an inviting gesture.

Emily reached over to him and slipped her arm about his waist, intending to embrace him.

"No, no," he murmured. "Come sit on my lap."

Emily knew she shouldn't, that it was wholly improper, but it seemed the most natural thing in the world to simply rise to her feet, settle herself on his lap, slide her feet to dangle over his legs, and nestle her head on his uninjured shoulder.

He was very strong and she felt completely safe in his arms. She buried her face into his neck and held back as many of her sobs as she could. A few escaped her, however, despite her efforts otherwise, and her tears soon dampened his shirt.

"There, there," he murmured, kissing her hair. "Sweet Em. My darling Emily. My outrageous Longcliffe."

At that she couldn't keep from chuckling a little and the

stranglehold on her chest and about her throat eased up. "I hadn't meant to become a watering pot."

"I don't mind," he responded. "After all, you're crying because you love me, and because you realize that if I died, you wouldn't be able to marry me."

His words, playfully spoken, brought a sudden stillness to Emily's spirit. She grew very quiet and a new sadness filled her.

She would never marry. She had told Kingsbridge as much, but it would seem he still didn't believe her. At the same time, the thought of living without the delight of his company seemed so unthinkable that she felt as though her feet had just become mired in a deep bog.

"Evan . . ." she began.

"No, no," he said emphatically. "I don't like the tone of your voice one whit, and I hasten to inform you that if you expect me to recover well from my wound, then you will withhold your thoughts from me—at least until we reach my home in Devonshire."

At that she leaned back and looked at him. "Whatever do you mean? Evan, I—I shouldn't go to Hollington Priory with you. Wouldn't that only serve to worsen the nature of our journey together?"

"Do but think," he said. "Your sister will be fixed in my house, along with Horatia and your cousin."

"I had forgotten as much," she said.

"Surely her presence will help to dispel whatever gossip might attend our scandalous adventure."

She blinked at him and thought that there ought to be a hundred reasons for telling him she had no intention of coming with him, but not one of these reasons came to mind to rescue her. "Very well," she responded.

The smile that grew in his hazel eyes caused a twinge of anxiety to wrap itself about her heart. Goodness, if she didn't know better she would think he had some scheme or other in mind. What was he thinking, she wondered.

She would have pressed him to explain the meaning in his eye, but at that moment a new scratching sounded on the door. Emily slid from Kingsbridge's lap just in time to watch her uncle push the door open and cast his gaze in a quick sweep over the chamber.

"Thank God we've found you all at last! We've been searching all the inns, day after day, for any sign of the Glossips. Only a few minutes ago, we heard that a kidnapping had been foiled at The Tudor House!"

Mr. Buxton followed closely on his heels. He was a tall, thick-chested man of some fifty years, bearing a snowy head of hair and black, piercing eyes.

"Teddy!" he called out to his son and heir. "Thank God you found her. What the devil happened here?"

Major Buxton explained, "I had just returned to The Hop Pole and learned that a man—who I now understand to be Lord Kingsbridge—had been inquiring about the Glossips. When I learned that a young woman had called to him from the street in an excited voice and that he had driven off pell-mell in his curricle, I knew that something untoward was going forward. By the heated responses of many witnesses on the street, I knew that they were heading toward The Tudor House."

Lord Trent caught sight of Kingsbridge's wound and paled visibly. "Good God! Kingsbridge! How did you come to be here and, and—good god, man, are you all right?"

"Yes, tolerably so. No, no! Don't fret. It's but a scratch, I assure you. As for how I came to be here, your niece asked me to help her search for your daughter and I agreed, given what seemed from the outset a dubious set of circumstances."

"Then you saved Evangeline," he murmured. "You and Emily."

"And Major Buxton as well. Never fear. Your daughter's abductors are in the buttery awaiting the magistrate."

"Good, good," he responded, nodding briskly. "I should

like you to meet my neighbor and friend, Mr. Buxton. Buxton—I would like to present my niece, Miss Emily Longcliffe, and the Marquess of Kingsbridge."

Mr. Buxton murmured his thanks through tightly pinched lips as he worked to restrain his emotions. Tears however soon reddened his eyes as he clasped each of their hands in turn and thanked them for their part in rescuing Evangeline.

By the time he finished his broken speeches, Lord Trent had crossed the chamber and taken up his daughter in his arms. He held her fast to his chest, as tears rolled down his cheeks and fresh ones, down hers.

Emily bit her lip and moved to stand just behind Kingsbridge. She placed her hand gently on his right shoulder. He covered her hand with his own and gave it a gentle squeeze. Evangeline's sobs could now be heard distinctly.

When her tears subsided, Emily and Kingsbridge approached the somber party.

"Uncle," Emily said, moving forward and also receiving a warm embrace for her efforts. "Have you been in Tewkesbury the entire time? Since I left you a sennight past?"

He nodded. "We have waited days on end, not knowing what to do or where to go. We were afraid of leaving lest the Glossips arrived—besides, where would we have gone?"

"I take it you did not receive my missive?"

"No," he responded, bemused.

Emily took a deep breath. "When I left Aldwark Manor, I returned to Kegworth and found that Kingsbridge had seen Evangeline and the Glossips pass through the village—but not toward the southwest as they should have gone, but northwest. I sent word to the manor to that effect, but I was convinced you would probably have already left for Tewkesbury, before my missive could reach you. That was why I decided to follow immediately in her wake."

He nodded. "Evangeline has just told me that she saw you in Kendal and Grasmere. What I don't understand is why she was taken to the Lake District, when the ransom letter distinctly indicated that the ten thousand pounds was to be delivered to The Black Bear in Tewkesbury."

"As to that," Kingsbridge interjected, "I could only conclude that they intended to demand a great deal more for her return than a mere ten thousand." He glanced at Mr. Buxton, who nodded his agreement.

"I would gladly have paid ten times as much for her safe return," the tradesman stated, his voice breaking.

"As would I," Lord Trent murmured. He then glanced from Emily to Kingsbridge and awareness dawned on him. "My god," he murmured. "Have the pair of you been travelling together, alone, all this time?"

Emily felt a blush on her cheek, yet at the same time she could not repine. "With our servants, yes," she responded. "But I would do it all over again, for I could not have accomplished the journey without him."

Her uncle nodded and took each of their hands in his. "Thank you, both," he murmured. "You'll not hear a word of censure from me, nor will I permit a single disparaging word to be spoken in any quarter against either of you."

Emily was stunned. "I—I shall never forget your graciousness in this moment," she said.

"How could I be less so," he responded. "When I am convinced you have saved my daughter's life."

At that moment, Kingsbridge interjected quietly. "I wish you to understand, Lord Trent, that I am fully aware of my responsibility in this circumstance and that I am intent upon doing my duty. As it happens, Miss Longcliffe and I are to be married."

Lord Trent's brows shot up in some surprise. "Indeed," he murmured, "then I will only say that you've won yourself a great prize, and that I've little doubt my niece will make you the happiest of men." He turned toward Emily, "I wish you every joy, my dear."

"Th-thank you, Uncle," she murmured, stunned that Kingsbridge would have made such an announcement to her uncle, since it was wholly untrue. She wanted to refute him instantly, but to do so would be to cause an argument that could only be detrimental to her cousin's shattered condition.

"Yes, every happiness," Evangeline added.

"Thank you," Emily responded, forcing a smile to her lips she in no manner felt.

"Then all is settled," Lord Trent said, his eyes again filling with tears. He took Emily under one arm, and Evangeline under the other, appearing like a brood hen with her chicks. He hugged each of them several times in succession, kissing their foreheads and cheeks until his tears rolled down his face.

After a moment, Evangeline drew back from her father sufficiently to look up at him. "They—the Glossips—were not kind," she whispered slowly, her lips quivering. She turned to Emily, "I cannot tell you the hope you gave me when I first saw you in Kendal. I know you must have thought it odd in me to have turned away as I did, but I was so afraid that they would see you, and then didn't know what might happen."

"I understand why you felt compelled to look away," Emily responded quietly.

Major Buxton stepped forward and added his appreciation for their efforts as well, giving Kingsbridge a hearty shake of his hand and a promise that if ever he could be of service to him, or to Emily, that he would come from the ends of the earth to fulfill even the smallest request.

During the ensuing hour, Lord Trent occupied himself with the constable and the magistrate as to how precisely he wished for the affair to be handled. Since this discussion took place in another chamber, with Mr. Buxton attendant, the party was reduced to Major Buxton, Evangeline, Lord Kingsbridge, and herself.

Major Buxton expressed his affection for Evangeline in a dozen instances of attentive consideration. Was she warm, or chilled? Would she like a glass of sherry or a little tea,

perhaps? Was she wishful of retiring to a chamber by herself
for a time with a maid in attendance? What would she prefer
for dinner, boiled chicken or a nice venison?

Though it was fully July and the southwesterly town was
warm by northerly standards, he insisted a fire be lit and his
beloved settled in the chair she had previously occupied, an
afghan tucked around her legs, and her feet propped up gently on a footstool that displayed a kitten playing with yarn.

When she was thus disposed, he had the chamber cleared
of all evidence that the Glossips had formerly occupied the
room. Then he ordered a welcome repast. When these tasks
had been accomplished and fresh covers were laid by a host
of curious servants, and when the major's attention was again
fixed on Evangeline, only then did Emily address Kingsbridge's earlier announcement.

Drawing him toward the windows, the failing afternoon
light settling warmly on his features, she said, "It was not
at all necessary to tell a whisker."

He lifted his brow in surprise. "What do you mean, a
whisker?" he asked innocently.

"You know very well what I mean—that we are to be
married."

"Oh, that," he murmured. "Well, I've already told you
that we are to be wed—and I certainly didn't think there
needed to be further discussion."

Emily drew in a gasp, her mouth falling agape. "No further
discussion? Evan, have you gone mad? I've already told you
I have no intention of marrying anyone."

He feigned a considering expression, his brows drawn together sharply. "No—I don't recall your having said anything of the like."

She gasped again. "What do you mean—why, you! Oh,
you are teasing me again, you beast."

He leaned toward her. "That is much better. I like it when
you call me a beast. I shall expect you to do so every day
once we are married."

"We are not going to be married," she retorted.

"Don't you love me, Emily?" he asked, a hurt expression in his eyes. "Not even a little?"

At that Emily swallowed very hard. She felt herself to be on dangerous ground and wished that she could think of something very clever to say. He took up her hand and, because her back was to both the major and Evangeline, he lifted her fingers to his lips and placed a passionate kiss on the back of her hand.

She felt dizzy.

Damn and blast! Why must she always feel dizzy when he assaulted her. Why couldn't she feel disgusted or appalled or even a little bored. Instead, she watched his lips caressing her fingers in a series of whispery kisses, and a coo and a sigh escaped her lips.

"There, you see," he murmured, still stealing kisses in between his speech. "You love me."

"I like that you kiss me," she answered somewhat tersely. "Which is another matter entirely."

He shrugged, using his healthy shoulder to perform the gesture of indifference, and murmured, "Sufficiently close to the answer I wish to hear to satisfy me. Do you prefer to be married in a church or in my receiving room?"

When he spoke these words Emily felt herself pale. His tone might be teasing, earlier he might have been protecting her from society's judgment by telling Lord Trent that they were to be married, his eyes might be twinkling merrily, but she knew Kingsbridge—he was more than serious—and what was worse, she understood him to believe that he had but to persist and the day might be won.

"Evan," she said softly, "I pray you won't continue deluding yourself. I shan't marry—"

"Oh, there is your uncle now. Never fear—we'll discuss the matter later. For now, I am a little fatigued and greatly starved."

Emily let the matter drop, especially when upon scrutinizing his face, she could see that his expression was drawn and his complexion lacking its usual color and warmth. For all his delight in tormenting her, he was not entirely well.

Twenty-four

Two days later, Emily and Kingsbridge arrived at Hollington Priory.

"Bert!" Emily cried, leaping into her cousin's arms. He caught her up in an affectionate embrace, her feet and light green silk skirts flying out backward as he swung her about in a wide circle. She enjoyed his warm, enthusiastic greeting, her mind immediately culling forth at least a dozen fond memories of the Aldwark apple grove and the games they used to play together.

When he set her on her feet with a delightful dizziness clinging to her brain, she exclaimed, "So tell me, is it true? Has Horatia—I mean Mrs. Matford—been safely delivered of her child?"

He smiled broadly and sighed with great satisfaction as he took up her hands in his. "I've a daughter, Em. She is beautiful, the image of her mother, but she fusses a lot, so I have complete confidence that she also means to take after me. She is pink, her fingers and toes are all accounted for, and she even possesses a head of dark hair which Nurse insists she will not lose even though nine of ten babies are bald before they are three months."

Emily saw his pride and his delight in his new daughter, and was deeply pleased for her friend. "And Horatia—I mean, Mrs. Matford? Is she well?"

"Perfectly so—but you must call her Horatia. I have spoken of you so often that she is already used to hearing of you spoken of as Emily, and not Miss Emily or Miss Long-cliffe." He glanced at Kingsbridge, "But here, I say, how do you go on, Evan? I take it you've made the acquaintance of my cousin. Horatia's letter was timely, then?"

He stepped forward and shook Bertram's outstretched hand. Bert's forehead was creased, and Emily could see the strain in his eyes. "Yes, it was," Kingsbridge responded. "We finally found Evangeline in Tewkesbury. She is perfectly well, I promise you, and her captors have since been delivered to the local jail, where they will await trial. Major Buxton, your father, and Mr. Buxton are attending to Miss Matford. Though there was some trouble, all is settled and done with."

"This would explain your bruises then?" Bertram queried, glancing from one to the other, his brow furrowed more deeply still.

Emily nodded.

" 'Fraid so," Kingsbridge said.

Bertram was silent apace, shaking his head in utter dismay. Emily placed her hand on his arm. "Truly, we are both well, as is your sister. We left her in excellent health, I promise you, though you will be astonished to learn that she is betrothed, and will likely leave Tewkesbury a married woman."

At that his brows rose and his former agitation quit his face entirely. "Teddy?" he queried, his eyes lighting up in amusement.

Emily nodded.

"Good God," he murmured. "She used to brangle with him nine days out of ten. Do you tell me she is in love with him?"

"I believe the circumstances of her having spent the past fortnight in the hands of two unconscionable kidnappers has quite taken the wind from her eye. She is no longer half as proud and argumentative as she was a month ago. Major Buxton was extremely solicitous while we were with them, attending to her every comfort. She could no longer deny the truth of her sentiments toward him."

"You don't suppose that she was merely overset by her ordeal, and somehow has submitted to the wishes of my father and Mr. Buxton in light of her fears and distress?"

Emily shook her head. "By the time we bid farewell the following day, there was just such a look in her eye—of fondness, of affection, of wonder—that I could not doubt Evangeline knew herself to be in love with Teddy."

Bertram smiled. "I am satisfied, then," he said. Turning toward Kingsbridge, he added, "I am certain Horatia will be anxious to see you and also to hear news of Evangeline as well. By now she has been informed of your arrival and will be fretting if she does not see you on the instant. She can be found in the nursery, as you might expect."

Kingsbridge agreed, then bid the butler inform his housekeeper to prepare a room for Emily as well as for their servants, who would be arriving in two or three hours.

When these details had been attended to and Lord Kingsbridge had mounted the stairs to visit his sister in her bedchamber, Bertram drew Emily into the library on the ground floor just off the entrance hall.

The fine chamber opened onto a terrace of golden stone, revealing a vista nearly as pretty as Lord Winsford's in Windermere. Stretching out to the horizon in succession was a magnificent rose garden, a low-lying hedge, a pasture dotted with sheep, and in the far distance a shimmering blue line of the sea. A clear blue sky overhead could be seen from the windows, and the piping of gray-and-white gulls peppered the air.

The chamber was in soft hues of yellow, a pale orange, and brown, reflected in the draperies of yellow silk, the various summer covers of light brown twill or patterned calicoes in like colors, and in the Aubusson carpet in predominant yellows and browns.

The bookshelves were a glossy white, rose from the floor

to the tall ceiling, and contrasted beautifully with the fine dark leather of hundreds of tomes. The whole effect of the chamber was light and welcoming.

Emily entered the chamber and glanced round the room, pleased with all that she saw. The evident fine taste of Kingsbridge and his forebears could be seen in the simplicity of the decor, enhanced by a scattering of ancient maritime instruments made of brass.

She turned to Bertram. "Did you know Kingsbridge is about to embark on a trip 'round the world?"

A misty expression entered his eye. "Indeed. I have known of it ever since my nuptials, for Kingsbridge allowed us the use of his home for our honeymoon. I have even been to Falmouth, where the ship is at anchor. Oh, Em, it is everything we ever imagined. How much I envy him."

"I, too, but I didn't tell you, did I? When we were on our adventures together, I came to—what is it? Why do you stare at me as though I've gone mad."

"Emily, you are not going to tell me that you and Kingsbridge—I mean, you weren't travelling with him all this time?"

"Well, yes, I was, but it doesn't signify."

He opened his eyes wide and his mouth followed suit. But instead of words issuing forth, a rather shrill, stunned feminine voice greeted her ears from the direction of the doorway. "Emily! How could you!"

Emily turned and was shocked to see Meg standing and staring at her with a hand to her bosom. Her complexion had paled significantly, and her eyes were wide with horror. "All this time—in the company of that—that *rogue?*"

Bertram stiffened instantly. "Take a damper, Margaret," he cried. "You are speaking of your host."

"As to that," she said, entering the chamber and drawing the doors shut behind her, "if my host has all but ruined the reputation of my sister, then I will speak of him in whatever manner I deem proper." She drew close to Emily, her eyes blazing with outrage. "Have you no sense, Emily? Were you then telling me whiskers in London when I came to call on you?"

If Meg was outraged, then Emily was in nothing less than a passion. "Yes, I was telling whiskers," she countered unapologetically. "Of course I was, for if I had told you the truth—that Kingsbridge was even then waiting in the antechamber beyond the receiving room—you would never have left my house, and I was most anxious to be rid of you! I had a critical errand to despatch, the rescuing of my cousin which, if I might add, I was able to accomplish to a nicety."

Emily's speech nearly brought Meg's eyes popping from her head. "Of all the scrapes you've gotten into over the years, this is by far the worst, and I don't doubt that you will never recover from so much indiscretion. Did anyone see you together?"

"I don't give a fig if they did! Let the gossip fly, I don't care anymore, Meg. I can't be what you've wanted me to be all these years, or what Prudence or Sophia wanted. I have learned that much on my adventures—just as I was about to tell Bertram—so you might as well forget the rest of the lecture I see poised on your tongue, for it will avail nothing. I am four-and-twenty, do you really suppose I shall change my steps now?"

"Apparently not," Meg breathed, folding her arms over her chest in a protective manner. She sighed deeply and turned away from Emily, her countenance bespeaking her sense of failure. "Whatever will Mama and Papa say?" she murmured aloud, but more to herself than to either Bertram or Emily.

"Why tell them?" Emily suggested. "It would only serve to give Mama a fit of the vapors and push dear Papa into a fit of apoplexy. You can achieve nothing by revealing what has happened. Besides, the whole of this affair is a matter between Bertram's family and Kingsbridge's anyway."

She turned back to face Emily. "I just don't understand

you. Ever since you were a child, you were the most incorrigible little thing."

Emily felt compassion for her eldest sister, whose notions of proper conduct she suspected were even more rigid than either their mother's or father's "I understand your frustration, dearest," she said. "But perhaps it would be best if you relinquished your need to gather up the reins and hold them so tightly. I am not your responsibility. In fact, I am no longer the responsibility of our parents either. I am a grown woman, and as such I will make my decisions apart from you, my parents, or our sisters."

"But your decisions," Meg said forcefully, "like travelling in Kingsbridge's company, affect your entire family. You must admit that at least this much is true."

Emily nodded. "I have thought of that," she said, "which brings me to something I was just about to tell Bertram. The fact is, I intend to—"

"Emily."

Emily turned toward the doors of the library and saw that Lord Kingsbridge had quietly opened the door and was now standing on the threshold, an extremely teasing expression on his face. "Have you told them our great good news yet?"

She did not like the twinkle in his eye. She did not like it one whit.

"What are you talking about, Evan? You don't mean to bring forward that absurd matter—" But she got no further.

Both Meg and Bertram glanced sharply at Emily and, as one, cried, *"Evan?"*

"You address the Marquess of Kingsbridge by his Christian name," Meg cried, horrified.

Emily felt a blush creep up her cheeks.

Kingsbridge entered the chamber on a quick tread. Emily glanced at him, her bravado failing under the piercing stares of both her cousin and her sister.

"Lady Chaddeley, I hope you will forgive me for having given your sister permission to address me in such a familiar manner, but I am hoping that given the nature of our circumstances, you will be able to overlook the indiscretion."

"What circumstances?" Meg asked, a frown now creasing her brow.

"That your sister and I are to be married," he said in a rather flat, matter-of-fact voice.

At that Meg's mouth dropped to her chin. "Married?" she asked, appearing nearly as horrified as she had been when she learned that Emily had been travelling exclusively in his company for several days. She glanced at Emily and then at Kingsbridge and finally blinked, disbelievingly, at Bertram.

"I say," Bertram said, turning to look at Emily with a smile broadening more and more on his delighted face as each second surmounted the next. "Is that what you were about to tell me? Well, by Jove, if I don't think it's the match of the decade! Well done, Em. You'll be a marchioness! To think in the end you've beaten all your sisters to flinders!"

Emily wanted to refute Kingsbridge's announcement, but when Bertram made this statement she realized that what he was saying was true, and that never in a hundred years would Meg have believed that any of her younger siblings could have out-married her. When she saw the look of heavy disappointment and dismay on Meg's face, she was furious and disgusted all at once with her sister's silly hypocrisy.

"Yes, isn't that something, Meg," she said, facetiously, "to think that when we enter a room, I shall have to precede you?"

At that Meg appeared as though the top of her head was about to fly off. Her complexion paled in quick stages, and she opened and closed her mouth like a fish searching for food in the shallows. She was about to swoon.

"Come!" Kingsbridge stated sharply, addressing Meg. "You need to sit down and I shall bring you a glass of sherry." He quickly moved to stand beside her, hooked his arm under her elbow, and guided her to a waiting chair near the fireplace. He was fortunate to have done so, for Meg's knees gave way almost at the same time. He caught her up, however, and soon saw her settled in a winged chair.

"Th-thank you," she murmured.

Emily was trying very hard to feel sorry for her sister, but she couldn't. In her fury, at least for the present, she couldn't bring herself to tell Meg that Kingsbridge had just told her a rapper of no mean order. She had never quite understood her sister's pride before, though today she had seen more of it than she hoped she would ever have to see again.

Kingsbridge crossed the chamber to a table opposite the fireplace on which was situated a silver tray, a decanter of sherry, and several small glasses. He poured Meg a glass and took it to her, then seated himself beside her and began speaking to her in a flow of gentle conversation.

At that moment, the housekeeper arrived, informing Emily that her room was prepared and that if she was wishful she would escort her there now.

Emily was very wishful and left the chamber without acknowledging either Kingsbridge or her sister. She found she was angry with them both, and wished them well in the enjoyment of the conversation in which they were presently engaged.

After one of Kingsbridge's upper maids had helped her restore her flattened locks to some semblance of order, Emily visited Horatia.

The new mother was seated in a chair, a glow upon her pretty features. Beside her was a large cradle, draped with white silk and gathered up in festoons with an abundance of pink ribbons, in which a sleeping infant rested comfortably. Horatia was gowned in a flowing frock of a pretty light blue silk, a color that enhanced the light blue of her eyes.

There was much in her countenance and in her visage to put Emily in mind of Kingsbridge. But they were sufficiently different to give Horatia a gentle, feminine beauty. Her hair was dark brown and caught up in a swirl of curls atop her head, through which was wound a white ribbon. Her complexion was a trifle pale from her recent ordeal, but her cheeks bore a faint pink color that promised a quick recovery.

Emily crossed the room to stand beside the cradle and stare down at the sleeping infant. The baby was swaddled in a soft knit blanket of what seemed to be a fine cashmere, a tuft of dark hair giving an appearance of unearned age.

She glanced at Horatia. "Bertram did not tell me—what is her name? Oh, but she is so very beautiful!"

"Quite like her namesake, I believe," Horatia responded, smiling.

"Indeed?" Emily queried.

"Actually, both her namesakes, for she is to be christened Emily Evangeline Matford in a week or so."

Emily blinked as the compliment and honor of the moment struck her. "Emily?" she queried. Odd tears touched her eyes as she glanced back at the sleeping babe. She stroked the silky tuft of dark hair and whispered, "You might bear my name, little one, but I would recommend you adopt your mama's temperament."

She heard Horatio giggle and knew that her words had been appreciated.

"Do come sit beside me, Emily. There is so much I wish to ask you, not least of which is how you were able to win my brother, when so many have failed."

At that, Emily felt herself pale. She drew back from the cradle and took up the seat beside Horatia, which she realized had been placed just for her.

Emily sat down, adjusting her green silk skirts not so much with the purpose of keeping the fabric from wrinkling as with the hopes she could quickly order her thoughts and find some manner in which to tell Horatia the truth.

"I see by your face that you are not entirely comfortable with marrying Evan," Horatia said. "I hope you believe me when I say that I am delighted with his choice. Bertram has told me so much about you, that I have already come to think of you as a sister. And—" here she paused and cleared her throat slightly. "And I assure you I don't think less of you for having travelled in Evan's company for so many days and nights without benefit of a chaperone."

At that, Emily met Horatia's gaze. Where to begin, she wondered. In the end, she decided to lay the truth before Horatia, so that not even the smallest misapprehension would mar their relationship. "We are not to be married, Horatia. Yes, yes, I know it is what Evan—that is—Kingsbridge told you, but he is laboring under a terrible delusion, which I can only attribute to his pride in refusing to accept that I have no wish to marry him."

Emily saw the raw disappointment in Horatia's eyes, a flickering of pain that brought a twinge of regret to her. She continued. "I can see that I've given you a shock—"

"You have indeed, but not for the reason you suspect. I do not quarrel with your disinclination to marry my brother. It is just that, well, Evan was convinced, completely, of your love for him, and when he spoke of his sentiments toward you, my word, I have never seen him so enraptured! Emily, you would think he had found a lady who, besides being quite beautiful and possessing every quality he had longed to find in a mate, also bore the wings of angels!"

"He did not say so," Emily breathed, astonished.

"Not precisely," she said, smiling in her sweet, soft manner again. "But he did prose on and on about your every virtue, and especially your ability to travel unfatigued."

At that, Emily could not help but smile. "We brangled often. I am surprised he did not say as much."

"He was too happy to waste even a moment recounting your faults. I have never seen Evan *aux anges* before. His eyes were glowing when he spoke of your future together. Well, I am sorry, for I can see that you are well suited to my brother. What are your plans then?"

Emily found herself trusting the young matron implicitly, and understood how it had come about that Bertram had tumbled so completely in love with Horatia. Therefore, she did not hesitate to share her most recent scheme with her. "I intend to go to the Colonies—to America—and tour the wilderness to my heart's content. I have long been wanting, passionately so, to set off on an adventure of my own. When I determined that I would follow after Evangeline, I did not know that what I would discover uppermost in my journeys was the depth of my need to leave England, to see what the rest of the world is about, to visit the numerous ports that Bertram and I plotted on our maps so many years ago."

Horatia's light blue eyes were shining with something akin to wonder. She nodded at Emily's enthusiasm as though she had for years been just such a heartfelt listener to another's daring plans and schemes. "I can see that you are intent upon your course," she said at last. "So I will wish you well and wish you joy. Pray don't repine for Kingsbridge. Perhaps I shouldn't mention it, but he told me that there was a measure of doubt about your nuptials and, if the worst should come to pass, he had already planned to offer for a lady of your acquaintance—Lady Alison, I believe her name is—the daughter of the Duchess of Amesbury."

At the mention of her good friend, Emily felt herself pale, and a strange dizziness overtook her. "Lady Alison?" she queried between oddly stiff lips.

"Mmm," Horatia responded, lowering her gaze and sighing deeply. "I met her once. I remember her as a thoroughly vivacious young woman, which of course must always appeal to a man of my brother's stamp, but do you think she would make him an excellent wife?"

No.

Emily heard the thought barked sharply within the recesses of her mind, but she couldn't offer her opinion so blatantly. "I—I don't know," she murmured. "I suppose she would, but I have never thought of her in such a capacity before. Are you—but are you certain he said Lady Alison?"

Horatia nodded. "Yes, he spoke of her as the young woman who had attended the Scarswell masquerade with you."

"That would be her."

"Evan said that she was lively and adventurous; and naturally since he will undoubtedly want to travel a great deal—you do know that he has a ship waiting for him at Falmouth, don't you?"

Emily nodded.

"Then you know that his wife will need to be energetic and vivacious in order to accompany him on at least some of his journeys. Lady Alison seems perfectly well suited."

"She probably would suffer no small degree of seasickness," Emily muttered ungenerously, her gaze sliding away from Horatia to the fine carpet of the nursery.

"You are probably right. Do you suffer seasickness?"

"Not a bit," Emily responded, lifting her chin proudly. "I have crossed the channel three times and, while all of my sisters were below deck, er, casting up their accounts, I was standing with my face to the salty breeze."

She glanced back at Horatia and saw the glow in her eyes. She realized suddenly that she was being humbugged a little, and felt silly that she had so neatly revealed her jealousy to Horatia.

The baby stirred and let out a whimper. Horatia turned her gaze toward the cradle and sighed deeply. Her thoughts were clearly directed toward her new daughter, and Emily thought it time to withdraw.

She rose from her chair, offered her hand to Horatia, and was pleased when she took it and gave her a gentle, affectionate squeeze. "I hope you will find what you are looking for, Emily," she said. "Before you leave for the Americas, be sure to visit me at least once more."

Emily promised that she would, then left the nursery wondering why the image of Kingsbridge taking Lady Alison tightly in his arms made her want to scratch the eyes out of her dear friend. She ought to be happy that Evan would know some consolation in her own rejection of his hand in marriage. Instead, she felt as though little balls of fire were springing their way through her veins until her hands clenched every time she thought of Lady Alison.

Twenty-five

Two days later, Emily stood in her bedchamber at Kingsbridge's house and stared in disbelief at her maid. "What do you mean, you are leaving my service?" she asked, stunned beyond belief.

Gwendolyn smiled shyly. "We—Egbert and I—were forced to travel together so often in Lord Kingsbridge's coach that we, that is, I, that is, he and I," she gulped visibly, "fell in love."

Emily blinked, and blinked again. "I don't understand."

"His lordship gave us permission t'marry and t'live aboard 'is ship."

"What?" Emily cried, horrified.

The whole of it was unheard-of, and she sensed somewhere in the depths of this revelation that *his lordship* was again putting enormous pressure on her to finally acquiesce to his desire to make her his wife. "I don't believe it."

"You must," she said solemnly. "For we're departin' tomorrow fer Falmouth. I've asked the housekeeper t'recommend another servant fer your employ. Please forgive me for the brief notice, but," here she smiled, "Cupid has struck and my heart must answer."

Emily could not argue with Gwendolyn. To what purpose? Besides, what could she offer her abigail but an uncertain future in America. "You must follow your own path," she said quietly, much subdued. "I wish you every happiness, truly I do."

She watched Gwendolyn swallow hard. "And I you," she responded. "I'm only sorry that your heart is not inclined to wed Kingsbridge."

She shook her head. "I love him," she responded. "But I will not marry him, or anyone."

Gwendolyn nodded her understanding and the subject was dropped.

When Emily had let it be known that far from having accepted Kingsbridge's hand in marriage, she was intending instead on a different course altogether, Bertram had called her a bird-witted ninnyhammer. Kingsbridge had merely smiled at her as though he knew in the end she would marry him, and Meg had been utterly torn into two neat parts.

Her sister wanted to insist on a marriage because of the scandalous journey she had undertaken with Kingsbridge; on the other hand she was having great difficulty in accepting that such a marriage would push her baby sister into higher social circles than even her own.

Therefore, Meg kept silent and, without her pressure, the subject was let drop.

On the following day, Emily awoke with a headache. The skies were leaden, promising rain, and as she crawled from her bed to look out the windows toward the sea, she knew that today Kingsbridge would travel to Falmouth and from her life forever.

Of course she was still fully resolved on her own course, and indeed had already made plans to leave Devonshire for Bristol the next day. Therefore she could not precisely account for her low spirits, since she was truly excited about charting her own course.

Perhaps it was just the headache then that accounted for the blue-devils which now beset her.

But as she sat in a deep purple chair by the window, one foot curled up beneath her, she released a sigh so laden with emotion that she surprised even herself. A gull dipped, rose, then dipped again in the inconstant bursts of wind. The skies darkened, and in the distance a line of rain could be seen near the seashore.

A scratching sounded on the door and, supposing that her maid, whom she had summoned, had arrived, she bid Gwendolyn enter.

She kept her gaze fixed to the sky beyond and for that reason did not immediately comprehend just who had entered her bedchamber. Only the sound of several footsteps caused her to turn in mild curiosity toward the door.

At the very same moment that she felt a pair of hands capture her shoulders, she spied Gwendolyn's nervous visage as she stood nearby wringing her hands, and a moment later felt a kerchief—or something like a kerchief—cross over her mouth and slip between her lips. She cried out, but it was too late. The gag was firmly tied at the back of her head.

A pair of strong, familiar hands slid under her arms and hoisted her to her feet, catching her hands at the same time, pulling them behind her back and tying them together in quick, decisive jerks. Only then did she realize that she was being taken prisoner.

Thus bound, she was pushed slightly away from the chair and whirled to face her captor.

Kingsbridge stood before her, dressed for travel on the gray July day, in a black coat and waistcoat, black pantaloons, Hessians with silver tassels dangling at the *v*, a perfectly tied neckcloth, moderate and neatly starched shirtpoints, and a several-caped greatcoat clinging to his broad shoulders. A hat of black beaver felt sat at a jaunty, roguish angle across his dark brown locks, he wore gloves of fine York tan, and his hazel eyes danced with merriment.

The worst of it was she couldn't even argue, scream, or brangle with the man, for he had effectively gagged her. She stamped her foot and growled, but the simple motion brought a new awareness dawning on her. She was dressed only in her nightgown. Even her feet were bare.

"Come," he said peremptorily. He snapped his fingers and

two footmen entered the room, their complexions high, their expressions nervous—as well they should be! Good god, had the entire household gone mad! Were any of these servants aware that they were in effect *kidnapping* her?

Emily eyed the footmen with intense hostility as they approached her. She stamped her foot again, glaring hotly at the men, so much so that they paused in their tracks, like a pair of frightened deer.

Kingsbridge stepped forward, forcing her to look at him. "You would do well, Miss Longcliffe, to permit them to escort you to my carriage, otherwise I shall have your legs bound and your entire body tied up in a sheet and carried out in exactly that manner. Your choice, of course. It makes no difference whatsoever to me, since I have made up my mind that you are coming to Falmouth with me."

Emily swallowed hard. She could not believe what she was seeing or hearing. She would never have thought Kingsbridge could be so very bad. In a thousand years she would never have believed he would kidnap her. Yet, what did she know of him anyway? From the outset she had known of his reputation, yet she had chosen to ignore it, and here was the result. He was abducting her entirely against her will!

She considered his words and the decisive sound of his voice and she could only conclude that he was not bluffing, that he meant what he said, and that unless she wished to be dragged bodily from her bedchamber, down the wide staircase, and out to his waiting coach, she had best acquiesce.

Taking a deep breath, therefore, she strode forward, setting her face away from the wicked marquess and allowing the footmen to each take an arm gently in hand. She set her mind to determining precisely how she would escape her captor.

When she reached the top of the stairs, however, she was met with a sight that broke her efforts at planning her escape, for awaiting her were Bertram, Meg, and Horatia with her baby in her arms.

She was never more startled, nor more chagrined. Her cheeks grew hot with mortification as Kingsbridge urged her forward, her feet padding down the carpet runner.

When she reached the entrance hall floor, Bertram greeted her first. He moved toward her and slipped his arms about her, placing a kiss on her cheek at the same time. "You've gotten your wish," he whispered.

Horatia then joined him, her eyes also dancing merrily, so much so that certain doubts began to flood her mind of the precise nature of this particular kidnapping. "You will be inordinately happy," she said, smiling and leaning forward carefully to salute her other cheek. Emily looked down at the baby whose newborn eyes watched her uncertainly. She knew she was saying goodbye to them all for a long time. She felt it in the deepest part of her being.

But that was silly! She would escape Kingsbridge before the ship could sail from Falmouth. She would find a way. She would!

Lastly, Meg addressed her. How stiff her sister was, her chin lifted in defiance of the ridiculous nature of the situation. "I don't approve," she said, "of either you or Kingsbridge. But in this, I am in agreement with the man who will shortly become your husband. You've lived scandalously with him for the past sennight and more, and this end is the only honorable answer. You have only yourself to blame for the fix in which you now find yourself." Emily shook her head, then to her surprise a quirk of a smile appeared at the very corner of her sister's mouth, blossoming fully in the next moment as she stepped forward, tears in her eyes, and caught up her youngest sister in her arms.

"Oh, the devil take it," Meg murmured.

Emily was shocked. She had never heard Meg curse in her entire existence!

Meg continued on a small sob. "I believe you will be the

happiest of us all. You always were. God keep you, Emily, and don't be a fool and jump ship at the last moment."

With that her sister released her, the footmen again caught up her arms, and she was ushered quickly out the door, across the gravel drive, and into the waiting coach. A second coach, bearing what she now understood was her newly married maid and Kingsbridge's valet, was harnessed behind.

The coach wheels touched the cobbles of Falmouth as evening fell. Kingsbridge had long since removed the gag as well as the bindings about her arms, but no matter how much she railed at him, she could not cull a single response from him except that only when they were aboard his ship would he listen to her complaints or her arguments.

The journey had been swift, and the shades had been drawn the entire time against prying eyes. She had never once been permitted to leave the coach, enjoying all the treatment of an invalid. Kingsbridge had provided a hamper of food for the journey, so, essentially, she could not complain overly much of her treatment—except that the whole of it was utterly against her will.

"The docks are not far," he said, as the wheels spun slowly over the lumpy cobbles. "You'll approve of the *Admiral Briton*," he added. "She is a refurbished East Indiaman which I bought at auction two years past. I've had her refitted for a journey which I expect will require three years to complete. She is fully manned, her guns are operational, but on board you will find yourself in company with a physician as well as his wife, a chaplain, and twelve scientists. Gwendolyn, of course, will serve in attendance on you. You will be required to take lemon juice three times a day as a preventative against scurvy, as will my entire staff and crew. The ship itself is quite beautiful, the hull is in the old beak-bow fashion, she bears a flat stern with a square counter, but no piled-up poop. She sits low in the water, and her sheer is so perfectly balanced that she looks almost straight. She has a simple sail plan, limited to lower and upper topsails, a massive, steeply tilted bowsprit, a jibboom of new design, as well as a jib and a forestay sail. But the mizzen is quite unique—but that I leave you to see for yourself."

Emily was astounded, since these were the first words he had spoken to her not only since leaving his home, but of his projected journey. Yet what was more astonishing was the matter-of-fact quality of his voice, as though he was assuming that she would be delighted with the news he imparted to her.

For that reason, she merely glared at him when he finished his speech, crossed her arms over her chest, and turned to glare at the drawn shades next to her. She heard him chuckle, however, a circumstance that set her heart and her will completely against him.

Yes, she would simply throw herself into the sea and swim to shore once the ship had set sail.

A few minutes later, the coach reached the dock, which due to the lateness of the hour saw the wharf bereft of activity. Only the distant sounds of a squeeze-box, the faint, though jaunty singing voices of deep-chested sailors, and the creakings and groaning of the ships could be heard.

When the wheels stopped rolling and Kingsbridge peered out the window, Emily's heart began to thrum strongly in her chest.

She had never been aboard an East Indiaman before.

Not that she wanted to see this one! Not when she had been brought to Falmouth utterly against her will.

And yet . . .

Several times she had made the crossing to Calais from Dover on the small, uninteresting packets. Once she had even sailed on Lord Trent's yacht. But never anything bigger or grander than these.

The thought of actually stepping aboard an East Indiaman, which had most certainly seen many of the ports in the China

Sea, the Bay of Bengal, and the Arabian Sea, was, just as Bertram had hinted, a dream come true.

Her thoughts had taken her so far away from the interior of the coach that only as she returned to the present did she realize Kingsbridge was watching her with a warm light in his eye and a crooked smile. "She's beautiful," he said teasingly, enticingly, seductively.

Emily merely licked her lips. She refused to allow him even the smallest portion of satisfaction, but wished like anything that he would please just open the door and let her out!

As though reading her mind, he smiled fully and gave the door a strong shove. Before he could even descend the coach, however, she found herself leaning eagerly over his shoulder for the first glimpse of the *Admiral Briton*.

Emily caught sight of the vessel, which she could see at a glance must have been over a thousand tons, and nearly swooned.

"Oh, dear god!" she cried. "She's magnificent. She must have cost a fortune."

"I've a few pounds invested in her, but once I bring her home I intend to put her up at auction. We've also been invested by several private parties who have scientific and geographical interests at stake."

Emily felt the cold, damp cobbles beneath her feet, but scarcely cared that she was still in her nightgown. All thoughts, except the beauteous nature of the ship, were obliterated. She shivered and the next moment Kingsbridge whisked his caped-greatcoat from off his shoulders and settled the heavy garment over her.

She did not wait for his invitation or for a supporting arm, but began to run barefooted down the length of the dock, which was considerable given the size of the ship.

"I don't believe it!" she cried, glancing back at him. "This is *your* ship? I can't believe it. I mean, I know you said you meant to journey 'round the world, but I never supposed you would have purchased an East Indiaman!"

He seemed pleased as she met his gaze. In fact, he was grinning.

All along the dock, lanterns burned brightly, reflecting in the water below and on the new paint of the ship. The *Admiral Briton* stood tall against the cloudy night sky.

A breeze buffeted Emily's cheeks as she trotted toward the gangplank. Her heart was in her throat, tears brimmed in her eyes.

Kingsbridge's ship.

Scientists aboard. A physician and his wife.

Lemon juice and scurvy.

Topsails, bowsprit, mizzen.

Africa, India, the Spice Islands, China, the Japannes, Russian America, South America, the West Indies, the Colonies.

She began to ascend the gangplank and, with each step, as the dock and the earth began to slip away, she felt as though she was climbing to the top of the apple tree once more. The wind grew stronger; her heart beat as though urging her forward more quickly with each step. Her feet must have had several splinters by now, but she couldn't feel them. She couldn't feel anything except a roar of excitement that rushed about wildly in her ears.

A moment more and she leaped onto the deck, much to the astonishment of a sailor on watch. "Oh!" he cried, catching sight of Kingsbridge. "Good evening, me lord."

Kingsbridge nodded. "A carriage will be following in due course, probably several hours yet, bearing the lady's maid and my valet. You will admit them."

"Yes, sir, very good, me lord."

Emily paid no heed to the astonished light in the guard's eye as he glanced at her. She paid no heed to anything except to the ship's fine points. Kingsbridge, seeing her interest, did not fail to begin enlightening her and gave her a steady tour, bow to stern, that must have lasted an hour, but which seemed to Emily to have been a mere five minutes.

In the end, she found herself alone with the marquess, in

his quarters with a view of the harbor and the numerous ships anchored on the quiet waters. Lanterns dotted the skyline, hanging from masts and appearing like distant lighted windows on a darkened country hillside. A small lantern burned on the center of the table. Emily shrugged off the heavy coat and laid it carefully across a chair at the table.

She felt as though for the past hour a strong wind had been blowing, gale force, through her mind, but had finally passed on to farther reaches. The quiet which now settled in her brain bore a fuzzy quality and did not make it easy for her to order her thoughts.

What a hypocrite she was, she thought distractedly as she moved to stare out the windows that opened onto the sea.

Why go to America, when she could sail with Kingsbridge?

A bolt of fear pierced her neatly and she folded her arms across her chest, the soft linen of her nightgown ineffectual in preventing a shiver from cascading down her neck, back, and legs.

"You are grown chilled," Kingsbridge murmured. She thought he might return his greatcoat to her shoulders, instead he moved to stand behind her, very close, and slipped his arms about her. He cradled her gently and placed a kiss on her ear.

She drew in a deep breath and felt like sobbing.

"Come with me," he whispered.

"Do I have a choice?" she queried. "After all, you kidnapped me from your house. Why would I suppose now that you would release me?"

She felt his chuckle rumble through her back and he embraced her more fully, settling his cheek against hers. A slight swell rocked the ship.

"You were never my prisoner," he murmured, again placing a kiss on her ear and another on her cheek. She felt a ripple of desire steal into her chest. He had not kissed her in a long time, not in four days.

"Then why did you feel you must needs steal me from my bed?"

"I did no such thing. As I recall, you were seated by the window when your abigail and I entered your chamber."

"Well, you might as well have stolen me from my bed, since I am standing here in my nightgown."

"Yes," he murmured hoarsely. "I am well aware of that!"

Emily drew in a quick breath. She was aware as well, but tried not to dwell on it overly much.

He continued, "So what do you say, Miss Longcliffe? Are you still determined not to wed me? Or has the sight of my ship been sufficient to persuade you that we are meant to be together, you and I, to feel the ocean spray on our faces, to explore each continent as pleases us, to be husband and wife on an adventure unparalleled. Tell me that this kidnapping has turned your heart, your mind, your spirit toward me even a little."

Emily understood him now and she smiled, then laughed. "You have been planning this since Kendal," she stated.

He kissed her cheek softly and slowly. In a whisper, he responded, "I believe I have been dreaming of this since seeing you peep from behind the curtain at the masquerade. I had never witnessed such a lively pair of eyes before, so mischievous, so spirited, so determined. Then, when I gave you chase and afterward caught you in the orangery, I remember feeling a curious emptiness in my chest. By god, if I didn't lose my heart then and there! Dearest Em, please put me out of misery, and say you'll make me the happiest of men and marry me!"

His speech had gone straight to her heart. She knew herself to be understood at last, and to be loved even for all her vagaries. She turned within his arms, he received her, catching her tightly against himself and kissing her full upon the lips.

Another slight swell lifted the ship, ever so gently.

How sweet his mouth was upon hers, searching and tasting

in a rich, sensual manner. She belonged to him, and she finally comprehended how completely he belonged to her.

She drew bask slightly. "The wind is in the trees," she whispered.

He nodded, lifting a hand to touch her cheek lightly with his fingers. "Indeed," he murmured. "And as God is my witness, I shall strive every day of our lives together to keep it blowing strong and full, for your sake as well as for mine. I comprehend your disinclination to marry, especially since before I met you I was of a similar mind. But together, we'll make an adventure of it. What do you say?"

He kissed her again. Another swell jostled the East Indiaman. The ship responded with a warm creak and a groan. His kiss deepened. Her heart rose to meet his.

She drew back just a little. "I'll marry you, Evan. Indeed, I would like it above all things."

And together they would roam the seas until they had both had their fill.

ABOUT THE AUTHOR

Valerie King lives with her family in Glendale, Arizona. She is the author of seventeen Regency romances, including *A Summer Courtship* and *Bewitching Hearts,* and two historical Regency romances—*Vanquished* and *Vignette.* Valerie is currently working on her next Regency romance, to be published in June 1998. She loves hearing from her readers and you may write to her c/o Zebra Books. Please include a self-addressed stamped envelope if you wish a response.

LOOK FOR THESE REGENCY ROMANCES